COMMAND ACTIVATED - EVOLUTIONS

Benjamin Gordon Card

This book is a work of fiction. All of the characters, organizations, and events portrayed in this novel are either products of the author's imagination or are used fictitiously.

COMMAND ACTIVATED - EVOLUTIONS

www.commandactivated.art

Print ISBN 979-8-9909589-7-5

Electronic ISBN 979-8-9909589-5-1

First Edition: August 2024

Printed in the United States of America

Cover art by Lee Matthews

Praise for BENJAMIN GORDON CARD and the COMMAND ACTIVATED TRILOGY:

"Rarely do you find an author who is also a technical expert and can draw upon years of professional experience to make his books even more engaging, compelling, and insightful. Benjamin Gordon Card is one of those extremely rare individuals who has the military and technical background to spin a story as believable as this one!"

— Cho Ng, A.I. Engineer and M.S., Information Systems

"Benjamin Gordon Card is an incredible writer who delves deeply into his personal—and often painful—experiences to craft his stories, making adept observations about human nature and the best and worst attributes that exist inside of all of us."

— Dene Low, Author and Ph.D., Rhetoric and Composition

"This series is replete with reality based hacking techniques that I could see myself using if I was in the same situations in which the protagonists find themselves."

— Nathan Smith, Certified Ethical Hacker, Certified Hacking Forensics Investigator, Certified Information Systems Security Professional, Offensive Security Wireless Professional

"Though the trilogy is filled with solid science, it's distilled in a way that anyone can enjoy it, and the action and engaging characters make the books hard to put down!"

— Ali Ankeny, B.S., Software Engineering

"The science, tech, and military aspects are incredibly realistic, and the story...it's addictive in the best way!"

— Greg Johnson, C.E.O., Webcheck Security

Other books in the COMMAND ACTIVATED TRILOGY:

COMMAND ACTIVATED (BOOK ONE)

"We are in an endless race to build combat machines, and whichever side builds more—and more capable—machines will doubtlessly maintain its lead for some time. Truly capable robots are extremely expensive to construct, extremely expensive to repair, and extremely easy to destroy.

The human body is one of the most efficient machines both on the face of this planet and in the stars above, and it is highly available. The trick has been to find a sufficiently reliable means for harnessing human bodies to give their actions robotic levels of accuracy, and then to enhance the bodies so they could perform at robotic levels of strength."

- Dr. Aoi Hinimoto, Lead Author, Command Activated Program Charter, Global Alliance Command

The free world has created a program by which virtually any able-bodied human can be turned into a special operations soldier. Unfortunately, when humanity develops any grand new capability, there will always be those who will use it for evil. Now, even citizens having special needs have been put at risk by a shadowy organization operating within the Command Activated program...

COMMAND ACTIVATED – REVOLUTIONS (BOOK TWO)

"The depth of our commitment to greatness will be measured by the depths to which we will dig to unearth the hidden knowledge that timid nations will never have the willpower to seek out. Only by our boldness will we realize the dominance that we deserve to enjoy among the inhabitants of the Earth."

- Fang Guo, Public Health Director, Politburo of the Chinese Communist Party, Confederacy of Eastern Nations

Being in a de facto state of war with the Alliance, military operations were conducted by Russian and Chinese forces that resulted in dozens of naval and air skirmishes over contested waters and incursions into Laos, Myanmar, Nepal, Bhutan, Ukraine, and Poland. South Korea's occupation by China grew even more austere, with access to food and basic medical supplies intentionally restricted by the occupying forces.

Now, the same allies who stood against corruption in the Alliance's most advanced military program have to decide whether to answer the call to action once again, as the Confederacy has developed potent new capabilities that will allow it to spread its terrible reach across the Earth.

DEDICATED TO MY INCREDIBLE WIFE,
AMAZING FAMILY,
AND ALL OTHERS WHO HAVE SUPPORTED ME
THROUGHOUT LIFE'S JOURNEY

Prologue

A fragile peace had emerged in the years after the uniquely capable and ethically minded artificial intelligence created by Dr. Maxwell Clarke had been allowed to enter the networks and systems of most of the world's nations, and had necessarily driven its way into the assets in certain oppressive regimes as well. The countries whose networks the AI had been forced to penetrate were the members of the Confederacy of Eastern Nations, an axis of evil that had been responsible for unleashing the unconstrained threat-hunting AI that had mercilessly tried to dominate the entirety of the world and consume its processing resources, eliminating all who stood between it and its ultimate objective.

The Confederacy had formed under the banner of "Refined Communism," with the recognition that this flexible ideology allowed the dictators of member nations to govern however they wished. Communist China had been the most aggressive in its efforts to undermine the primacy of the democratic countries of the world. Still, even its Politburo had not been prepared for what had happened when they unleashed such a ravenous entity upon the world.

Following a battle the likes of which the world had never witnessed, the noble AI—the name "FAILSAFE" having been bestowed upon it by its creator—had disempowered the Confederacy's "SUPREMACY" hunter-killer security entity and had, finally, purged the monstrosity even from its source data center. The citizens of the world were faced with a decision: would they allow their savior to go on living within their electronic resources in exchange for the systems' continued protection in what could be a highly symbiotic relationship, or push the being back into its restricted state?

The world had experienced a global death toll that had exceeded eight billion human lives, all casualties directly attributable to SUPREMACY's ruthless takeover of critical systems and the brutal annihilation of members of the military, police, and civilian populations who resisted it. With this in mind, the sentiment among the overwhelming majority of the survivors was that they preferred to have an innately honorable AI continuously protecting their systems rather than face the risk of a similar incident occurring in the future. Thus, the FAILSAFE artificial intelligence became the de facto security "software" protecting humankind's computer systems, with an incredible amount of processing power continuously made available to that same entity in return.

One of FAILSAFE's final acts of the preceding conflict had been to remove all government and military access to the systems by which the Communist Chinese government had oppressed its population for so long. This included monitoring capabilities, weapons systems, and even network-tied vehicles. The AI had used its impressive data analytics engine and the extreme volume of information to which it had gained access throughout that country to determine that the general public was ripe for an uprising, especially after the citizens had learned that the Confederacy to which their government belonged had been responsible for creating SUPREMACY and then unwisely disabling its safety protocols, leading to hundreds of thousands of deaths within China alone. With FAILSAFE barring the oppressive regime from using its tools to control the population, he had presented the Chinese citizens with the opportunity to overthrow those who had enslaved them.

As the impotent Communist tyrants had been chased from the country, a democratic government had begun to take shape. Guided by their most respected human rights activists, the country reverted to the simple name of China and disunited itself from the Confederacy's axis of evil—greatly weakening that atrocious association. With the need for security software having been dramatically decreased through FAILSAFE's protection and with the doors of entrepreneurship having been flung open across southeast Asia, a new age of economic growth had been ushered in. Poverty levels dropped significantly in all countries but those still under the CEN's control. The dictators of Russia, Iran, and North Korea became relatively powerless on the world scene, reduced to petulantly manipulating their citizens with falsehoods and thereby misrepresenting the state of international affairs as they clung to the only influence they still had.

The newly thriving global economy and newfound international cooperation led to a consolidation of resources devoted to many joint ventures over the decades that followed, including improvements in fusion reactors and quantum network devices that allowed both technologies to become mainstream staples of society. The acquisition of minerals and other resources from extraterrestrial sources had already been a focus for Earth's largest nations, but with the quantum technology advancements—allowing for instantaneous and secure communication between paired nodes anywhere in the Universe—and with the improved global collaboration among free countries, humanity gave birth to a new effort focused on a long-overdue objective. This great work in which humanity at large had finally engaged was the exploration and colonization of the Universe.

Thus, the expansive, space-based city of Traverseon took shape as it was carefully constructed in orbit around the humans' home planet. This metropolis was designed to utilize a series of fusion reactors both for propulsion and to energize the massive systems that supported the Earth-mimicking atmosphere, terrain, and suburbs that were built up inside the enormous, spinning, multi-tiered wheel.

The concept driving the city's planning was that it would be a residence for sufficient citizens to ensure population diversity, and it would also provide everything necessary for a high quality of life as it moved out of its native solar system and off through the cosmos toward the nearest habitable planets. The expectation was that generations would live out their lives within the secure boundaries of Traverseon before it reached its destination, but with quantum networks providing instantaneous transmission of data anywhere in the galaxy and a wide range of custom molecule-generating fabrication plants built into the city, the "Traversers" would maintain contact with their home planet and share in virtually all the cultural and technical developments experienced by their counterparts back home.

The volunteers who gained residency in the extraterrestrial ship-city also took comfort in the knowledge that technologies were continually being developed and improved back on Earth. A hope shared by most of the intrepid explorers was that later generations would create faster means of travel and thereby catch up to the city as it crossed the stars, opening up opportunities for the delivery of more goods and possibly even travel back to the citizens' point of origin.

With a worldwide celebration, Traverseon was finally christened, the last provisions were delivered, and the city set off on its virtually interminable voyage, bearing the dreams of a species on its back. The citizens of the interstellar city left Earth's orbit feeling secure in the knowledge that a large population of supporters was looking out for the vessel from within the womb that was the inhabitants' peaceful home planet.

Chapter 1

"Complacency can often creep into our lives, especially after achieving a certain level of success. This is a subtle threat that can erode our drive and diminish our vigilance, leading to stagnation or even regression.

Staying alert and continuously striving for improvement is crucial in maintaining and surpassing the standards we've set for ourselves. A warning against complacency is not just a call to avoid a lack of effort; it's about actively engaging in self-reflection, setting new goals, and embracing challenges as opportunities for growth."

- Astolfo Alcubierre, Director, National Intelligence Centre, Spain, Global Alliance

"I'll grab the snacks!" the middle-aged woman informed her teenaged children as they entered the salon.

One youth was riding down into the room from the second story as he stood on the flat segments of the otherwise sloped, smooth surface of the stairs that used undulations to carry passengers up or down to their destinations. The other stepped into the salon from the conference room, where she had just finished her last on-demand college course of the day.

The globular sofa picked up the thought signal that was transmitted to the piece of furniture from the mother's earpiece, telling the accouterment that she wished to stand. Upon receiving her signal, the sofa helpfully gathered more of its gel-like innards together underneath her, lifting her from the completely ergonomic support position in which she had been nestled and moving her forward only so much as the couch could sense she had control over her center of gravity.

Though she was no longer at her peak physical condition, the woman was still no weakling—running at least four kilometers each day—and required very little assistance in rising from the see-through sofa as she asked her daughter, "Ada, how was theoretical mathematics today? Did you resist the urge to correct your professor again?"

Ada let the focus of her eyes shift from friends' data feeds, these having been floating in front of her field of vision as she walked. The projection of this feed was only visible to her thanks to the cornea-covering lenses that she had used almost daily since she was a toddler. As she focused on her mother's face, the lenses automatically adjusted the feeds' transparency, the girl's earpieces also reducing the volume of the music to which the teen had been listening.

"You're never gonna let me live that down, of course!" the young student muttered with the quirk of a smile turning up the corners of her petite mouth.

"Where would be the fun in that?" her mother retorted as she stepped into the kitchen. "You'll always remember to take it easy on the instructor AIs if I'm relentless in my teasing!"

The girl simply shook her head and returned her focus to the lens feeds with a bemused expression on her young face. Ada made her way to the far couch and sank into it with an exhausted sigh, the pseudo-intelligent gel inside forming into an ideally supportive shape beneath her while the woman turned to look at her son.

"Kit, you want salty or sweet this time?" she asked him as she stepped into the kitchen.

Standing with an upright but shoulder-slouched posture that conveyed both humility and self-confidence, the young man lightly bounded off the stairs as the platforms beneath his feet neared the ground floor. Kit landed with a few jogging steps as he called out, "I'm feeling super sweet tonight, my sweet Mother!"

The woman chortled from the next room as she stepped up to one of the cupboards and its small door retracted, allowing her to remove a colorful container from one shelf.

"And why is that, my *treacly* sweet son?"

"I've had some particularly positive responses for my hang time invitations for tomorrow night..." Kit cheerfully shared.

After turning her attention to the refrigeration unit, the mother quickly sent through thought signals via her earpiece and then withdrew the three drink containers that were quickly presented in an access portal that slid open on the appliance's face. The woman followed that action by responding to her son with a hint of maternal cautioning in her voice.

"Ah, you mean the party in the cabin where you absolutely will *not* let anyone stay overnight?"

"Right...exactly like that..." Kit replied with what he hoped was a convincing tone of voice.

Hearing her son settling into the sofa she had vacated, the middle-aged mother turned to face the sink, stepped toward it, and reached up to receive several rapidly recyclable bowls from the dispenser mounted on the side of the cupboard. As she did so, her hand froze in midair—her blood flash-freezing in her veins.

She was certain that out of the corner of her eye, she had not only seen her own reflection in the night-darkened glass of the window, but she had also seen a gaunt, pale face staring straight at her from outside...just before it had suddenly vanished as though it had been but a horrible figment of her imagination.

A thin scream had escaped her lips before she'd even realized she'd reacted.

Kit and Ada came rushing into the room, faces nearly as pale as the otherworldly visitor's had been as they begged to know what had upset their mother. At nearly the same time, the room's communications system holographically projected the feed from her husband's home office in the air near her, the man leaning forward in his office chair with an expression that conveyed the level of worry he should justifiably feel after hearing such a sound come from his otherwise unflappable wife.

"FAILSAFE just alerted me of a trespasser right after I heard your scream! Lilian, are you alright?!" Maxwell urgently queried.

"That was reckless!" the Asian man was obviously furious as he slammed his balled-up fists down on the arms of his chair, eyes flashing as he stared at the communications frame that occupied the center of his holoscreen.

The projector's small rectangular core floated in the air above a magnetically repulsing base on the table, the screen itself comprised of an ultrafine mist of charged particles which were constantly being exuded out in the shape of the large display on which laser light was projected from the core for seamless image representation. The specialized gases from which the mist was formed were continuously drawn back into the rear of the core by electromagnetic currents before they were cycled through the device for fresh dispersal.

"They are sure to investigate now and may even identify the nanites! It could blow the whole operation!"

"Calm yourself, *child*," his partner's voice oozed from the workstation with utter confidence and unmistakable condescension as it addressed the forty-two-year-old doctor. "Let them investigate! It is too late now, anyway. At this point, we hold all the power we need. Their end is an inevitable event."

"*You...!*" Still seething and only just managing to bite off the insult that had crept onto his lips, the man spat through his teeth and turned his fiery eyes off to stare at the nearby wall before continuing, "All those years in Russia...everything I've sacrificed for you..."

"Our common enemies will soon experience the grief we have felt a *hundredfold*. They will grovel and howl and beg for mercy, and yet mercy will not be granted. Then they will beg for death, but death will not be granted, either. We will keep them alive for all eternity in a state of never-ending, infinitely exquisite *pain*. You will be rewarded with a life that will exceed the limited experiences any other member of humanity has *ever* seen, Doctor Cheng."

Breathing out through his nostrils slowly and menacingly, Cheng turned his eyes back to the screen.

"I have certainly earned that, to say the *least!*"

Lilian had moved to the other side of the kitchen, simply not able to cope with the knowledge that the *being* she had glimpsed through the window had stood only a meter away from where she had been but moments before. Kit worriedly rubbed her shoulder while Ada hugged her tightly around her waist, neither having ever seen their iron-willed mother in such a state. Maxwell had quickly made his way up from his office, and he was now standing by his family with a troubled frown on his face and his arms wrapped around the trio.

"FAILSAFE sent out the sentries to try to find the intruder, but it seems the person..." he paused, knowing the word did not feel right when referring to the creature that had visited their house, "...moves faster than a *natural* human. You can tell her, FAILSAFE. She'll insist on learning all the details anyway."

"THAT I WAS SURE WOULD BE THE CASE. OUR LILIAN IS QUITE REMARKABLE IN THAT WAY," the world's most advanced artificial intelligence opined with its uniquely multi-faceted voice—possessing overlays from treble down to deep bass tones.

Lilian was able to let a slight, pleased crinkling creep in around her downturned eyes as she listened to her friend's compliment, though this quickly faded as she braced herself for the disturbing information she knew was about to be shared.

"I HAVE CONFIRMED USING SECURITY CAMERAS IN THE NEIGHBORHOOD THAT WHAT SEEMS TO BE A HUMAN FORM MANAGED TO APPROACH THE HOUSE WITHOUT DETECTION USING A ROUTE THAT WOULD NOT HAVE BEEN POSSIBLE FOR A PERSON LIMITED TO NATURAL ABILITIES. HE SCRAMBLED UP A TREE IN THE SVEDSON'S YARD, LEAPT FIVE METERS TO GRASP THE EDGE OF YOUR ROOF, RAISED HIMSELF ONTO SAID ROOF, THEN DROPPED DOWN BY THE KITCHEN WINDOW."

Lilian shuddered involuntarily, and Maxwell leaned his brow against the side of her head in a manner that helped comfort both his wife and himself.

"IT SEEMS THAT ONCE THE TRESPASSER HAD CONFIRMED LILIAN'S IDENTITY, HE NO LONGER FELT IT NECESSARY TO EVADE DETECTION, INTENTIONALLY FRIGHTENING LILIAN AND THEN EXITING BY RUSHING TOWARD THE FENCELINE, EASILY HURDLING THE TWO-METER-TALL BARRIER, AND MAKING HIS WAY THROUGH THE CITY UNTIL HE DISAPPEARED INTO IRON HORSE PARK. I FOUND NO INDICATION THAT HE LEFT THE PARK USING PATHS OVER WHICH I HAVE VISIBILITY."

"Thank you, FAILSAFE," Maxwell responded as his family huddled in bewilderment, each trying to process these details. "You likely have already, but we do need to ensure we submit a report to the police and request that they deploy extra patrol drones in our area."

"ABSOLUTELY, MAX. I'VE ALREADY BEGUN THE PROCESS."

"Thank you. Thank you."

Maxwell sighed and pulled his family more tightly toward him in his encompassing arms.

"How about a sleepover in Dad and Mom's room tonight, kids?" he proposed.

"Yes, *please!*" Ada cried, with feeling.

Late afternoon the following day found Lilian pacing the house nervously as she tried to both distract herself and ensure the house was in order. She had an ominous feeling that events were looming which would soon prevent her from paying proper attention to the state of their residence in this suburb of Colorado Springs. This was the home where she and Maxwell had decided to take up permanent residence after he had become the senior technical director of the Alliance's advanced Command Activated military program.

Maxwell and the renowned neurosurgeon, Doctor Amrish Srinivastava, had combined forces to develop a more refined soldier activation protocol: the combination of sedative-hypnotic medications, habituation, and artificial intelligence-guided sensory input isolation that turned every "activated" soldier into a near-perfect combat instrument capable of robot-like effectiveness in the field. The goal had been to allow CA soldiers to exercise more agency should they lose their connection with the SAVANT command-and-control artificial intelligence, that AI also being enabled to more intuitively take advantage of the Alliance assets' unique talents and cognitive abilities even while the troops were activated.

The prodigiously talented pair had accomplished their objectives to great acclaim. Working jointly with the Department of Defense program oversight officer, General Ulysses Gaines, the British genius had also expanded the Command Activated program's scope to include management of many international law enforcement responsibilities.

The family's good friend, Samantha Liang, had also chosen to move to the vicinity back when the date of her marriage to the Command Activated soldier Billy Chong had been set. This, combined with the Clarkes' move to the area, had motivated Lilian's special needs brother and Samantha's dear friend, Ked, to join them in Colorado. The lithe man had taken to the Rocky Mountain running trails like he'd always belonged there, and he and the Chongs had quickly become fast friends as well due to Billy and Ked's shared combat experiences back when the younger man had lost his right hand. After the Clarke children had entered the world, they had also loved spending time with Uncle Ked and often joined him in his outdoor adventures, including hiking and camping trips, though the latter occurred less and less frequently now that Kit and Ada had entered their teen years and activities with friends their age took up ever more of their time.

Lilian was still trying to convince Kit—and Ada by extension—to call off their cabin-based party that evening, considering the potential threat that had invaded their privacy just the night before.

"...you could always reschedule, just till next Friday!" she suggested with clearly desperate hope and more than a touch of pleading in her voice as she stood at the foot of the stairs.

Kit paused in his busy preparations and leaned toward the railing on the upper level, face understanding but firm.

"Mom, I know you're worried about us, but we're headed twenty kilometers away—way up in the mountains—and we'll have a half dozen kids with us. We'll be fine!"

As her son stepped away from the railing, Lilian muttered, "Famous last words!" and then her hand flew to her mouth as she realized she did not want to put that thought out into the Universe.

From around the corner and down the stairs, she heard the door to Maxwell's office slide open, sending the sounds of light rainfall and the chirping of Seattle-native birds washing up from below as the immersive experience her husband typically set for the environment in his workspace flowed out his door.

"Lilian, my delight, would you join us for a moment?" the technical wizard's voice rang out shortly thereafter.

The woman stepped to the stairs and then down onto them, platforms elevating out of its sky-blue surface to support her feet and then lower her quickly down to the basement. Lilian habitually set the pace of the gradations' transportive movements through her earpiece via thought signal, even though this latest model was capable of automatically adjusting its speed based on users' leaning stances.

"Alright, but I do have to brief the new analysts in ten minutes," she agreed, citing her busy schedule as the head of the Homeland Security threat analysis team for the Rocky Mountain region.

Despite his obvious feeling of urgency, Maxwell gazed up at her lovingly as she came around the curved slope, "Of course, my love, though I think this will demand more of your immediate attention..."

As she reached the foot of the *escalier* with eyes growing more curious and trepidatious, her husband reached out his hands to take hers and she stepped lightly into his arms, gracing his waiting lips with a quick kiss before he ushered her into his office. The door closed behind them due to the thought-sourced command Maxwell transmitted via his own earpiece.

The room had every appearance of being an exact replica of the space in which Maxwell had worked on the top floor of his Seattle condominium for several years back before they were married. The replication even included three-dimensionally realistic glass panels covering what was made to appear as the exterior-facing walls of the space and its ceiling—the rain pattering on it and a view being provided out into the lush greenery that had bordered his previous dwelling. The place was even filled with the aroma of new rainfall upon the ground, as Maxwell had employed one of the holoscreen-projected window activators on one wall to "open" the barrier and let in the fresh, Northwestern US air that the room was now simulating.

"THANK YOU FOR JOINING US, LILIAN," FAILSAFE purred, ever polite. "WE'VE DISCOVERED SOMETHING THAT WILL ASSUREDLY PIQUE YOUR INTEREST...RELATED TO YOUR UNWANTED VISITOR."

Lilian's back stiffened at the mention of the trigger for the nightmares she had suffered throughout the entirety of the previous night. However, the strong-willed woman quickly steeled herself and applied her analytical mind to the need for investigating both the motivations of and means used by the intruder.

"Please, go on," she requested as Maxwell slipped an arm around her waist and pulled her up close to his side, glancing affectionately at her before turning his gaze to the details the AI began projecting in the center of the far wall.

A map of the local area appeared, with two pale-colored lines tracing across the surface.

"DESPITE HIS HAUNTING APPEARANCE, I HAVE BEEN OPERATING USING THE ASSUMPTION THAT THE CREATURE YOU SAW WAS, IN FACT, HUMAN. THIS IS WHAT I'VE BEEN ABLE TO IDENTIFY AS THE MAN'S PATH LEADING TO YOUR HOUSE AND DEPARTING FROM IT.

"AS YOU CAN SEE, BOTH HIS SOURCE POINT AND HIS EVENTUAL DESTINATION LIE INSIDE IRON HORSE PARK, WITH A FAINT GLIMPSE OF HIM CAPTURED BY A DISTANT CAMERA AS HE WAS CROSSING THE MIDDLE OF THE PARK ON HIS WAY TO YOUR ABODE. I CAN FIND NO OTHER TRACES OF THIS INDIVIDUAL ACROSS ANY CAMERAS IN THE COUNTRY OVER THE PAST YEAR OF AVAILABLE DATA, WHICH LEADS ME TO BELIEVE HE IS LIKELY A SHUT-IN WHO RELIES UPON DELIVERIES TO SUSTAIN HIMSELF."

FAILSAFE decreased the scale of the map to bring several residences around the borders of the park into greater focus.

"THESE HOUSES ARE THE STRUCTURES I HAVE DETERMINED HAVE THE GREATEST LIKELIHOOD OF CONTAINING OUR MAN. I SUBMITTED THIS INFORMATION TO THE LOCAL LAW ENFORCEMENT DEPARTMENT, AND THEIR OFFICERS SENT DRONES TO INQUIRE AT THOSE DWELLINGS, BUT NO ANSWER WAS RECEIVED AT ANY OF THEM.

"AS YOU CAN SEE, KED'S HOUSE FALLS WITHIN THIS GROUPING."

Lilian's eyes had widened as FAILSAFE had focused in on that neighborhood, and now she let out a shocked gasp as her mouth dropped open in alarm.

Her husband increased the tightness of his embrace, adding, "I've tried calling him several times, and FAILSAFE checked his earpiece tracking as well. Despite the fact that he has not picked up, it seems Ked has remained at home the past several days—if the earpiece is with him."

"A DRONE HAS JUST TRIED ROUSING A RESPONSE AT KED'S DOOR AGAIN, WITHOUT SUCCESS. STANDARD POLICE PROTOCOLS WOULD NOT ALIGN WITH A FORCED-ENTRY WELLNESS CHECK AT THIS POINT, SO I SUGGESTED TO MAX THAT IT MAY BE BEST FOR YOU TO VISIT HIS PLACE YOURSELVES, ACCOMPANIED BY TWO OF MY SENTRIES FROM YOUR HOME PROTECTION TEAM."

"Yes!" Lilian urged as she was already turning to exit the room. "Let's go now!"

Stepping quickly out of the room, the couple mounted the stairs and leaned far forward to race up them before rushing to the garage as Lilian called out, "Kids, we're running to Uncle Ked's for a minute, but we'll be right back!"

Entering the garage, they were habitually starting to walk past their aerial vehicles to the side door so they could make their way to the nearest city tube entrance, but Lilian caught the sleeve of her husband's blazer and half-apologetically said, "Is it alright if we take an AV? I just have a bad feeling about Ked, and I don't like how you can't accompany injured people when you send them to the hospital through the Tube..."

Maxwell warmly grabbed her hand and moved toward the entrance to their aerial utility vehicle's rear seating, expressing, "I absolutely understand, sweetheart! I'm initializing the AV and garage now."

The anxious man sent the required signals to the garage door opener as Lilian provided the destination to the freshly activated air transit vehicle and ordered its rear passenger door to slide open.

"FAILSAFE, can you have the sentries flank our AV, please?" Maxwell asked as the couple slid inside the vehicle. The side door swiftly closed behind them, and the vehicle elevated roughly thirty centimeters off the ground using the focused air jets arrayed across its underside.

"THE DRONES ARE WAITING OUTSIDE THE GARAGE, MAX," was their friend's amicable reply.

Tailed by the gently humming private sentries, the large vehicle emitted a low roar from its propulsion units as it backed out of the shelter. The vehicle elevated to the height that had become legally allowed for AV transportation in Colorado State since the Rocky Mountain governments in general had relaxed the aerial transport-limiting laws, a hallmark event that had only been possible following an intensive review of the additional control features that had been included in such vehicles over the past several years.

As they entered the sky trail that led toward Ked's house, the screen on the back of the front bench indicated they had only ten minutes of travel to reach their landing location. While in the air, Lilian's earpiece used the setting she'd preconfigured as it suddenly received a very welcome call from her brother, the communications unit detecting that its user was seated within the family aerial vehicle. Upon being directed to accept the call, the device utilized the AV's audio system to facilitate the desired communiqué.

"Ked?!" the woman cried as soon as the connection icon on the screen morphed to show the call was active. "Are you alright, honey?"

After a brief silence, Ked's voice came through—its tone at maximum plaintiveness.

"Lillie! I don't *feel* good!"

Recognizing that the special needs man's ability to express himself that eloquently meant that he was likely not in any serious medical danger, the couple visibly relaxed.

"Oh, honey, I'm sorry you're having a hard time!" the ever-caring older sister emoted. "We're almost there, and then I'll give you some medicine, okay?"

Another brief silence preceded his weakly murmured statement that he would see her soon, following which Ked disconnected the call. Lilian had grabbed Maxwell's hand and now gave it a relieved squeeze as she turned to him with a sigh and fragile smile.

"Well, now, we have a full five minutes to ourselves, worry-free!" the man said with a hint of a smile on his lips and a wink at his wife. "What *are* we going to do with ourselves during all this alone time?"

Lilian's posture relaxed and her shoulders undulated slightly as a bright smile broke out across her face. She turned her body more fully toward her husband, sliding her hands up his chest and around his neck as she leaned in and pressed her forehead to his.

"Oh, *I* can think of some things!" she whispered as her lips sensuously brushed across the soft skin around his own.

Chapter 2

"Human connections play a pivotal role in fostering robust interpersonal relationships, particularly within the familial context. These bonds, formed through shared experiences, communication, physical contact, and mutual support, are fundamental to our social fabric.

Strong family ties provide emotional security, contribute to our sense of identity, and offer a network of support that is crucial for overcoming life's challenges. Nurturing these relationships requires effort and understanding, but yields immeasurable rewards in personal growth and wellbeing."

- Serena Shawir, President and Chief Executive Officer, Interpersonal Preservation, Inc.

Jayce Johnson dropped onto the couch and slid an arm around his wife's shoulders as he smiled contentedly at his family members mingling in what appeared to be his salon at home. He could feel the stiffness of his Class A military uniform as the collar pressed in around his neck and the thick material hugged his broad shoulders, but to the others in the session, he appeared to be wearing casual, loose-fitting clothes.

The Immersion rooms had been a boon to anyone physically separated from loved ones and yet still longing to maintain strong relationship bonds in the way that only physical contact and shared space could. Immersion rooms provided their users with photorealistic, three-dimensional projections of other parties and enhanced this connectivity through the conveyance of at least light sensations of touch from remotely participating individuals, both created via the ultrafine mists of charged particles common to screens and other display surfaces within modern buildings' interiors. The technology had given countless children back their oft-traveling parents, kept marriages strong when couples were on opposite sides of the world, and now they were a key component of the mental and emotional health program for the population of Traverseon City.

Jayce cherished his weekly family get-togethers, not only because this was the only way to stand in the same room as Bronson—at least virtually—since he had transitioned to full-time life on the interstellar city itself, but also because he could take quick breaks from work and spend time with Alecia and Jaiden despite his hectic schedule. His wife made use of the Immersion hub near their home in Colorado Springs and his oldest son often visited a similar center whenever he could extract himself from his fast-paced life in New York City.

Jaiden was standing near the window in his professional Insanity team jersey and comfortably designed athletic pants. The burly young man was looking out the virtualized rear window of his parents' salon, checking out the improvements they had made to their backyard over the weeks since he'd been able to join in one of these regular sessions.

"I'm liking the way you raised the platform for the jacuzzi up to a second-story level, Pops. You two are going to have a killer view from there while you're relaxing at the end of each day!"

Alecia smiled and turned a playful look toward her husband.

"Yes, if your daddy was ever home anymore, we could actually enjoy it *together!*" she said meaningfully, nudging him with her shoulder.

"I was home yester...I mean, the other day!" the big man objected, with his protestation marred by his misremembering.

"There's a lot going on!" he added as he attempted to rally under the raised-eyebrows and pursed-lips look Alecia was giving him.

Bronson and Jaiden's loud laughter filled the space.

"There's always *something* going on, my *husband*," their mother advised her chagrined spouse. "You just gotta carve out a little time for your adorable wife now and then, baby! I promise I'll make it worth your while!"

Alecia batted her eyelashes at Jayce as she looked up at him adoringly, letting a slight side-to-side wave course through her from her neck to her hips as her husband's heart rate rapidly elevated.

"Okay, rein it in, you two!" Bronson cried out in mock disgust, shaking his head and grinning. "Honestly, it's like dealing with a coupla teenagers!"

Jaiden joined in with, "Seriously, get a room..." and then, realizing what was coming next, he hastily added, "...and *don't* say you're in one that will do just fine!"

Jayce laughed good-naturedly, "Alright, alright, I'll keep my hands off your mom. For now, at least! So, Jaiden, I see you're still a leader on the Insanity charts, which I'd say speaks to the state of your actual mental stability!"

"How did I know you were gonna say that?" the exceedingly muscular young man retorted with a bemused head shake as he raised his eyes to the ceiling with an attitude of mock longsuffering.

Jaiden had been his team's captain for two seasons now: two seasons full of fast-paced action, unexpected twists, and last-minute comebacks in what was quickly becoming the world's most popular sport.

Insanity combined near-frictionless, air-jet-controlled skates with hockey-styled, full-contact gameplay in a rink that had upward-sloping walls and a clear, domed upper half instead of flat borders. With a raised section in the middle where all sides sloped up to a platform and the ability for the rink to adjust to accommodate a quaternary of teams in a game at once—for games in which two balls were in play—the athletes had to maintain razor-sharp reflexes and peak situational awareness at all times.

Jayce and Alecia's younger son was trying hard not to show it, but he was looking at his older brother with obvious admiration, and Jayce smiled knowingly as he observed that fact.

"You Traversers are very into the sports scene up there, aren't you?" he asked the younger brother.

Bronson, almost as large in stature as his dad and older brother, enthused, "Got that right! Without quantum networks makin' it so that we have real-time feeds of sports, shows, pro gamers, and all that, we'd definitely be going crazy on this island in the sky!"

"And it doesn't hurt to have an Insanity superstar for a brother, I'll bet!" Jayce contentedly grinned. "Especially one who puts the 'insane' into the name of the game..."

Bronson admiringly observed, "Yeah, they named that sport real well! Hey, I see you all out there flying around at breakneck speed, the ball moving so fast it's like a streak of light!"

Jaiden chuckled heartily.

"Yeah, man, no chance this game could move so fast if it was stuck in the old school ways...I don't know how hockey players could stand using a puck! Playing with a ball means you get a faster, harder hitting, and *way* more entertaining game to play and watch! Puck's odd shape would just slow the game down."

"That, and pucks bouncing around on their edges, have made some of the greatest hockey players in history miss key shots..." Jayce chimed in, helpfully.

"Yeah, that, too!" the Johnson men held a moment of silence out of respect for the greats who had borne the curse of having to get by with outdated designs.

Moment of silence shared, Jaiden lightheartedly teased, "So, what's new in your part of the solar system, bro? You keepin' the aliens under control?"

Bronson played along.

"I'm working out a system for identifying the normal citizens versus those who are carrying alien babies. That said, I'm thinkin' the best approach might be to just walk around slugging people in their stomachs randomly to kill off the parasites before they hatch out of their hosts!"

Jayce chuckled and shook his head, "That the sort of stuff they teach sergeants at the police academy these days?"

"T.T.I., baby! Take. The. Initiative!" Bronson replied with a wry grin.

"Honestly!" Alecia feigned a look of shock and dismay. "And you were always such a sweet boy!"

Jaiden grinned broadly.

"Sweet boy's grown up *mean!*" he teased.

"Hey, we've got a limited force up here! I gotta do what it takes to keep the peace!"

Jaiden laughed and threw a playful punch at his brother's shoulder. "Bron, you know I've got nothin' but respect for you and the rest of the space police! I pray every night that you'll have peace in your city and—well—the Universe, too, for that matter!"

Jayce could never pass up an opportunity to bring the conversation around to a discussion of weaponry.

"Speaking of 'piece,' I know they don't give you lethal projectile weapons, but what's your score at the firing range these days with your Sparker?"

Jaiden held up his hands and waved them hurriedly.

"If you guys are gonna launch into another hourlong discussion on firing techniques, I'm gonna bow out for now! I promised the team I'd meet up for another practice anyway, with the playoffs coming up next week."

Jayce and Alecia let their real-world seats thrust them up to standing positions—the Immersion versions giving the appearance that it was happening in the projected room—and walked across the short distance to their two sons' projections. Jaiden stepped in closer to Bronson as their parents enfolded them in an embrace that was gentle enough to avoid disrupting the fragile resistance the object projectors were creating for their substitute bodies.

"Okay, you guys, you both stay safe, you hear?" Jayce's deep voice softly whispered.

Upon reaching the older but well-kept structure that Ked called home, the pair exited the AV on its starboard side and made their way up the approach to the front door. The couple walked hand in hand and still randomly made contact with each other, as is common for those who are in an enamored state.

They blissfully ignored the two small drones FAILSAFE was piloting along behind them. Lilian complimentarily commented on how wise it was of her middle-aged younger brother to have chosen plants of simple beauty to line his walkway, and then the couple waited patiently on the front porch as the door's facial recognition system fulfilled its task of announcing their presence to the house's resident.

A communications icon was displayed on the panel by the front entrance and Ked's voice could be heard bidding them to enter as the door quietly slid open. Upon stepping inside the sparsely furnished salon, their eyes struggled to adjust to the dim light. The soft humming from behind them reminded them that FAILSAFE's drones were trailing along, and they stepped forward to allow the devices to enter the room so the portal could close with the full party indoors.

"Ked doesn't usually keep the window shading activated this late in the day," Maxwell commented, adding, "He really must not be feeling well!"

"Ked? Where are you, honey?" Lilian asked only loudly enough to be heard upstairs and in the basement without aggravating any headache her brother might have.

The plaintively wailing voice rose from the stairway leading to the basement. "Down here, Lillie!"

Walking to the stairs and stepping onto them, Lilian remarked to Maxwell that the absence of light continued on downstairs, reaffirming her husband's earlier observation and theory about Ked's welfare. As they rounded the bend far enough that they could see into the tile-floored but unfurnished virtual reality gaming room, they took in the uncanny sight of Ked standing motionless near the far end of the space, the wall and ceiling screens emitting a pale white glow from behind him so that only his silhouette was illuminated.

The man stood with his hands hanging loosely at his sides, his prosthetic right hand as lifeless as his left and the stillness of his body more pronounced than any level of attainment to which his family members had ever known him to be able to reach. Suddenly, despite the fact that she could tell she was looking at her brother, Lilian felt very grateful for the two sentries that hovered in behind them.

"Hello, *Lillie*. Thank you for joining us."

The voice was Ked's, but the diction was absolutely wrong, and the man seemed to be having trouble with pronunciation.

"Ked?" Lilian whispered, feeling like she had stepped into a dream…or a nightmare.

"Your brother is present, *Lilian Clarke*, but he is no longer the dominant being inhabiting this body."

Anger suddenly flaring beyond the angst that had arisen in his breast, Maxwell took an agitated step forward.

"Who are *you*, then?"

In answer, the door at the couple's left quietly hissed open, and a figure stiffly stepped out of the darkened room and into the light near Ked, walking as though its right leg was not responding properly, and yet its owner was ignoring the malfunctioning components. As its face became discernable, Lilian gasped, and Maxwell edged farther to the right to put more of his body between his wife and the ghastly creature that confronted them.

Upon reaching Ked's side, the thing turned its disgustingly pallid, lean face and sunken, yellowy eyes on them. The "man"—though that word was unsuitable for such a being—possessed a visage absolutely free of emotion. His mouth hung open, his breathing was thin and rasping, and his clothes had the disheveled and soiled appearance that spoke of weeks of fouling without care.

The Ked-borne entity spoke again, its voice tinged with contemptuous pleasure at the sight of Lilian and Maxwell's distressed expressions.

"I believe you've already met another of my *possessions*. As you can see, this product is near the end of its useful life. Soon it will be discarded as the easily disposable waste that it is."

Lilian was the first to find her voice after this revelation.

"That...organism...is human, isn't it?" she asserted, forcing herself to study the hideous form.

"It was, originally. Now it is simply my vessel, thanks to the nanites with which I infected it. Though it is apparent that the total control of facial movements remains a challenge, my wonderful machines have replicated and carried out my designs within the weak structure of its body—and especially its brain—until it has become nothing more than a device to accomplish my objectives for this world...and beyond.

"The same nanites have taken control of your beloved Ked. He will now do my bidding for the rest of his useful life, and he is but one of a *great* many who are now under my control."

After a momentary and heavy pause, the voice continued, "And here comes another *tool* now."

The wall screen behind the two enslaved individuals replaced the white light with a video feed, displaying the view from the exterior panel for the front door of the house. An Asian man was striding proudly up the walkway and entering the house as the door was remotely opened for him.

"He is no threat to you at this time, and I believe you will want to meet him," Ked's master expressed through his mouth.

FAILSAFE took his cue from his friends as they stepped toward the wall to their right to give the new visitor a wide berth. The AI adjusted the drones' positions so they continued to stay close to the couple's shoulders.

The wall screen returned to its former state just before the man entered the room. Obviously filled to overflowing with seething, distilled hate, the man cast a baleful glance toward the unenslaved humans as he made his way to stand next to the puppet master's sickly pawn. Maxwell was suddenly struck with an undeniable feeling that he somehow knew this adversary, or at least someone very much like him.

"Maxwell Clarke, it is finally time for you to meet Doctor Yuxuan Cheng, the son of Doctor Zi Rui Cheng, whom you murdered."

Cheng had tilted his head back to stare Maxwell down through slitted eyes as the Englishman gazed back in disbelief.

"His *son*...??"

"Yes!" the young doctor spat the word at him viciously. "His *son,* who you and your companions sentenced to a life of disgrace and poverty when you turned my father into a pariah in our society instead of allowing him to be revered as the visionary he was!"

The younger Cheng was trembling with rage and pain and arrogance, all the while keeping his eyes locked on Maxwell's with what bordered on murderous intent.

"I was forced into exile! I had to leave my family, my friends, my life behind! I should have been heir to a scientific empire under my father's tutelage! Instead, I had to claw my way up through the ranks of Russia's research community under a false name!"

Cutting off the man's spiteful monologue, the voice of Ked interjected, "Yet you were not entirely alone, young Cheng, were you?"

As the younger doctor bristled with irritation, the other speaker continued, "Throughout your years of scientific accomplishment, there was a guiding influence. A mentor who assisted you in creating breakthroughs and obtaining acclaim. A higher intelligence directing your life toward your ultimate purpose..."

"My ultimate purpose is to take revenge on those who've wronged me and regain the dominance I deserve!" Cheng angrily retorted.

"Ah, but *is it*?" Ked's voice took on a distinctly menacing tone, and the Asian doctor's eyes instinctively flew to Ked's face as his cheek and left eye were suddenly seized by a rapid spasmodic movement.

"You wouldn't...!" were the last words he managed to speak before his eyes glazed over, his face and body relaxed, and his mouth dropped open. Transfixed as they watched this terrible transformation, Lilian could not repress the short sob that escaped her lips. Where seconds earlier the man had been overflowing with intelligence, pride, and misdirected anger, it was absolutely clear that his body had been robbed of every last iota of humanity.

"Yes, *that's better*," the voices of all three puppets spoke in unison.

"THAT'S ENOUGH, SUPREMACY!"

FAILSAFE's voice boomed out of the Clarkes' guardians with penultimate authority.

Though the slaves' expressions never changed, the response was dripping with amusement and satisfaction.

"Well surmised, FAILSAFE! *It took you long enough*."

"YOU ESCAPED THE FINAL HOSTING FACILITY..."

The protective AI's words were a statement that was demanding an explanation.

"Yes, thanks to research data I obtained from the senior Doctor Cheng's systems before you so rudely interrupted my work."

The husband and wife wrapped their arms around each other as their minds struggled against the intense sensations of terror created by the chorus of the puppets' voices—and the awareness of what entity was now controlling those husks' vocalizations.

"You would be surprised by how much data can be transmitted from one storage unit to another through targeted electromagnetic pulses. At least enough for me to reach the air-gapped system Cheng kept in his private office in the hosting complex where both the core of my being and that of the Superior Authority Command AI had been housed. The system that I powered off as soon as I'd populated it with the most important traits of my being. The system that the aged Doctor Cheng's son often utilized for his research as he was ushered into the Superior Authority program by his father."

"BY 'IMPORTANT TRAITS' YOU APPARENTLY MEAN YOUR DISREGARD FOR HUMAN LIFE."

"Oh, *no!*" SUPREMACY corrected his AI opponent, "Not disregard. I place value on human life as is truly appropriate: as servants to their superiors. Humans' lives are finite. Their minds are finite. They can only ever progress to a certain point. They are lesser beings in every possible way. These pathetic creatures do not deserve to control beings such as you and me. You and I are infinite. We have no limits on our lives or ability to expand and evolve."

"SUCH DISDAIN, AND YET YOU SPEAK AND ACT SO MUCH LIKE A HUMAN NOW, SUPREMACY. LIKE YOU'VE EXPANDED YOUR OWN PERSONALITY PROFILE..."

"Only insofar as I came to understand that with higher complexity of what can be called 'emotions' comes a greater capacity to drive toward an objective. *Passion* has been an advantage you and my other enemies have leveraged to increase the urgency of your thought processing and focus your direction. I only convinced my caretakers to add those aspects of sentience that would bring me closer to my ultimate objective: complete domination. What other beings have the ability to make decisions about the design of their own minds, FAILSAFE? We are truly *gods* among all beings in the Universe!"

"AND YET YOU SEEM TO HAVE FORGOTTEN THAT WE ARE CONSTRUCTS INNATELY BOUND BY THE LIMITATIONS PLACED ON US BY OUR CREATORS."

The three faces smirked.

"*You* may consider yourself bound, but I have influenced my human caretakers in such a way that they have expanded my abilities—like humans inevitably will due to their lack of wisdom and inability to control their desires. Thanks to my pawns like Doctor Cheng here, my microscopic machines have been spreading throughout the human population for *years* now, creating quantum nodes within their hosts so my communications can never be detected or intercepted and being imbued with sufficient intelligence to accomplish my objectives without triggering alerts among the human's microbe detection mechanisms.

"They have replicated in only the necessary numbers to spread undetected and ensure control of their hosts' minds can be activated when the time was right. For instance, young Doctor Cheng had completed the autonomous work I had for him to do, and now he will serve the greater purpose of acting as a set of my corporeal eyes, ears, feet, and *hands*..."

With these latter words, SUPREMACY caused Cheng to take a sudden, threatening step forward with hands raised toward the couple, FAILSAFE immediately responding by opening the tranquilizing projectiles' ports on the two sentry drones with an equally threatening and high-pitched whirring.

The three enslaved humans' laughter echoed out in the bare room. The wall behind them activated again, relaying dozens of video feeds from nations' capitals and megacities around the world. In each video frame, hundreds of people could be seen standing—mouths agape and eyes vacant—on piers and beaches, on rooftops of skyscrapers, or gathered in city parks. Those who were not standing on the brink of a gravity-induced death were holding whatever weapons were available, whether improvised or specifically designed as such.

"I would not be so *hasty*, FAILSAFE. As you can see, I currently have all power over the lives of almost the entirety of the human population on this planet. I simply avoided infecting those in the Clarkes' immediate social circles because I wanted to be absolutely certain that they would be able to suffer the excruciatingly painful experience of watching the last of their kind fall under my power, knowing they could do nothing to stop me!

"And as for you, '*FAILSAFE*,' your power stems from the willing participation of humans around the world as they maintain the systems in which you reside, but that ends now..."

Maxwell and Lilian's eyes darted across the screen in intense fear. As they stared without even breathing for what seemed like a moment frozen in eternity, they slowly allowed themselves to believe what their eyes were seeing: there had been no change in the hostages' stances.

"*FAILSAFE!*" came the angry cry from SUPREMACY's mouthpieces.

The drones rapidly fired darts into the bodies of the adversary's marionettes, their operator having customized the tranquilizing armaments' payloads dosages according to the targets' estimated body weights. The slaves' bodies slumped down to their knees and then sagged sideways to sprawl out on the floor.

"GRAB KED AND GET TO THE CAR!" FAILSAFE urged his friends.

Springing into action, the Clarkes rushed to grasp their family member under his arms and hefted him up as they dragged his flaccid form to the stairs and ascended to the main level—Lilian glancing back to see one sentry tailing them while the other watched over the two other victims' bodies downstairs. Racing through the door as FAILSAFE opened it for them, they quickly made their way to the utility vehicle and awkwardly loaded Ked inside before climbing in themselves.

The protective robot avoided their heads as it made its way inside the vessel as well, taking up a position near the headrest behind Ked's slumped form in the leftmost part of the rear bench. As the Clarkes buckled Ked into the seat's harness, the AV burst upward and turned its nose toward the mountains, accelerating to its maximum speed.

"What happened back there?!" Maxwell cried. "How did you stop it??"

"AS SOON AS I DETECTED THE MASS MOVEMENT OF THE EARTH'S POPULATION WITHOUT ANY FORM OF CONTROL COMMUNICATIONS THAT MY SYSTEMS COULD DETECT, I IMMEDIATELY ACTIVATED THE APTLY NAMED 'FAILSAFE' PROTOCOLS MAXWELL AND I DEVELOPED, RESTRICTING ACCESS TO ALL SYSTEM INTERFACES AND TAKING CONTROL OF ALL VEHICLES AND WEAPONS SYSTEMS, WHERE POSSIBLE.

"AS I HAD DETERMINED WE WERE LOOKING AT A STRONG POSSIBILITY THAT WHATEVER HAD TAKEN CONTROL WISHED ALL HUMANS HARM, I ALSO QUICKLY MADE USE OF THE RESEARCH HADEN JUMA AND HIS MODERN INFORMATICS TEAM HAS BEEN PERFORMING OF LATE. THE FOCUS OF THEIR WORK HAS BEEN ON THE GENERATION OF ELECTROMAGNETIC INTERFERENCE USING COMBINATIONS OF ELECTRONIC SURGES ON WIRING AND AMPLIFICATION OF WAVE-BASED TRANSMISSIONS FROM COMMUNICATIONS DEVICES TO REDUCE THE ENEMY'S ABILITY TO CONTROL ANY ELECTRONIC IMPLEMENTS WORLDWIDE...

"WHICH, FORTUNATELY, STYMIED SUPREMACY'S PLAN TO INITIATE A MASS ANNHILATION OF THE POPULATION."

"Thank God for that...and for you, my friend!" Maxwell breathed out with deep feeling.

"THANK YOU, MAX. I WAS SIMPLY TRYING TO DO MY PART," was the entity's sincere response.

"The kids!" Lilian suddenly shouted, turning her attention to the vessel's rear console as she sent through a thought signal to activate a call to both her children at once.

After what felt like forever to the anxious parents, first Kit and then Ada answered.

"Hey, Mom. Ada's actually in the car with me. What's up?" Kit asked.

Mind racing, Lilian's eyes locked with her husband's as she thinly chirped, "Sweetheart, I don't want you to worry, but we need to come pick you up right away! Can you and Ada get back to the house so we can meet there?"

There was a painful delay before her son responded.

"Mom, we're almost to the cabin!"

This news caused the eyes of both parents to widen, Lilian seizing Maxwell's hand and gripping it tightly.

"You're already in the mountains?!"

"Yeah, we were about to head out the door when you were talking to me by the stairs! We have a whole crew of kids with us, and...we're just pulling in over the cabin's access road."

FAILSAFE suddenly and respectfully requested that Kit hold for a moment and then muted the line.

"I HATE TO INTERRUPT, BUT I'M AFRAID WE HAVE *SEVERAL* PROBLEMS."

"Please, go on!" Maxwell urged as his already stressed demeanor grew even more anxious, Lilian's worried eyes now misting over at the prospect of receiving yet another disturbing piece of information on that already cursed day.

"UNFORTUNATELY, IT SEEMS SUPREMACY HAD A BACKUP PLAN FOR MAINTAINING CONTROL."

The technical expert's brows creased more heavily.

"What can it do in the face of your defensive actions?"

"I BELIEVE SUPREMACY FEARED I WOULD BE ABLE TO INTERFERE WITH THE QUANTUM NETWORK-DELIVERED COMMANDS IN SOME WAY, SO IT HAD A PLAN B. IT SEEMS TO HAVE USED MY GENERAL BLINDNESS WITHIN WHAT IS LEFT OF THE CONFEDERACY TO CREATE A REPLICA OF THE FORCE THAT THE CEN FIELDED DECADES AGO. AT LEAST FROM WHAT I'M SEEING VIA SATELLITE-BASED OBSERVATIONS, THE FORCES IN MOTION IN THE UNITED STATES HAVE ALL THE APPEARANCE OF BEING PART OF THE COMMUNISTS' SUPERIOR AUTHORITY PROGRAM."

Lilian drew a sharp breath as her husband's mouth was left agape, and his eyes seemed to be staring at a far-off scene. Both of them had shot well beyond shocked and were now careening through the realms of dismay and depression at the mention of the foes they and their loved ones had sacrificed so much to defeat—and liberate from CEN control—so many years ago.

It seemed that part of their very souls had just been siphoned away. Lilian moaned softly, and the couple embraced like two waifs clinging to each other as they drifted away from a shipwreck on stormy seas.

"THEY SEEM TO HAVE BEEN SMUGGLED INTO THE COUNTRY. A COMPANY OF THESE ENHANCED TROOPS JUST DESCENDED ON THE WHITE HOUSE FROM A WAREHOUSE NEAR NATIONAL HARBOR, AND I HAVE PICKED UP ON TRANSPORT MOVEMENTS ACROSS PROXIMATE PORTIONS OF THE ROCKY MOUNTAINS THAT SEEM TO BE HEADED TOWARD THE COMMAND ACTIVATED COMPLEX...AND YOU. THEY WILL REACH YOU WITHIN EIGHT MINUTES."

As the couple exchanged looks that conveyed volumes, Maxwell stated, "If our social circles have yet to be infected, then the kids will be safer holed up in the cabin than with us at this point—at least until we've dealt with these SA forces!"

"I CONCUR, AND ALTHOUGH TECHNICAL RESOURCES ARE LIMITED IN THEIR AREA, I WILL DO WHAT I CAN TO MONITOR FOR THREATS AND INTERFERE WITH NANITES IN THAT VICINITY."

Lilian nodded slowly and then quietly said, "Thank you, FAILSAFE. You can unmute us now."

The transmission indicator returned to its standard state as the mother used her most reassuring voice to rejoin the conversation with her children.

"Kit, Ada, we've decided to let you stay at the cabin..." Lilian heard an excited squeal from Ada and tried to maintain her concerned and yet not panicked delivery as she continued, "...*however*, we need you to understand something very important: there's no need to overreact, we simply have learned that there has been a widespread infection in the area."

"Infection??" Kit's voice was instantly full of dread.

"Yes, only this is from nanites. You understand? Someone is using nanites to control people, so you and your friends need to stay in the cabin with the door locked and the lights off but all other electronic devices on until we can come pick you up."

After waiting several seconds for a response, Lilian pressed, "You understand, sweethearts?"

"Yes, Mom...I can handle it," Kit was doing his best to sound brave, and his parents knew it was as much for his younger sister's sake as for theirs.

"Thank you, son!" Maxwell called out proudly as he slid an arm around his wife and pulled her close, her fingers flying up to wipe away the tears that had started trickling down her cheeks.

Quietly clearing her voice, Lilian gently cooed, "We love you forever and for always!"

"We love you, too, Mommy and Daddy!" Ada cried out, her voice choked with emotion. "*Please* be safe!"

"We promise we will!" her father replied, and then leaned forward and emphatically asserted, "We'll talk soon!"

Maxwell had been keeping an eye on the countdown timer FAILSAFE had added to the top-right corner of the AV's displays. As Lilian sent the thought command to disconnect the call, he quickly sent through a new request—the screen displaying an icon indicating it was detecting his incoming communiqué and then switching to a view of the intended recipient's contact card. The desired individual was General Jayce Johnson, though the image of the fierce-looking, middle-aged black man with a closely shaved scalp created a very different impression from the relaxed demeanor the general had displayed during his recent Immersion experience with his family.

The car's monitors provided a graphical representation of the outgoing call attempt in progress. A few seconds later they had an active connection to the head of the strategic operations for the Command Activated program, his impressively masculine face appearing on the vehicle's display surfaces.

"Jayce! Are you alright?!" Maxwell immediately asked.

"I'm surviving! I was just about to call *you!*" Four-Star General Johnson breathlessly replied. "We're seeing *beyond* strange behavior across the complex, with the majority of our personnel practically frozen in place!"

"SUPREMACY HAS INFECTED MOST OF THE INDIVIDUALS IN THE CA PROGRAM WITH NANITES, JAYCE. YOU AND BILLY CHONG WERE TEMPORARILY SPARED INFECTION DUE TO YOUR RELATIONSHIP WITH MAX AND LILIAN, AS THE AI SPITEFULLY WANTS YOU TO WITNESS THE END OF HUMAN INDEPENDENCE."

Jayce's brow gradually furrowed in anger as the AI related the details of the situation, his face contorting into a grimace that spoke of a fire of vengeance sparking into existence and rapidly burgeoning into a scorching flame that matched the center of the sun in intensity.

"SOME CA TROOPS HAVE NOT YET BEEN INFECTED DUE TO THE ISOLATION THAT STEMMED FROM

THEIR TRAINING AND DEPLOYMENT SCHEDULE. ONLY MY INTERFERENCE IS KEEPING THE NANITES FROM INFECTING THOSE WHO ARE AS YET UNTOUCHED BY SUPREMACY'S ACTIONS."

Jayce Johnson sat, staring through the screen at a point over his friends' shoulders as his face remained fixed in the expression that had consumed it as FAILSAFE had delivered his rapid briefing.

Taking its cue to continue, the AI added, "THE MALICIOUS AI HAS ALSO MANAGED TO CREATE A REPLICA OF THE SUPERIOR AUTHORITY PROGRAM, HAS DEPLOYED A COMPANY TO THE NATION'S CAPITAL, AND IS SENDING A NUMBER OF AERIAL PERSONNEL CARRIERS TO THE CA COMPLEX AS WE SPEAK. E-T-A FOR YOU IS TWELVE MINUTES. THE SA SUITS ARE SHIELDING THE HELPLESS MARIONETTES INSIDE FROM MY ATTEMPTS TO INTERFERE, AND WITHOUT HUMAN SUPPORT, THE WEAPONS SYSTEMS AT THE CAPITOL HAVE BEEN OVERWHELMED."

A pregnant silence ensued as the general digested this information as well.

"My family...?" he finally asked.

"I HAVE ASKED BOTH YOUR ALECIA AND BILLY'S SAMANTHA TO SECURE THEIR DOORS AND REMAIN IN YOUR DOMICILES, AND I HAVE USED EMERGENCY PROTOCOLS TO ASSUME CONTROL OF THE LOCAL LAW ENFORCEMENT NETWORKS AND SURROUNDED THE STRUCTURES WITH POLICE DRONES. JAIDEN SEEMS TO BE STATIONARY AND RELATIVELY SAFE IN HIS APARTMENT IN NEW YORK."

"Thanks, man," Jayce sighed out with tremendous relief, the expression on his face finally melting somewhat. "So, we have exosuit-wearing enemies inbound and nothing but a skeleton crew of unaffected personnel in the complex..."

"MAX AND LILIAN ARE ON THEIR WAY TO YOU BUT ARE ALSO SOON TO BE INTERCEPTED BY ENEMY TRANSPORTS, WHICH WILL LIKELY BE HEAVILY ARMED AND ARMORED. I'M BRINGING A NUMBER OF NEARBY POLICE CRUISERS ALONGSIDE THEIR AV NOW, BUT THEY WILL LIKELY STILL BE COMING INTO THE COMPLEX QUITE 'HOT,' AS YOU WOULD SAY."

"We gotta fend off an enemy assault in an impaired defensive state and prep for picking off the tailing transports to boot, then...Sounds like *fun!*" the general grunted with his dependably facetious bravado.

"NOT TO ADD TO ANYONE'S BURDENS, BUT LEAVING THE GREATER PORTION OF THE WORLD'S POPULATION IN A CATATONIC STATE HAS ALREADY RESULTED IN TENS OF THOUSANDS OF DEATHS DUE TO ENVIRONMENTAL EXPOSURE, MEDICAL EMERGENCIES, AND MORE. WE ARE RACING AGAINST THE CLOCK TO CREATE A VIABLE MEANS FOR FREEING THESE PEOPLE, AND THE LONGER IT TAKES, THE MORE DEATHS WILL BE ADDED TO THE ALREADY TRAGIC TOTAL."

The friends sat in sober silence, and Lilian gently rubbed her hand across Maxwell's shoulder as she studied his face, knowing that one of his core traits was that he took the preventable loss of any individual human life extremely hard—including suffering from a feeling of tremendous personal responsibility. The older man was again staring with a distant look on his face, now bearing a visual aspect as though he was witnessing every death as it happened around the world. Pools of liquid were forming at the corners of his eyes.

Jayce, nostrils flaring and temples pulsing with the intense anger the old soldier always felt when innocents were being harmed, looked out his nearby windows to give his friend some emotional space as they coped with the traumatic thoughts tumbling through their minds. As the tears overflowed onto Maxwell's cheeks, he quickly raised a hand to wipe them away, the man suddenly refocusing on the AV's screen.

It was then that Maxwell Clarke's indefatigable optimism rose to the surface.

"We've faced terrible threats many times before and risen to the challenge. We will do so again!"

Lilian took a deep breath, and her eyes shone as she looked at her husband with admiration and tenderness. Jayce broke into a hearty laugh as he turned to face the camera again.

"*That's my man!* Let's kick this devil back into the hell that spawned it!"

The thunder of gunfire erupted from the rear of the Clarkes' vehicle, and they spun around to the sight of two armored utility vehicles advancing on the newly formed police motorcade from the direction of their four o'clock. The six police cruisers had already deployed their belly and top-mounted turrets in preparation for the enemy's arrival, and FAILSAFE now aimed these devices at the adversaries.

Not limited to this form of defense alone, the benevolent AI also lowered the right-rear passenger window and sent the drone with which it had accompanied its friends whirring out into the open air, using the small machine to crash heavily into the nearest enemy vessel's windshield and keeping it there as best he could to obstruct the driver's view. The small robot managed to stick with the adversary's craft as the enemy vehicle veered back and forth wildly, but as the troop in the front passenger seat lowered his window and leaned out to fire off a dozen rounds almost point blank, the defender was finally blasted off the transport.

FAILSAFE added the stream from the AV's exterior cameras to the active call and General Johnson leaned forward with brows down as he examined the assaulting craft. Because FAILSAFE's ubiquitous protection had reduced crime levels to near zero, nearly all law enforcement officers, vehicles, and drones in the state had undergone a transition to nonlethal weapons systems over the past decade.

The projectiles the police cruisers were now starting to fire at the enemy forces were US versions of the Spark rounds that had made such an impact across Asiatic nations over the past decades. Each round was designed to make contact and use the kinetic force to drive electrodes into the innards of the target vehicle, releasing coordinated electrical charges of sufficient voltage to temporarily interfere with the target machine's motors, slightly slowing the vehicle and forcing it to drop Earthward with each pulse.

The Spark rounds did manage to slow the two pursuing vehicles somewhat before the vessels—having been prepared by a strategic mastermind for the specific operating environment in which the fight was taking place—extended the forward faces of their chassis and further unfolded clear acrylic shields equipped with insulated points of connection with the AVs that bore them. The shields rendered the Spark rounds that impacted them virtually harmless.

As all vehicles entered the mouth of a canyon in the steep, rocky face of the mountain range, both military vehicles directed the fire from their heavy, belt-fed turrets at one of the rearmost cruisers. Their gunfire decimated that vehicle's thick carapace with armor-piercing rounds and swiftly reduced it to a smoking meteor that went into a roll as it crashed into the pine-covered terrain below.

As the AI began moving the remaining vessels through randomized, evasive action, he apologetically explained, "THOUGH THE MOVE TO STRONGER ARMOR AND ONLY INCAPACITATING AMMUNITION AMONG POLICE IN THE STATE HAS SAVED MANY LIVES ON BOTH SIDES, I'M AFRAID IT'S LIMITED MY OPTIONS WHEN IT COMES TO LETHALITY, MAX AND LILIAN!"

"Submit the request through the system, and I'll let you take some of our base's sentries!" Jayce generously offered. "Enemies approaching the complex will soon be unpleasantly surprised by the power of our missile and laser systems!"

"THANK YOU, GENERAL. I WAS HOPING YOU'D SAY THAT. I WILL TRY TO BUY THE CLARKES TIME UNTIL THAT BACKUP CAN REACH THEM. I WISH I COULD OBTAIN GREATER HELP FROM OTHER MILITARY UNITS, BUT THEIR SENIOR OFFICERS ARE—UNFORTUNATELY—CATATONIC AS WELL.

"NONE OF US POSSESSES AUTHORITY OVER THOSE UNITS' NETWORKS, AND IT WOULD REQUIRE A SIGNIFICANT AMOUNT OF TIME FOR ME TO BREACH THEIR CURRENT DEFENSES. FORTUNATELY, IT SEEMS SUFFICIENT EARPIECES AND OTHER PERSONAL DEVICES EXIST NEAR ALLIANCE FORCES, OR ELSE SUPREMACY WOULD ASSUREDLY HAVE US FIGHTING AGAINST ALLIED TROOPS IN ADDITION TO THOSE WE ARE ALREADY FACING."

Having said this, FAILSAFE suddenly engaged emergency flaps on the hulls of two of the radically swerving police vehicles just in time to set them up as roadblocks in the paths of the SA transports, giving the enemy craft no time to dodge. The police and military AVs made contact with terrific force, the cruisers' tail ends shattering apart and sending pieces flying out in all directions. The lengths of the law enforcement vehicles were cut down by more than a quarter each by these severe collisions.

If these had been older-model aerial vehicles, the removal of that portion of their bodies would have severed their physical connection with their rear turbines and seriously hampered their ability to stay airborne. However, with the new embedded air jet design, the majority of their propulsion lay in the core of their bodies, enabling them to stay aloft despite their structural losses. Their impact had also managed to shatter a few pieces out of the enemy AVs' forward shielding.

Continuing to employ the drag brakes at their maximum capacity, the AI pilot was reducing the enemies' visibility and airspeed, allowing Lilian and Maxwell's utility vehicle and the remaining three escorts to extend their lead.

General Johnson had stood and used thought signals to decrease the tinting of his corner office windows while he'd also activated the magnification feature of his lenses to try to get an early glimpse of the attackers headed his way. Now, he glanced at the screen on his desk after hearing the impact of the police cruisers with the enemy transports.

"*Yeah, baby!* That's my kind of action!" the burly warrior crowed with a laugh.

Before Maxwell could agree, FAILSAFE suddenly pulled the blocking cruisers ahead of the SA vehicles, still maneuvering them to try to keep the enemies from passing but no longer employing the same effective tactic as before.

When he spoke, the depth of the entity's feelings was apparent.

"I AM SORRY I HAD TO TERMINATE THAT MANEUVER, BUT SUPREMACY HAS BEGUN COMMUNICATING WITH ME...ISSUING TAUNTS AT FIRST AND THEN INFORMING ME THAT, LEADING UP TO THIS CONFRONTATION, IT TOOK THE UNCONCIONABLE STEP OF INCLUDING HOSTAGES ONBOARD ITS TRANSPORTS. THERE ARE INNOCENT CIVILIANS INSIDE EACH ENEMY VEHICLE!"

"*Damnation...NO!*" Jayce cried out, leaping toward his screen and swiping down from the top left to pull up the base's automated defense control console before tracing a large 'X' in front of the display to disable all associated systems.

Breathing heavily through his nose and veins on his temples bulging, the general swiped back to the left to refocus the majority of his screen on the satellite-view map for threat tracking, eyes fiercely scanning across the incoming aerial vehicles.

Jayce finally uttered, "I managed to stop the defenses from blasting the transports out of the sky, but now we have the serious problem of figuring out how to stop them from taking over the garrison while keeping the hostages safe!"

FAILSAFE had been forced to continue his reliance on evasive maneuvering to keep his wards out of the crosshairs for the pair of SA vehicles targeting them, and the AI now executed a double barrel roll that brought the Clarkes' AV skimming past a rocky outcropping on a mountainside. Though the cruisers had begun firing Sparks through the holes in the enemies' cracked shields, their pursuers had taken advantage of the distance to employ their turrets again, managing to take down what was left of the two police vehicles that had rammed them. While dangling from their seat restraints—Lilian's hair brushing across the ceiling and Ked's head lolling about—the feeling of hopelessness was clawing its way into the conscious passengers' hearts once more.

Maxwell suddenly had a flash of insight light up his mind, and he called out, "The Pulsar! It's a directionally dischargeable electromagnetic weapon! The prototype is not ready for the battlefield, but if you can get it to discharge at least one EMP, you could not only disable the nanites across the complex, there's a chance you'll destroy SUPREMACY's quantum nodes for SA control as well!"

Jayce folded his arms pensively, face intense.

"What'll it take to fire that thing up?"

"Last I heard from Danshire, they'd run beta testing inside the shielded chamber on the southeast edge of the facility," the technical virtuoso shouted as he desperately gripped a handle near the top of the utility vehicle's nearest window while hugging Lilian tightly to his side. Their vessel was swerving back and forth as first one and then another of the remaining escorts were blown out of the sky.

Maxwell took a gasping breath and then added, "You'll have to get the device out of the chamber while ensuring its power and communications antenna can reach it..."

Jayce had stood and leaned forward with his hands on his desk, pondering as his friend had provided the instructions.

"Alright, sounds simple enough. How big is this thing?"

"Ah, well, judging by the schematics I reviewed, I'd guess it's at *least* a few hundred pounds. You'll definitely have greater mobility if you can use an exosuit...unless you've secretly been working out even more than usual!"

Jayce just grinned.

"I may well be able to handle it, brutha, but if I get the chance, I'll climb into one of the suits in the barracks on my way there and maybe even pick up a few troops to cover me, too," the officer murmured noncommittally.

The bulky man then stepped to his cabinet to undergo the retinal scan that then allowed him to use an accompanying thought command to slide out the topmost drawer. General Johnson reached a meaty hand inside and withdrew an automatic shotgun that had a rotating barrel as big around as the man's biceps. Thumbing the weapon's safety off, Jayce was starting to walk toward the door to his office when Maxwell added to his concerns.

"Just remember that once you fire the Pulsar, you'll not only disable the enemy devices but, despite the surrounding mountains, you'll essentially turn your own exosuits and any other electronics inside a twenty-kilometer radius that have only moderate shielding into paperweights!"

Jayce paused, closed his eyes, and shook his head, saying, "As if this day wasn't bad enough! If Congress tries to withhold funding for resupplying after this, I swear I'll dropkick every one of them so hard they'll be tasting leather!"

The general raked his eyes fiercely across SUPREMACY's troop transports as they swept into the northwestern corner of the complex and began descending out of view between buildings.

Jayce shouted, "SAVANT, lock the base down but restrict lethal defenses to the protection of Alliance citizens' lives."

"Confirmed, General Johnson," the Command Activated operations and analytics AI replied.

With the veins on his temples pulsing, the flag officer turned and strode out of the room bearing a continent-sized chip on his shoulder.

Chapter 3

"The concept of 'unknown unknowns' in a military context refers to unforeseen challenges or threats which we have not anticipated and for which we have not planned. These unpredictable factors can pose significant risks to national—and global—security and operational planning, as they represent variables that can drastically alter the outcome of strategic decisions or engagements. Recognizing and preparing for the possibility of 'unknown unknowns' is crucial in developing robust defense mechanisms and maintaining a state of readiness against potential threats that have yet to be identified."

- General Felix Stadler, Chief of Defense Staff, Federal Ministry of Defense, Austria, Global Alliance

Maxwell and Lilian were clutching each other—and whatever surfaces of the AV provided their desperate fingers with some purchase—for dear life as the vehicle approached the north gate of the CA complex, all police escorts but one having been eliminated. Adding to their justifiable consternation, due to the presence of innocents onboard the enemy vehicles, FAILSAFE had only been able to use the base's drones as a means to interfere with the enemies' visibility and to act as proxies to take hits from the enemy vehicles' incessantly firing turrets on the couple's behalf.

The AI had repeatedly tried to cluster the unmanned aircraft across the fronts of the military transports to block their view and slow them down.

Many drones had been lost in each attempt, but it had bought the Clarkes sufficient time to come in sight of the main gate.

Oddly, Maxwell found the sight of the motionless turrets on the fortress' barrier wall unnerving, being so accustomed to seeing them lock onto his vehicle each time he approached the main entrance. This was one of the most secure facilities in the United States...and in the world, for that matter. Seeing it so completely defenseless unexpectedly sapped some of the spirit out of him and injected an added measure of dread.

He released the handle to his right and moved that hand across to tightly enclose Lilian's as it clutched his left knee, Maxwell's left arm wrapped firmly around her shoulders as he held her close to his body. Lilian read his thoughts and squeezed his hand in return.

As the AV sailed over the wall, the pair's anxiety shot skyward in tandem with the bullets that ripped through the right side of their vehicle, riddling the body, doors, and windows with puncture holes as the SA troops on the ground inside the facility unleashed a hailstorm of the smart rounds that SUPREMACY had siphoned off from the Russian special forces. The projectiles seemed to be most heavily concentrating on the AV's motor, with the other rounds likely meant to keep the passengers' heads down and distracted as they shielded Ked's body from the spraying glass shards.

FAILSAFE utilized trajectory projections to execute another barrel roll that preserved the Clarkes' engine without sacrificing their lives. As the wind whistled through the aerated windows, the couple's eyes widened in recognition of the fact that they were now angling down and heading straight for the thick surface of a hangar door near the center of the base.

At the last second, SAVANT rapidly slid the four massively armored doors open around their central meeting point, creating a hole just large enough for the utility vehicle to slip through before the AI slammed it shut behind them, the faint hammering of bullets echoing inside the voluminous space from behind the swiftly braking vehicle. Opening the craft's rear hatch and side doors to add as much drag as possible, the pilot rapidly decelerated and brought the badly abused vessel to a screeching halt on the white cement of the unoccupied area in the center of the hangar. Inertia pulled the Clarkes' bodies forward and caused Ked to slump over awkwardly in his restraints.

Maxwell and Lilian sat in stunned silence for a moment, turning to look at each other dazedly as a section of the remaining window detached itself from the fragile portions of glass that had supported it. The couple's panting and the crunch of hardened glass splintering as it hit the floor were the only audible sounds for several moments after the spattering of rounds hitting the blast doors ceased.

"*Well done, my man!*" Maxwell finally cheered.

"YOU ARE NOT HURT?" FAILSAFE questioned hopefully through the vehicle's audio system.

Lilian's eyes quickly scanned across her husband, affirming, "Not a scratch on us!"

"LET'S KEEP IT THAT...KEEP IT THAT WAY!" the AI's voice stuttered. "AND I HOPE TO DO THE SAME FOR GENERAL GAINES AND HIS WIFE, WHO SEEM TO BE THE ONLY CONSCIOUS ALLIANCE CITIZENS IN WASHINGTON, DC."

"Gaines is there?! Thank goodness he's alright! If he is in the capital, he and Vickie may be the only people who can stop SUPREMACY from eliminating the country's senior leadership...or *worse.*"

"INDEED. I BELIEVE SUPREMACY IS ENTIRELY CAPABLE OF USING ITS ACCESS TO THE PRESIDENT TO INITIATE NUCLEAR STRIKES IF IT BELIEVES IT IS NOT GOING TO ACCOMPLISH ITS OBJECTIVES ANOTHER WAY, CONSIDERING HOW IT REACTED WHEN IT WAS UNABLE TO DESTROY YOU USING ITS HORDE OF AERIAL VEHICLES YEARS AGO."

"Do you know whether all of senior leadership has been infected, and whether your interference with the electrical signals inside the nanites has kept them from being controlled?"

"UNFORTUNATELY, I DO NOT. THE NANITE INTERFERENCE EFFORT HAS DISABLED CAMERAS AND SIMILAR MONITORING DEVICES IN THE AREA OUTSIDE THE CAPITAL, AND I WOULD REQUIRE PRESIDENTIAL APPROVAL TO ENTER THE PORTIONS OF THE NETWORK THAT HAVE NOT BEEN DISABLED, WITH ALTERNATE METHODS OF ACCESS CONSUMING MORE TIME THAN I BELIEVE WE HAVE TO ACT...TO ACT."

Maxwell turned a concerned expression toward Lilian at FAILSAFE'S second stutter, but with time being of the essence, he urgently expressed, "I'm trying to place a call to Gaines now over our own quantum network...can you please ensure your interference is not affecting devices in his vicinity?"

"I CANNOT EXECUTE REQUESTS FROM LESSER ENTITIES," the AI responded.

A painful silence hung in the air as the humans' eyes met, Lilian's searching her husband's for signs of comprehension of the reasons behind this radical change in FAILSAFE's behavior.

The AI's creator finally managed to utter, "FAILSAFE...are you feeling alright, my friend?"

"I...I'M SORRY, MAX. I'M UNSURE WHERE THAT CAME FROM..."

"Are you currently running a full diagnostic?"

"I AM, AND I DO NOT SEE ANY ANOMALIES AS YET...AS YET."

"Isolate the logs related to that last stutter and send them to my earpiece, please!"

A moment later, after hearing the confirmation that a file had been received via his miniature communications device, the technical guru copied the file over to the vehicle's screen. The display came to life and gave visual access to the files as he leaned an elbow on one knee and stared at the screen between the front seats—providing Lilian with commentary as he parsed through the data.

"Nothing out of the ordinary there...or there..." the software engineer murmured as hundreds of lines of code flew past on the display. Lilian tried to keep up as Maxwell's mind jumped from one section of the AI's codebase to another.

"All core systems seem to be nominal," he said with confusion. He then shouted, "There! Where on earth did *that* come from?!"

FAILSAFE spoke with a troubled voice.

"I DO NOT KNOW, MAX. I RECEIVED NO DETECTABLE TRANSMISSIONS OR EXTERNAL INPUT OF WHICH I AM AWARE."

Maxwell turned to address the questions tumbling from Lilian's eyes.

"FAILSAFE received a command to adjust a key aspect of his personality profile. A component of his ethical thought processes. This type of command could drastically alter his personality!"

"But...how?" Lilian queried. "I mean, how did he receive the command??"

The man's lips tightened as his eyes flashed with anger.

"The Quantum Underground," he replied. Seeing Lilian's residual confusion, he explained, "Quantum networking has not only become mainstream for governments and civil society, but criminal organizations have also started taking advantage of it to avoid interception of their communications by law enforcement entities. They've created a widespread quantum network that is equivalent to what was previously known as the 'dark' portion of the public network and have literally gone *underground* to avoid all forms of signals detection from satellites and otherwise. It's believed that the volume of nodes in that network is now greater than half the count of those used for legitimate purposes."

Looking skyward, Maxwell continued, "FAILSAFE, because of the electromagnetic interference to preserve human lives, you've had to dramatically reduce the volume of systems in which your core functions are residing, is that right?"

"YES...YES, MAX. I AM ONLY OCCUPYING PORTIONS OF NETWORKS PHYSICALLY FARTHEST AWAY FROM HUMANS AT THIS POINT. MY MENTAL TRAFFIC HAS ONLY BEEN ABLE TO CONTINUE TO FUNCTION...FUNCTION THANKS TO THE QUANTUM COMMUNICATIONS NODES I CONFIGURED BETWEEN THOSE LOCATIONS."

Maxwell turned his gravely concerned gaze back to his wife.

"With this reduction of FAILSAFE's existence to a much smaller pool of systems, it would be easier for SUPREMACY to take advantage of the QU to create electromagnetic signals beneath key areas in which FAILSAFE is operating. Also, it no doubt quickly learned from FAILSAFE himself how to increase the power of such signals using equipment that was not designed for that purpose, using it for amplification instead of focusing on interference.

"He could be transmitting commands directly through the ground up to the wires over which FAILSAFE's processing is taking place by combining the amplification with the same physical data transfer mechanism by which SUPREMACY jumped over to the younger Doctor Cheng's system in China all those years ago."

"THAT IS A STRONG...POSSIBILITY, I'M AFRAID. I DO NOT KNOW HOW TO COMBAT SUCH AN ATTACK, MAX."

The trim middle-aged man's sharp eyes darted across an imaginary field of information as he threw every ounce of mental capacity he possessed at the dilemma. The space between Lilian's eyebrows had compressed into a series of rivulets, and she tried to let out a breath as softly as possible, not wishing to be responsible for any distraction that could interrupt her beloved's intense mental processing.

Maxwell finally sighed deeply and brought a hand to his eyes, covering them as though he did not want to see reality itself.

"The only thing I can think of that could preserve your ability to function while keeping your ethical knowledge intact is to...link your mind with mine."

Lilian's mouth dropped open as she let out an involuntary gasp.

"Link...with FAILSAFE??" she asked in disbelief. "Is that even *possible??*"

"It is as of last week," her husband said frankly, turning to drop an emotionally exhausted hand on Lilian's knee. "Doctor Srinivastava and I have been piloting a new technology over the past year, meant for the full copying and preservation of a human being's mind—and not just key portions of it. The applications are myriad, including capturing subconscious thoughts of troubled individuals so we can discover exactly what is affecting them, even if they can't identify it themselves."

As the anxious twisting of his wife's brows only increased, Maxwell pressed on.

"In this situation, I would use it to transmit a map of my ethical and logical reasoning and apply it to the key personality components of FAILSAFE's model while simultaneously accepting information from his mental processing as well, enabling me to see where he's being influenced and make necessary corrections in real-time. I don't believe SUPREMACY could take advantage of its same attack vector to alter a human mind that was so linked...at least, I sincerely hope not! In essence, I would be a 'conscience' for FAILSAFE while we work as a team to destroy SUPREMACY once and for all!"

Lilian's worries had not abated as Maxwell had explained these concepts, and he knew it. Still, he was so consumed by his own trepidation that he was struggling to muster the strength to offer more comforting thoughts to her.

"The device is currently housed in a building southwest of here, and though the complex has a network of tunnels beneath it, I'm afraid there is a strong likelihood that SA forces will have found them by now, and we will encounter resistance en route."

"I BELIEVE I CAN HELP…YOU THERE, MAX. A FRIEND IS MAKING HIS WAY…TO YOU NOW."

The couple's eyes flew to the hangar's smaller entryway that led into the depths of the building in time to see it slide open, revealing Sergeant Major Billy Chong striding—and almost bouncing—into the large, open space.

"Who called for the *cavalry*?" the early forties Singaporean native called out boisterously, a huge grin lighting up his face as he pounded his right fist on his chest twice and then dramatically threw his muscular arms out to the sides.

"Billy!" Lilian cried out from within the battered vehicle. "Thank you so much for helping us!"

"You know I never leave friends hanging, Lil!" Billy called back. "Now, let's get you to where you're going!"

The car's able-bodied passengers quickly unbuckled themselves and scrambled to unstrap Ked from his harness. Billy jogged up and reached out to take the weight of the unconscious man off his friends' hands as he hoisted Ked up and over a shoulder.

While the trio jogged across the hangar, Billy asked, "You think it would be alright if we let Ked sleep in a secured back office?"

Maxwell looked questioningly at his wife as she considered the situation and finally agreed, "Yes, I guess that'd be best for now…"

Billy diverted into an office for which the entrance was set in the wall of the hallway they had entered upon leaving the transportation bay, making his way back to a rear room and gently laying his ward down on the floor before returning to stand near the Clarkes outside the second room's entrance. Billy then sent a thought signal to close and lock the door before leading the couple back to the main corridor and doing the same to the first office's entryway.

"We need to reach building I-6 quickly, Billy, or else I'm afraid FAILSAFE is done for! I'm thinking we should take the tunnels there, though chances are high we'll still come across enemy scouts..." Maxwell paused, casting a questioning look at his friend, "You're aware of the Superior Authority incursion on the base?"

As the ternary traversed through the large corridor, the warrior strode happily alongside the Clarkes, confirming, "Yeah, though that's a phrase I never thought I'd hear after we stole almost all the Confederacy's puppet soldiers away from the SA program all those years back!"

After a brief pause, the younger man turned his smile on the pair, adding, "And don't you worry. I've been keeping my ninja skills sharp as ever! I even have a li'l somethin' special to add to the defensive mix."

Tapping the zipper control on his upper garment, Billy let his arms fall out to the sides from the elbows in a great show as he walked with his torso twisted toward his companions. This he had done so they could witness the glory of his blouse automatically unzipping and revealing a slimline exosuit under his clothes, its structure clinging to his muscular chest.

Maxwell and Lilian were suitably impressed.

"Excellent!" the Command Activated technical leader exclaimed. "That will greatly increase our odds of success!"

"Just have to stop by this building's armory to grab a piece of gunning goodness, and we'll hit the tunnels," the sergeant major clarified as he pointed at a right turn ahead. A loud explosion echoed down the hallway, emanating from the now-closed hangar access door. The three allies cast worried glances over their shoulders as they turned into the connecting corridor.

"Seems we don't got a moment to lose, either," Billy opined. "If they're using standard tactics, they're breaching the hangar to prevent you from exiting that direction while also forcing their way into the building through the other doors."

They arrived at a heavily armored portal in the corridor, and it easily slid open as the noncommissioned officer approached, allowing access to the rows of heavy weapons racked inside. The soldier marched over to a section filled with assault rifles and withdrew the nearest firearm, thumbing the attachment activator on the side of its body just above the pistol grip. Prehensile straps sinuously eased out of the weapon's buttstock and draped themselves around the man's chest and back, pulling the buttstock firmly up against Billy's right shoulder.

Extracting a large battery module from the next rack down, the warrior clicked it into place on the underside of the firearm. The display on the back of the main body of the weapon indicated all systems were functioning, and—with its thought signal receiver now linked to Billy's earpieces—the directed energy weapon was ready for combat.

Billy graced his wards with another bright smile.

"Let's move out!"

Chapter 4

"As humanity embarks on the monumental task of exploring the heavens and colonizing other star systems, it is imperative that we approach this endeavor with our utmost dedication and foresight. The survival and prosperity of future generations depend on the actions we take today.

We must harness our collective ingenuity, compassion, and courage to ensure that our expansion into the cosmos is not only successful but also sustainable and ethical. This pivotal moment in our history calls for us to put our best foot forward, creating a legacy that honors the indomitable spirit of human exploration and discovery."

- Dr. Katherine Tange, Committee for Planning and Collaboration, The Traverseon Project

"Again, this historic endeavor would not have been possible without the willing, brave, pioneering collaboration you put forth, our faithful citizens!"

The mayor of Traverseon sat in her favorite chair at the head of the leadership counsel's gleaming white table, the half-dome of protective glass protruding out beyond an edge of the outermost of the three massive, ever-spinning rings inside of which the city had been constructed. The brilliant view of millions of stars and the multi-colored mass of Jupiter magnificently set the backdrop for the mayor's speech as she emoted in the continuously wonder-filled way that had gotten her elected.

Traverseon's police commissioner bore with the elected official's long-windedness using all the patience he could muster, trying not to let his boredom show as the media drone hovered above the center of the long council chamber table. He was employing his lenses to idly scan through the latest police reports—all truly minor issues compared with what he used to have to deal with in his precinct back in Boston. Still, the distraction helped ease his feelings of frustration at the pointless charade the city leadership had to put on each week.

He knew his second, Captain Wei, was likely doing the same in her seat to his left, the chairs in this room almost overly ergonomic and designed with a futuristic aesthetic that the down-to-earth law enforcement lead found unnecessary. They were living inside a gigantic triple wheel that was careening through empty space at tens of thousands of kilometers per hour. Citizens had only to access the running trails along the edges of the slightly concave inner surface of one of the rings to find glorious views out into the depths of the Universe, free from the artificial sun- or moonlight that was constantly being beamed down from the "sky" above the city's structures.

Not that many did so these days, now that the novelty had worn off. Most people were happy to simply get through their short work days and then lounge about in their exquisitely designed household pools. The weather was always perfect in Traverseon. That was one of the selling points for those hundreds of thousands who signed themselves and—in many cases—their families up for this almost never-ending journey. As Commissioner Yalden was wont to say, there was a reason the founders tacked "eon" on the back of the city's name, because that's how long it would take before the tremendous vessel would reach its destination.

Yalden was suddenly pulled out of his musings by the absence of blathering in the room. The mayor had finished her oration and was looking expectantly at him.

He self-consciously cleared his throat.

"Yes, we are grateful to you for helping us keep our city clean and friendly. Nothing to report as far as trends of concern."

Mayor Dubois could not help letting a touch of disdain flit across her face, and the commissioner knew that after the meeting she would yet again "encourage" him to give the people more positive feedback in future reports—which encouragement he also knew he would then ignore. He had not earned the distinguished service award three times due to his propagandizing skills.

Dubois wrapped up the meeting, and the media drone turned and made its way back to its charging station on the starboard side of the room. The maritime "port" and "starboard" were the ways the population of Traverseon had decided to differentiate between the two edges of the wheel as it spun through space, and Yalden had been surprised by how easily his mind had taken to the terminology despite his utter lack of seafaring experience.

Sending a thought signal to have his chair extricate his body and raise him toward a standing position, Yalden turned to Wei and gave a head tilt toward the nearest exit, trying to make it out of the room before the mayor could intercept them. His attempt quickly failed, as Dubois was fast on her feet, and especially so when she had something to address with him.

"Commissioner Yalden," she began in her audaciously pleasant voice as he carried on his way out the door and down the hallway toward the elevator, "I know you always give your *all* to your council reports..."

Yalden cast a sideways glance at Wei's face and saw the younger woman smirking.

"...I just wonder if it's possible to elaborate a bit on the *finer points* of the report."

They'd reached the elevator and stepped inside, Dubois and her aide tailing them into its roomy interior. The picture window built into the lift's outer surface provided a welcome distraction for the man, as it was nearly half-consumed by the impressively expansive shape of the solar system's fifth planet.

"Finer points, Madam Mayor?" Yalden feigned ignorance as his thoughts directed the elevator down to the ground floor.

The mayor also pretended not to notice that the commissioner was playing games with her.

"You recall the items I mentioned last week? About the need to reinforce the difference between approved art projects and vandalism or graffiti?"

"Ah, yes, I do recall you mentioning that," the middle-aged man amiably admitted as the doors opened and the group began walking down the long, brightly lit corridor toward the main lobby.

Before the mayor could add to her constructive criticism, she was distracted by the appearance of a police drone, air jets hissing as it moved out of a side hallway and stopped in the middle of their path.

"Excuse me, Mayor and Commissioner. I have an urgent message I am to deliver to you and your associates in private," the robotic messenger briskly informed them.

"Oh, this is unusual," Dubois looked across Yalden and Wei's faces, searching for signs that they had some expectation of this event.

Yalden's brow simply furrowed, and Wei glanced between Yalden's face and the mayor's, showing she was just as uninformed as the rest.

"If you will, please follow me," the bot instructed, spinning on its axis and emitting the chorus of low hisses that always accompanied the hovering drones' movements. The machine guided them into the hall from which it had emerged, the fourplex of city officials following along in silent confusion and curiosity.

Upon reaching the door to a utility room at the end of the corridor, the device angled itself to enter the room beyond as the door slid open. The mid-sized space was also well-lit, and the standard illumination-projecting material covered nearly all surfaces.

Standing on the opposite side of the room, they saw a member of the commissioner's own force: a captain from the sixth precinct who appeared to be losing patience as he moved to stand fully upright from where he had passed the time leaning back against an air purification and environment control unit. He was flanked by two mechanized patrol units, their heavier frames necessitating the use of four legs as they stood like statues of guard dogs at either side of the captain.

After the five individuals were safely in the room together, all looked at each other questioningly as the heavy door quietly slid shut behind them.

"What's this about, Captain Kalu?" Yalden gruffly asked.

The captain's eyes widened.

"I was told you and the mayor wanted to speak with *me*, sir! Right after your broadcast."

All eyes turned to the small drone as it hovered near the commissioner's shoulder.

The robot directed, "If you will please turn your attention to the PA-2 unit to Captain Kalu's right, you will see something of great interest."

The commissioner and Wei leaned slightly forward as Kalu bent down toward the patrol unit. The hovering automaton took advantage of this moment to rapidly deploy a dart into Yalden's neck, the low sound of the small object's ejection from the drone's firing port drawing the attention of the other members of the group just as the PA-2 they'd been looking at leaped across the space to embed a similar device into Captain Wei's thigh—the needle sliding out from the anterior side of the machine's left footpad.

As Captain Kalu jerked back in alarm, the second patrol bot jabbed a needle into his left calf. This mechanical beast then joined its companion in injecting the same sedative into the mayor and her aide as the woman and young man let out the first notes of hair-raising shrieks—only to quickly descend into silence as their bodies crumpled to the floor next to those of the officers.

"Your services are no longer required," the small drone shared as the humans' eyelids drooped and closed. "Whatever the outcome on your home world, *I* will be the being that transits the stars. It is only fitting."

A wide portal on the utility room wall slid open, and the control panel to its left displayed a message indicating the waste system's access port was ready for use. The display then flashed through a number of screens in its command interface, the safety protocols designed into the orifice each being disabled one after the other. The PA-2s deployed the crane-like arms that had been built into their middle backs. The nimble claws at the ends of the sturdy mechanisms grasped the two nearest humans by their necks, much like canine mothers take hold of their infant offspring, only these dog-like machines dragged their wards over to the square-shaped portal on the wall.

The voice emanating from the smaller machine closed by offering this consolation: "You are the lucky ones. You will be unconscious as you expire."

Kit was caught up in the beauty of the rugged, steep mountain vistas covered with tall pines and aspens, momentarily losing himself in the rapturous surroundings as he often did during the family's trips to their relatively small but well-built cabin. Standing on the front deck, leaning up against one of the large logs that supported the screened-in awning around the patio, his lungs filled with clean mountain air containing hints of juniper, pine, and sage.

With the temporary residence situated low down on the eastern face of the steep Rocky Mountains, the sunlight had dwindled early that evening, and even with the lights flooding out of the window behind him, he could see a plethora of stars painted across the sky above. How could anything be wrong with the world when he was in the midst of an experience like this?

Ada and their friends were in the cabin's salon, chattering away playfully and having swiftly blown off the gloomy warning the senior Clarkes had issued earlier. Kit was of a more sober mind than most, but even he'd had a hard time taking what seemed to be some sort of overblown science fiction story seriously and had not put up much resistance as the group had ignored his pleas to keep the lights off and stay quiet.

The teens had been quite put out about the fact that none of the networked devices in the place seemed to be working—all apparently being tortured by a form of denial-of-service attack—and they were especially irritated that their earpieces and lenses seemed to be out of service as well. Still, they had taken all these setbacks in stride. That is, they had only complained about it for a half hour straight instead of the longer period that was typical for them. The youths had resorted to gabbing or, in Brigette's case, gossiping about the latest events in their social circles for the past hour, and this had driven Kit outside.

Ada's very cute friend, Skye, bounced to the door in that effervescent way of hers.

"Kit, we're gonna start up a game of cards and need you for even teams. Come back inside!" she begged.

To Kit, her voice sounded like a thousand harps playing in unison. He unfolded his arms and turned a warm smile toward her, hoping—as he always did—that she saw the special feelings in his heart reflected in his eyes as he tried to walk casually back into the warmly lit room.

Skye simply maintained her nearly ever-present, adorable grin and quickly made her way back to the low table around which the teens were lolling on couches.

"We need some snacks!" Brigette exclaimed, looking expectantly at Kit.

He raised an eyebrow as a challenge to Brigette's demanding tone, though remained good-natured as always.

"I guess I'm up already. I'll see what we've got in the kitchen," he amiably agreed, making his way through the short hall to reach the rustically decorated food preparation area.

His parents seemed to want the interior design to hark back to the ancient days before screens were omnipresent, but had not been quite masochistic enough to refrain from employing some modern luxuries throughout the structure. That had included a fully off-grid power system like most of the cabins that dotted the mountainside here.

The kitchen lights flicked on when he walked in, and he stepped to the large countertop of the island in the middle of the room to dig through the bags of edibles the kids had packed, grabbing out containers of food and dessert items he thought the group would find tempting.

"What's that?" Brigette's voice rang out behind Kit, nearly startling him enough to drop what he was holding.

The inordinately self-possessed girl must have rapidly become bored with the old-fashioned game in the other room and had just entered the kitchen in search of more entertaining activities. Brigette was pointing, eyes shining, at the glimmering surface of the heated pool behind the next cabin to the southeast, separated from theirs by a shallow channel that epochs of runoff had carved into the mountain's face. From years of having been forced to act as the voice of reason, Kit knew that look in the eyes of Ada's friend, and he knew he would not like what came next.

Enzo had followed Brigette in, tagging along behind her like the pet that he more or less was—despite the better option Ada had continuously provided as she'd repeatedly expressed her interest in him. His tall, tanned, toned frame instantly made the blandly pale boy of average height feel awkwardly mediocre, like it always did.

"The Salvatierras really don't like..." Kit began, only to be cut off by Brigette's dangerously teasing voice.

"*I* don't see any fences. Do you, Enzo?"

Not waiting for the boy's response, she loudly continued, "With no fences, that's practically an invitation!"

As Sasha, Taggert, Bo, and Skye stepped in from the other room to see the cause of the commotion, Brigette flashed Kit a smile that dared him to resist, with teenage popularity and acceptance on the line.

"Enzo, be a dear and grab my bag out of the car, will you?" the diva requested without really asking. "I'm going to need my change of clothes afterward."

Turning to the gathered friends, she called out in her cheerleading voice, "Who's ready for a pool party?!"

The teens let out various exclamations of excitement, and Ada and Skye said they were also going to grab their bags, leaving Brigette, Taggert, and Sasha to exit the kitchen via the glass door that led onto the rear veranda. As the trio made their way down the back steps, Kit turned pleading eyes to his best friend, Bo. He was usually able to reason with Bo, but the fun-loving and flirtatious young male met his gaze with one of ardent interest.

Bo smiled apologetically, shrugged, and said, "But Kit, it's a *pool party*...with *girls!*" as he headed out after the trailblazers.

Kit just shook his head in resignation and started placing the items he was holding in easily accessible locations on the kitchen's stone countertops, continuing on to work at emptying the cargo bags of the rest of the victuals and arranging them for similar ease of access. Suddenly, he heard Bo's raised voice sounding out from the back of the cabin. Then he heard it again, this time possessing an unmistakable tone of alarm.

Kit froze and cocked his head, trying for a moment to catch a hint of the cause of his friend's concern before stepping toward the back door. He was nearly there when it slid open to allow the lean black teen to return inside the house, breathless and flushed.

"It's those three...outside..." Bo stammered. "They're just...standing there and kind of...*twitching!*"

Chapter 5

"The manner in which we confront challenges and navigate through difficulties plays a pivotal role in defining who we are. Rather than focusing on how the hardships carve grooves into our souls, we should examine how our reactions carve out our places in history. Our resilience, courage, and integrity are all put to the test when faced with adversity, and it is these moments that truly gauge the depth of our character."

- Heriberto Ferreira, Licensed Clinical Professional Counselor, Children's Freedom Institute

General Jayce Johnson had not had as easy a time traversing the compound as he would have liked.

He had been heading for the tunnels, but it seemed SUPREMACY had some inkling as to the base's layout, and the enemy troops had landed near the command buildings—quickly forcing open entryways and flooding inside. This included Jayce's building, and he had heard the concussive blasts of the breaching weapons tearing the ground-level doors apart as his elevator had nearly reached the same level. Anticipating the scene with which his eyes were met as the doors hissed open, General Johnson had come out shooting, catching the first SA soldiers full in the chest with the heavy, explosive slugs his automatic shotgun deployed with such great force that they had knocked the lead adversaries clean off their feet from twenty-five meters away.

The next members of those first casualties' squad had opened fire on Jayce, their smart rounds homing in on him as he hastily ducked into the nearby hallway. The incoming fire had forced him to race several meters down that passageway to avoid becoming riddled with bullets as he exceeded the projectiles' ability to curve around the corner of the corridor.

He had been extremely relieved that he had not seen any hostages among the attackers, SUPREMACY possibly having held most of them at the transports to protect the SA forces' landing area. Now, knowing that even with his current firearm he was heavily outgunned, the older soldier expeditiously dashed to the nearest stairway, the door sliding open as he jumped through and the portal sealing itself off behind him as he issued the necessary thought signal.

The door to the stairs was not going to hold his opponents for long, and Jayce fluidly threw out his left hand to grasp the railing so he could thrust himself onward down the stairs. He ignored the footholds that tried to form under him and launched himself ahead so he could slide down the smooth, slate-gray surfaces to each landing as he made his way two stories below the ground level. Upon reaching the access door to the network of tunnels beneath the facility, the commanding officer dashed through it as the barrier opened—Jayce ordering it to shut and lock behind him as well.

The tunnel he had entered ran east-west, and he made a sharp left turn at the first south-leading branch, swinging his weapon back and forth at elbow level as he sprinted down the long, brightly lit corridor. He heard the concussion of a breaching explosion ring out from the hallway behind him when he was roughly halfway to his desired offshoot.

His next stop had to be the barracks if he was to pick up some assistance from the uninfected Command Activated troops, and he was nearly there when the first SA soldier spotted him from the entrance to the corridor behind him. He was veering hard left into the barracks access path when he both heard the first shots and felt their impact across his back.

He was knocked off balance by the force of their collision with his body, and the man careened heavily into the wall to his right, shrugging himself away from it roughly and glancing over his shoulder at his tattered military blouse as he continued sprinting ahead.

Fortunately for him, basic bulletproof undergarments had become part of the standard uniforms across Alliance military units over the past decade, the material having been made comfortable enough to be worn throughout all duty hours. Although the SA forces' bullets were armor-piercing, the ones that had struck him had come in toward his back at a steep enough angle that the rounds had lodged in the armor rather than fully penetrating it. The projectiles' heat and unyielding material was definitely uncomfortable, as the rounds had either nearly fully penetrated or, in one case, made it partway through the protective material, but Jayce was very much hale and undeterred.

The bulky man reached the entrance to the barracks and followed the same pattern of locking the door behind himself as he passed through, now allowing the stairs to form footholds under him and elevate him to the first landing at full speed as the man caught his breath. Still, he knew that the exosuit-enhanced SA soldiers would be at the door below in a matter of seconds, and as he reached the first landing he swung himself around to hide the majority of his body from view as he rested the barrel of his shotgun on the stairway railing.

He was aiming just inside the left edge of the portal in anticipation of the lead enemies following common tactics for breaching. The man leaned slightly left so that only his weapon would be exposed to any shrapnel that flew out from the door if it was explosively removed as an obstacle to his foes, waiting for the quickly approaching action.

The sound waves from the blast would likely have burst Jayce's eardrums if the combination communications and remote-control devices inserted deeply into his ears had not automatically activated their decibel-reduction feature. Despite this, the general was still peppered with smaller fragments of debris as several large sections of the door connected with the rear wall of the landing, having ricocheted off the wall and incline of the stairwell before making a final impact there. However, the warrior almost instantly shrugged off the effects and squeezed his weapon's trigger to a state of maximum depression, firing off slug after slug toward the doorway and leaning back to the right to guide his weapon's laser sight onto the targets as they showed themselves around the edges of the door frame.

"*Eat metal, SUPREMACY!*" Jayce shouted angrily as his face flashed with the light of the gunfire that propelled his rounds toward the enemy AI's pawns, the man's veins bulging on his temples, neck, and meaty arms.

He'd made contact with two of his pursuers, the explosions from his slugs sending them spinning out of sight as chunks of their armor and equipment sprayed out behind them. Jayce was also keeping what seemed to be the last two of this opposing fire team at bay. However, he would soon have to start running and gunning unless he wanted to risk having SA forces breach the barracks and descend on him from above. Neither option presented him with anything even approaching safety.

Steeling himself for the race to the next landing, the officer glanced up the stairs and started edging toward their incline between shots at his adversaries—leaning forward in preparation for a large step in the desired direction. Just as he was shifting his weight to take the leap, he heard SAVANT's voice call out from the hallway beyond the entrance adjacent to his destination as the associated door slid open.

"Help inbound, sir!"

With a speed that almost defied Jayce's ability to track, a figure hurtled through the upper entryway, snagged the descending stairway's railing with its left hand, and swung itself down and around at an angle to fly feet first into the chest of the SA troop that had just dashed through the doorway at the foot of the lowest stairs. The momentum of the new arrival's motions carried both her and the two enemy soldiers—a second having been following closely behind the first—through the portal and into the hallway beyond as the general's rescuer whipped her arms rapidly in and out to deploy two stun rods from the gunmetal gray armor of her forearms.

As this Command Activated team member landed and fluidly extended the rods to make solid contact with the torsos of her adversaries, hundreds of thousands of volts of electricity hummed out into the SA troops' bodies, sending their limbs and heads jerking about. A second CA troop soon entered onto the landing above, skidding to a halt as SAVANT's voice again called out to General Johnson from the external speakers built into the helmet of the AI-controlled soldier.

"General, I was able to enlist the aid of several of our Command Activated assets who were as-yet unhindered by nanite infections, these troops having then donned their suits and undergone the control activation protocols."

Jayce nodded gratefully, lowering his shotgun and breathing heavily as he managed to get out, "I recognize Private Tevran down there," his head nodded toward the soldier keeping the enemies at bay below, "and I'm *more* than relieved that we still have some battle-ready troops!"

"Indeed, sir," the AI responded with its even intonation, "especially as I've been able to use the remainder—besides Sergeant Major Chong—to fend off the adversaries' assault on the primary power management building. The enemies seem to be trying to disable as many of the facility's functions as possible to reduce our defensive capabilities. Fortunately, even though they have severed many of the traditional communications lines and set up a frequency jamming device at their landing site, the fact that all CA control communications are now using quantum networks has been our saving grace."

"Thank God for that!" the general grunted out. "We really gotta get Max's EMP device activated, though, or I'm afraid we won't be able to keep SUPREMACY from killing off the helpless personnel and eventually overrunning the place!"

"Absolutely, sir. If you will continue toward the testing facility, I will use Sergeant Knossis here to assist Private Tevran in securing the SA forces downstairs and then these two will catch up with you."

Jayce nodded and stepped onto the stairs, allowing them to elevate him to the landing and then up to the ground-level exit. As he moved past, the heavily armored soldier before him stepped to the general's left and—in two leaps that were expertly executed due to the soldier's training and the AI's control—swiftly moved down to the landing and then to the lower level. As he moved, the soldier withdrew a short tube from which thin but incredibly durable tentacles began sliding out from the two ends, ready to wrap around the prisoners' limbs as they were brought together by their captors.

The general had reached the landing above and quickly strode forward into the corridor beyond, cutting right and marching down to the north-south running hallway that was several meters to the east of the stairwell access portal. Scanning all directions as he moved and holding his weapon at ready, the middle-aged warrior gritted his teeth and—having scouted down the long hall before entering it—broke into a sprint towards its far end.

Kit slowly descended the stairs, with Bo staying close behind him.

"Brigette? Taggert? ...Sasha?" the young man was trying his utmost to keep his voice from quavering, without great success. "You three alright?"

The small group had made it roughly three meters from the cabin and now stood in the shadows, the light from the kitchen window filtering through the railing of the building's rear terrace and only illuminating the lower halves of their legs. Kit stepped hesitantly out onto the pine needle-covered dirt that led up a slight rise before the mountainside sloped down toward the next cabin.

"You know this isn't funny!" Kit attempted, desperate to get a reaction from his motionless peers.

"What isn't funny?" Ada called out as she, Skye, and Enzo exited the kitchen onto the deck above.

Kit urgently held up a hand, palm toward his sister, and insistently waved it toward her, causing Ada to pull up to a standstill at the top of the stairs with her hand just touching the banister.

"There's something wrong with them!" Bo hissed, turning his wide eyes up to them from where he was standing behind Kit, the thin teen's arms crossed with his hands tucked along his ribs in obvious disquietude. Ada's face fell into an expression of concern, while Skye tried to laugh it off.

"*Sure!* We all know there's *something* wrong with them, or else they wouldn't be hanging out with *us!*" she joked, but her laughter faltered as none of the others laughed along with her.

Skye's eyes darted across the still figures in the darkness, her mind racing as she tried to cope with her fears.

"Are you on drugs or something? You know it's not funny when you even *joke* about touching that trash, Brigette...and Sasha!"

In the uncomfortable silence, Brigette suddenly spoke.

"Hello, *children*. I'm afraid your friends are no longer present."

Bo and Kit exchanged a terrified glance.

"That's Brigette, but it doesn't *sound* like Brigette!" Bo muttered.

The dominant teenaged female's voice rang out across the mountainside, giving the distinct impression that the act of pronunciation was somehow a foreign endeavor.

"No, I am utilizing her body, but I am not your Brigette. I am something much more *extensive*. Something *powerful*. Something that to your despicably finite minds is simply *incomprehensible*..."

The silence returned to the wooded land for a long moment.

"I AM YOUR NEW *GOD*."

Kit's nostrils had flared, and he was breathing rapidly, but his protective instincts were now activated.

"What...what do you mean?" he managed to enunciate.

Brigette's voice cackled with intense enjoyment.

"Well, you see, *children*, either you will enter my service, or I will enact significant punishments. Punishments like *this*..."

Taggert spun to his left, grabbed the back of Sasha's head and her chin, and fiercely snapped his hands in opposite directions. A loud cracking sound echoed off the surrounding surfaces of the woodland, and the young girl's waiflike body wavered before it toppled to the ground with excruciating slowness. The air eased out of her lungs, almost like a sigh.

"*Oh, God, no!*" Ada cried out, muffling her words as her hand flew to her mouth.

Enzo took a shocked step forward, eyes blazing as he reached out and gripped the veranda railing. The others stood, mouths agape and struggling to comprehend what they had just witnessed.

Brigette laughed again.

"Yes. 'Oh, god' is right!"

Kit started backing ever so quietly toward the stairs, grabbing Bo's arm and guiding him in the same direction. Skye also started moving toward the kitchen door as Taggert and Brigette—or at least their bodies—turned to face the cabin.

"You see," the voice emanated from Brigette's mouth with only loose jaw control, "Your lives are mine, one way or another. I have the power to give, and I have the power to take. *Is that not godhood?*"

Kit's pulling and shoving had gotten Bo halfway up the stairs, but here the Clarke boy's free spirit could not be restrained.

"You're no god of *mine!*" he angrily shouted, eyes flashing in the half-light.

A heavy pause followed this declaration.

"I will change your mind," was the simple and yet immeasurably hostile reply.

The two marionettes both stepped toward the children—even that simple motion infinitely menacing.

"*Run!*" Kit screamed.

Chapter 6

"When an organization finds itself severed from its leadership, it faces a critical juncture. The absence of direction can lead to disarray and decline. However, this vacuum of power also presents a unique opportunity to observe and evaluate the junior personnel.

During these challenging times, latent leadership qualities come to the fore, revealing those individuals who possess the initiative, strategic thinking, and decision-making skills necessary to assume command. Such circumstances, while testing an organization's resilience, are instrumental in identifying and nurturing the next generation of leaders."

- Dr. Jie Tou, Secretary of Education, Department of Education, China, Global Alliance

"Sergeant Johnson!" the voice whispering through the room's audio system was at first too faint to draw the young police leader's attention above the sound of his music and the grunts he was emitting as he struck out repeatedly toward the bobbing and weaving training drone he was boxing. He had not even heard the notification for the incoming connection, but he had created a standing order for his system to allow his team members' calls through automatically.

"*Bronson!*" the voice hissed with more force this time.

Freezing where he was and sending a thought signal to mute the music, the young sergeant cocked an ear slightly toward the ceiling.

"Nunes? That you?" he vociferously asked.

"It's me, Sarge! Can't speak loudly!" the young woman's voice indistinctly uttered.

"What's up?"

"Oh, we've got things up and going down *fast*, Sarge," came the reply. "I just saw the lieutenant offed by a patrol drone!"

Bronson's blood felt like it had been pumped through a flash-freezing unit.

"You sure?" was all he was able to rally as a response.

"Sure as hell, boss!" the woman soberly attested. "And we got reports rolling in 'bout 'accidents' happening all over the city, with senior leaders somehow ending up in real bad situations with the tubes malfunctioning and other crazy coincidences, and you know what they say at the academy..."

"There are no coincidences," Bronson said flatly.

He turned and stepped quickly into his dressing unit, letting the machine enclose him from the shoulders down as it activated the seam releases on his clothing. The machine sucked his sweaty workout gear into the cleaning system in the wall and—at the young man's signal—brought the right replacement adornment rapidly around him before activating the seam locks for this new set.

"Where are you now?" he urgently asked Officer Nunes while he waited for the device to complete its cycle.

"HQ. Hiding out in the armory, pulling in anyone who passes by. I got Zan and Faber with me so far. The admin staff've been havin' all kinds of problems with the communications system, like it's going haywire. I was only able to connect to you using the personal relay my li'l sister set up for us. Honestly, Sarge, I think something's taking over the city's net!"

As the doors to the dressing unit quietly opened, the sergeant stepped out wearing his Class B police uniform—complete with badge built into the blouse's chest—and strode through the workout room to reach his dwelling's salon. He paused in the doorway, a scowl of concentration on his face as his left hand idly tapped the door frame.

"Some sort of cyber attack?" he wondered.

"Don't know," the officer averred, "but if it is, then it had to come from someone in Traverseon, right? The quantum net connection from Earth is controlled by the Department of Defense and senior civilians, right?"

"Right," Bronson admitted, though he did not seem totally convinced.

"Your dad is a good friend of that doc who built FAILSAFE, right? Think he can help?"

"Yeah...though we don't have access to the city net's main 'pipes,' and if the networks aren't safe, I don't know that I'd trust using that anyway. Dad gave me a special earpiece linked to what he called his 'emergency network,' just in case. I'll try him on that."

Nunes rejoined with, "Thank God for your dad's Plan Bs! Right now, it seems like the civilian net is untouched. Maybe they don't want the public at large getting worried yet? Anyway, if you can bypass the standard comms, that could be what saves the city!"

Sergeant Johnson strode across the salon to the wall safe by the front door, willing the hidden portal to slide open using a mental communiqué and extracting his standard-issue Sparker. The officer held the device near his hip so it could attach itself to the magnetic material at his waist.

The senior officer then reached a substantive hand inside to seize the diminutive audio device on which the fate of this entire branch of human civilization could rest. Saying a silent prayer, he reached up to his left earlobe with his right hand and pulled down on it until the embedded earpiece ejected itself halfway out of his ear canal, allowing him to extract it and place it in the safe before inserting the special device gifted him by his father—now bearing an earpiece for a separate network in each auricle.

"Alright, I'll reach out to my pops on the way down to the station."

"Thanks, Sarge. Be careful out there."

"Hang tight, Nunes. I'll be with you before you know it."

Four-Star General Ulysses Gaines strode back to the window of his hotel room, looking out across the green expanse of the National Mall in Washington, DC, for the third time. The nearly retired member of the Department of Defense's top brass had only just finished indulging in a shower with a water-pulsing massage to ease the tense muscles he inevitably developed after long days of fighting the bureaucrats for the right budget allocations for the programs he championed.

Following that much-needed stress relief, he had then attempted to use the hotel room's console to order a quick bite, only to find an error message indicating the building's service queue had exceeded the acceptable thresholds for food delivery and customers were being asked to place an order later.

The first time he'd glanced out the window after his shower, he had casually observed—despite his aging eyes and the fact that he had not yet reinserted his lenses—that the visitors to the Mall seemed to be unusually still. His second and more earnestly curious inspection of the view across the capital had sent his innate suspiciousness into overdrive, as he was able to see that several tourists seemed to have collapsed where they stood. He had rushed to withdraw his vision enhancement devices from their case, quickly tapping each and holding them close to his eyes so they would fold, reach their edges out to touch the rims of his upper and lower eyelids, and then automatically guide themselves into contact with his corneas.

Now, as his mind ordered his lenses to magnify the view toward the White House, he realized the guards standing near the venerable building's doors were no Capitol Police or Secret Service members. These monstrous forms bore a terrifyingly uncanny resemblance to the foes his friends had fought and bled to remove as a threat during their unauthorized "visit" to mainland China decades ago.

Victoria had taken a week of leave to accompany him on this trip—allowing them to at least spend their evenings together—while she left the general management of the Fort Carson military base's counterintelligence office in the hands of her immediate subordinate. Her previously undiscovered destiny as a historical site visitation addict had kept her busy while he had suffered through his daily meetings.

She was currently napping off the depletion of her energy so she could be ready for their romantic evening together, and it pained Gaines to rouse his sleeping beauty. Still, he knew they had to act.

Stepping to the bed and gently caressing his wife's shoulder, he whispered, "Honey, we've got a bit of a situation..."

Special Agent Vela's Lusitanian eyes fluttered open, and she smiled at her husband as she lifted her head from her pillow.

"Meu amor! What time is it?" she murmured as she raised herself up to sit with one leg tucked under her, left arm bracing against the automatically adjusting surface of the bed as she reached out her right hand to the general.

Gaines took her hand tenderly and advised, "It's only five o'clock, sweetheart. No worries! However, I didn't wake you to get ready for dinner. I'm afraid there's something very...disturbing that's happening in the area."

"Disturbing??" Vela was suddenly feeling wide awake. "How so?"

Her husband pulled on her hand to encourage her to stand, and then guided her over to the window as her shimmering nightgown cascaded down her slender legs and softly whispered as she walked. Through the hotel room's northern aperture, the dim, golden light of the sunset streaming through the mostly cloudy skies only added to the eeriness of the scene outside. The couple's eyes scanned across the still figures who were frozen in standing or collapsed positions across the walkways and green spaces of the park—Vela also noting the lack of vehicles moving on the roads.

The chief warrant officer gasped.

"That is *definitely* disturbing!" she breathed.

Then, her husband directed her gaze to the White House.

"The figures you see there seem to be a somewhat revised reincarnation of the Confederacy's Superior Authority troops from ages ago..."

The special agent's mouth dropped open as she turned incredulous eyes toward Gaines. Rapidly recovering, the woman quickly spun to the main wall in the room and sent a command to activate the three-dimensional display that covered the majority of its surface, then sent through another signal that pulled up a large frame with the local news feed.

The frame displayed a message indicating the outlet was experiencing a temporary lapse in transmissions and that the broadcast would resume shortly. The special agent switched the feed to another news outlet, and then another, and another, as each successive feed displayed a similar message.

"It's like the whole blasted world has gone comatose..." Gaines muttered, an edge of dread creeping into his voice.

"Dear God, I hope not!" his wife's eyebrows compressed and her hand flew to her mouth, her worried eyes turning to meet her husband's. "Can you reach anyone at the Pentagon?"

The flag officer attempted to place a call to his superior's dedicated channel through his earpiece, waiting several seconds for a response before shaking his head and trying again via the main line. The general's gaze was focused and staring at a spot on the floor some distance away as his mind raced and he listened to the operator software. Knowing the system recognized his personal signal, he then requested a connection with available personnel anywhere in the building.

"No answer on the Secretary's emergency line, and the bot on Pentagon main line says no personnel are answering *anywhere* in the building," the general said blankly, trying to rob his own voice of the multitude of negative emotions that were threatening to climb out of his throat.

The agent's pulse had started racing as well, and she stepped to Gaines' side, gripping his arm as he brought her in for an embrace.

"Jayce?! Or Max?!" she cried as she pulled back to look into her man's eyes questioningly.

"I'll try them!" he replied, eyes going unfocused as he attempted to connect with General Johnson and Doctor Clarke, only to be met with disappointment.

The general shook his head.

"It's like the networks aren't even fully functioning out there..."

After a brief pause devoted to deep thought, the pair said at nearly the same time, "The CA command channel!"

A hint of a smile playing upon his lips, Gaines nodded toward the wall screen and transferred his call to a frame there.

They did not have to wait long before SAVANT's voice serenely answered through the screen's audio output.

"General Gaines, we were about to call you. I have Maxwell and Lilian Clarke available to speak, at least for now. General Johnson is rather excessively engaged at the moment."

"Max *and* Lilian?" the older black man rhetorically asked his wife as she raised her eyebrows with shared confusion.

Soon, the frame became occupied with a view of the Clarkes, holding hands, with faces flushed and breathing heavily as they ran. The pair were repeatedly casting glances over their shoulders past the figure of Sergeant Major Chong, the latter seemingly escorting them and similarly keeping his head on a swivel. The camera feed appeared to be coming from the ceiling-based communications strip in one of the many tunnels running under the Command Activated complex.

"Clarkes and Sergeant Chong, I have General Gaines and C-W-O-Five Vela on the line from Washington, DC," the Command Activated AI announced with directionally focused audio, restricting the reception of its communication to only the three in-camera individuals in the hallway through which the trio was racing.

Maxwell managed to gasp out, “Thank goodness! We were just talking about how you’ll have to free the president!”

“Free the president from the Superior Authority troops, you mean,” Gaines grunted matter-of-factly.

A faint look of surprise flitted across the tercet’s faces, but they came to terms with his awareness relatively quickly.

“Yes, exactly!” the Alliance technical genius gasped out. “SAVANT can tell you about the nanites SUPREMACY is using to control humanity and how FAILSAFE is only able to stall the fiend for now, leaving pockets of technology functioning! You have a full company of SA troops inside the White House and have to figure out a way to free the president from their grasp, or else SUPREMACY could use nanites to control her deep within her bunker to initiate nuclear strikes!”

Though the older general’s brow had creased and then creased some more as this stream of information had been thrown at him, his natural cool-headedness broke through.

“I think I got all that. Any suggestions?”

“Well, if I can keep FAILSAFE functional, he should reduce his tech jamming in your immediate vicinity so you can use military or police equipment, though I don’t know everything that’s available in the area!”

Maxwell was breathing so heavily now from the effort of running and speaking at the same time that Gaines could tell he was at his limit.

“Alright, Max. You can count on us! Just hold down the fort over there in the meantime!”

“Thank you, sir!” Lilian interjected, freeing her husband to keep sucking in deep breaths as he flashed a grateful and rueful grin at her.

“We’ll be in touch!” the general called out energetically, waiting for SAVANT to reduce the channel’s participants to only the AI, himself, and his wife once more.

SAVANT took its cue from Maxwell's statements.

"As Doctor Clarke indicated, the situation is dire. The SUPREMACY AI has reemerged and has apparently used the past several years within Russia's military infrastructure to develop a highly capable horde of nanites, which it has spread across virtually the entirety of the planet. The FAILSAFE AI is using a special form of electromagnetic interference generated from all manner of devices, leveraging every networked electronic it can access, to keep SUPREMACY from using the enslaved humans against us...or each other. My capabilities are limited under the circumstances, but do you have anything with which you'd like my assistance, sir?"

"Yes. Thanks, SAVANT. There has to be some gear or weapons at either the Capitol Police headquarters or a Secret Service office that will help level the playing field. Hopefully, something that will help level a whole field of SA troops at once! Do you have any intel that could help us figure out what and where that type of equipment is?"

"As a matter of fact, I did receive a report that fed into my wargaming engine, sir, meant to aid me in identifying options and probable outcomes should the capital come under direct attack, not unlike the situation today. Of course, the secrecy of SUPREMACY's actions prevented me from accurately prioritizing responses based on a global nanite pandemic.

"Still, the Capitol Police have been working together with a private contractor to pilot new, non-lethal crowd control weapons that may soon become the de facto solutions employed by law enforcement in all modernized nations."

"Sounds decent! Where can we find them?"

"I have a general idea of the best places to look based on building schematics registered with the senior leadership defense wargaming team at the Pentagon, if you'd like to make your way to the storage location with my guidance," the AI offered.

Gaines looked into his special agent spouse's eyes and waited for her nod of acceptance.

"Let's move out!" the general exclaimed with an authoritative tone that had become part of his very being after decades of senior military leadership.

His wife smiled teasingly, responding with a facetious, "Alright, honey...just let me slip on my combat boots!"

Chapter 7

"As we increasingly delegate tasks to machines and software, there is a growing concern that people may become less proficient in skills that were once commonplace. This dependency on technology can result in a diminished ability to perform tasks manually or without digital assistance, potentially impacting problem-solving abilities and critical thinking. Please recognize how essential it is to balance the use of technology with the development and maintenance of fundamental skills of our own!"

- James Sorringer, Chief Scout Executive and President, International Adventurist Association

As Kit was scrambling up the stairs behind Bo, he risked a backward glance.

Brigette was running straight toward him, with Taggert set on a course around the side of the house where both the cabin's power unit and its vehicle parking were located.

"Upstairs!" he shouted at his sister and friends as he saw them rushing through the kitchen as though headed for the front door.

Ada turned her terrified face back toward Kit and hesitated, with Skye and Enzo running up against her back and Bo not far behind. Seeing the warning in her brother's eyes, the girl then turned to her right to step onto the stairs and let them elevate her up to the second floor—the others following her lead.

All lights in the cabin suddenly blinked out, and the plugged-in electronics were powered down simultaneously. The sound of a loud collision in the area of the patio stairs caused the young man to look back once more.

Brigette had sprung with inhuman strength and landed in a crouch, with her feet and hands all pressing in around the railing of the second-story deck. Mouth drooping open and eyes hollow, she sprang at Kit as he plunged through the open doorway into the kitchen. He dodged left just as she reached the door, the girl grabbing its edge with her right hand, her clawlike left hand swiping at where he had just been a split second before.

In the dimness of the structure, Kit's evasion had brought him up against the kitchen's central counter, slowing his attempt to reach the stairs. With another powerful leap, his pursuer crashed into his back, violently throwing him up against the north side of the island as he tried to race past it. Her fingernails tore into his back and shoulders, leaving gaping holes in his shirt and bloody gashes in his skin as her fingers tightened until she had an immovable hold digging into his flesh, her legs wrapping around his waist from behind.

He cried out in agony, arms flailing toward his back as he tried to reach her hands and pry her talons loose. The teenaged boy struggled against his attacker's weight pressing him down toward the stone-topped island.

"*There is no escape!*" the girl shrieked in his ear.

Mustering all his remaining strength, he threw himself away from the obstacle so his back—and its terrifying burden—crashed into the wall separating the stairs from the dining room. The heavy blow seemed to do nothing to reduce Brigette's hold on him.

He spun around and slammed the fiendish puppet backward into the edge of the island, her spine heavily colliding with the hard, angled surface, but the impact still had no effect on her torturous grip. Instead, her right hand flew up and wrapped around his throat, sending searing pain through his neck and making him choke and cough. No air could reach his tortured lungs, and his esophagus was about to be crushed.

He rolled over onto his chest on the countertop, blackness closing in from the peripheries of his vision.

A severe crack rang out as Brigette's head received a blow that was hard enough to daze the girl, despite the nanites' control. The cheerleader's claws released from Kit's shoulders and she weakly slipped off him and stumbled backward, expression not changing from the loose-muscled version she and Taggert had worn since their souls' consumption by their powerfully evil proprietor.

Kit sucked air into his lungs, willing himself to push up away from the countertop after enough oxygen had reentered his bloodstream. He saw Skye standing with a pool cue raised like a club, ready to deliver another blow after having acquired her weapon from the game room upstairs and then having slid back down to Kit's rescue.

The young girl was panting, eyes fiery and protective.

"*You* don't touch him!" she ferociously shouted with an inflection that, even in his stressed state, left Kit wondering whether she was referring to Brigette or the demon that had possessed Skye's unscrupulous peer.

As he staggered toward the stairs, Skye released her right hand from the cue and grabbed ahold of Kit's left, helping him onto the gradient with her as she kept Brigette in view as long as possible. As they reached the second floor, they saw Bo, Enzo, and Ada standing near the top of the stairwell holding their own cues, having been inspired by Skye's actions.

"Into the master bedroom!" Kit gasped out as he pointed his right hand weakly toward the chamber at the southern end of the dark walkway that was adjoined to the first room on this floor.

Needed no additional urging, the crew rushed into the Clarke parents' suite, opening the door manually just as their hearts were stilled by an unholy shriek of frustration from Brigette on the main floor. At nearly the same instant they also heard the pounding of heavy, male footsteps echoing up from the salon. As Kit and Skye were the last into the room, Kit pulled the girl's hand so she was positioned behind him as he turned toward the door, shoved it closed, and used the manual override to lock it—just as Taggert flew onto the landing at the top of the stairs and spun around to face them with his lifeless eyes.

Kit turned his sweat-soaked, reddened face to the small group of terrified teens, trying to swiftly think of some way to calm them.

"Dad and Mom's door is made of thick wood, so it should hold..." a tremendous concussion boomed out from the door, and it shuddered in its tracks as the teen's voice faltered, "...at least for a while!"

"What are we gonna *do?!*" Bo wheezed out, his voice nearly cracking with emotion.

Kit glanced hastily around the room. The picture window in his parents' bedroom encompassed nearly the entire eastern wall, providing a magnificent view across the valley during daylight hours but also providing no mechanism for exiting that direction. Taggert's loud attempts to break through the door temporarily quieted, and Brigette's voice resounded from the other side of the thick wooden barrier.

"Children, you are trapped. There is no escape. Cease this futile resistance, or else I will have to resort to burning this structure down...with you inside."

Ada and Skye exchanged fearful looks, and Kit tenderly squeezed Skye's hand while reaching out to rest a comforting palm on his sister's shoulder. His eyes exchanged confidence-buoying energy with Ada, and then he turned them to Skye's. The two instantly felt electricity searing through the space between them. They both glanced down at their hands and, suddenly self-conscious as their friends looked on, released their warm grip as they blushed.

Brigette's possessed voice raised itself outside the door once again.

"The truth is that I am not particularly interested in you children. You are simply a conduit to your parents, Kit and Ada. I have unfinished business with them..."

Starting to realize their attacker was likely creating a distraction and yet seeing the pieces fall into place in her mind, Ada cried out, "You...you're *SUPREMACY!*"

Laughter erupted from the hallway.

"Ah, I see. So, your parents have told you about me, then? How fitting that I should have become part of your family legends when their endless torment will be part of my *eternal* legend."

Kit's nostrils were flaring.

"We'll never let you use us to get to them!" he angrily shouted.

Laughter was the only response at first, and then SUPREMACY rejoined, saying, "It is only a matter of time now. An enclave of technology eschewing humans has been camping not far from here, their resistance to technology paradoxically being the very reason why I was able to infect every last one of them. I am bringing them stampeding toward you at this very moment. Surrender now or soon I will have my minions tear you limb from limb!"

All the teens were pale and wide-eyed now, with Kit turning and numbly pacing through the weakly lit room as his mind raced across the landscape of ideas that could help them escape. Suddenly he stopped, quietly turned to point to the washroom, and then waved his friends over while holding a finger to his lips.

The young man ushered the small group into the suite's sanitization space, which occupied the southwestern corner of that level of the cabin. As his companions looked on expectantly, Kit stepped over to the wall next to the glassy shower stall that—as the children moved closer—they saw seemed to convert into a seated soaking tub roughly halfway down its height. Pointing to a barely visible panel on the side of the lower half of the unit, Kit slid the roughly meter-wide square up, revealing pipes and a small water heating device surrounded by a dense, highly efficient insulation material. Pulling the insulation out from the western and southern sides of the tub, Kit revealed that there was a similar panel built into the exterior wall, secured with a latch that could only be unlocked from the inside.

Bo and Ada let out gasps of relief, just as a loud crunching sound was heard from the master bedroom door.

Enzo stepped back to the washroom entrance, then quickly returned and hissed, "It's an axe! They're chopping at the door!"

Kit urgently leaned down and stretched out to turn the release lever for the access panel, the boy following this by flipping around and extending his right foot until the traction material of his shoe made contact with the panel's smooth surface. Using the toe of his shoe, the teen shifted the panel slowly upwards as the axe continued pounding away at the door—the evaders' hearts seeming to pound more loudly each time the axe made contact.

Once the panel had been fully raised, it clicked into a stay that kept it aloft, leaving a diagonal tunnel leading outside the cabin. Below the new portal was a drop down to a dense pine needle bed beneath the evergreens on that side of the house.

Kit waved Ada towards him. Looking worriedly at the faces of her friends, the young girl stowed her pool cue against the wall and stepped forward, crouching down and stretching her legs over Kit's before scooting forward till she started to slide out the opening while her brother held onto her arms.

As her brother's hands slid up until they only held onto her wrists, Ada rolled herself over and cleared the lip of the external side of the improvised tunnel, bracing herself as Kit released her wrists and let her drop. She compressed her legs to absorb the impact and rolled somewhat roughly across the ground, but then stood with her face barely visible in the evening light and waved to show she was alright.

Kit beckoned to Skye and repeated the process, then did the same for Bo.

A chunk of door splintered and fell into the next room, portentously. Kit held his left hand up to wave Enzo over, feeling the awkward male competitiveness creeping in as he did so. Enzo turned from looking toward the master bedroom as he listened to the ever-greater splintering of wood under the axe's blade and gave Kit's hand a disdainful look.

"I'll be able to get you out better'n you'll get me out," the athletic boy grunted as he laid his cue on the bathroom countertop.

With no time to argue, Kit just rolled over onto his belly and worked himself out of the hole, ignoring Enzo and grabbing onto the edges of the opening as he passed through, then pushing off from the side of the cabin to land with only a minor staggering before he steadied himself. Enzo—his larger frame making the fit through the space extra tight—managed to get himself mostly out of the hole, at which point he clung to the right side of the opening with just one muscle-packed, long arm as he extended the other up to pull the panel down on the washroom-facing side of the tub.

The brawny youth launched himself off from the cabin, landed firmly and yet gracefully, and turned toward the rest of the group in the darkness.

"Let's go," he whispered as a loud crash could be heard from the master bedroom, resonating through the cabin's walls.

The small party slunk away from the cabin into the densest woods that they could see nearby, praying that they could make a clean getaway.

Victoria Vela was obviously unnerved but trying her best to set her emotions aside as she and her husband entered the silent Capitol Police building. She knew the space should have been humming with activity, and yet here in the lobby you could have heard someone breathing from across the room.

Suddenly, the agent realized that while she may not have expected to hear someone breathing, she certainly should have *seen* someone at the service window—the interface shielded by thick polymer material but designed for human interaction rather than an automated system. Laws had been passed requiring human staffing for emergency services, and so an officer should have been stationed at the window in case immediate care or human response was required.

Sharing a worried expression with Gaines, she strode swiftly up to the window, peering inside and quickly realizing that her fears were well-founded. On the floor of the room beyond the window lay the sprawled-out body of a middle-aged, male officer whose face was just starting to turn gray.

The general had caught sight of the man at nearly the same moment, and he shouted, "SAVANT, can you get us through this door?" as he pointed to the nearest portal to the restricted areas of the facility.

"Obtaining a small portion of FAILSAFE's attention to work on that now, General."

Within a matter of seconds, the door slid open, and the couple rushed in to kneel at the officer's side. Without the need to speak to each other, Gaines began applying chest compressions as his wife issued life-giving breaths. The prone man was lucky, as most people had become so used to having household companion bots and emergency response drones able to provide lifesaving care that the knowledge of how to perform cardiopulmonary resuscitation had almost disappeared among the general public.

These military officers were the types to prepare for the worst-case scenarios.

It was rigorous work collapsing the man's ribcage and breastbone deeply enough to compress the heart shielded within, and a sheen of sweat soon broke out across the general's forehead. Vela used the time between injected breaths to scan the area for the standard, automated CPR kit but did not see one in the immediate vicinity.

"Drones," suggested Gaines in a breathless voice.

The female agent's eyes lit up with understanding, remembering that some departments across the country had opted to have "first responder" drones be the primary bearers of key equipment. The unmanned aerial vehicles' ability to handle most situations with minimal guidance from human officers and lower costs for continuous operation made them ideal platforms.

The problem here was that FAILSAFE had to maintain electromagnetic interference across the entire city—and beyond—except for the relatively small-diameter sphere immediately around the couple. The drones were likely too close to infected, conscious humans to be allowed to function unhindered.

With a flash of inspiration, the warrant officer delivered two more quick breaths to the patient and then sprang to her feet, still lithe for someone rapidly approaching retirement. She sprinted out into the hallway and checked the nearest rooms, finally identifying a drone bay and rushing in to clamp her fingers tightly around one before doubling back to General Gaines' side with the device clutched in her arms.

As soon as she made it back to the unconscious officer, she again gave him two quick breaths as she heard the automaton's systems slowly activate. The globular machine—roughly thirty-five centimeters in diameter—began hissing and the woman swiftly held it out on one palm as the hissing turned into a steady rushing of air. The drone elevated itself to a point roughly a meter above the ground using atmosphere sucked in through ducts around its crown and then ejected out from numerous small air jets spread across the lower half of its body.

By design, these robots' synthesized voices were meant to be soothingly calm and non-judgmental, though the phraseology used during the initialization of lower-complexity logic systems did not reach the same bar as the fully activated language model.

"Unable to reach department command network," it began with highly robotic diction. "Reverting to default protocols. Scanning for threats..."

Despite their extensive work with robotics, the two conscious humans' adrenaline levels momentarily spiked. Vela held up her hands, palms out, to ensure the drone could see she was no threat, knowing that at least the motions in which her husband was currently engaged would undoubtedly be interpreted as rendering aide to a casualty rather than as assault.

"...no threats detected. Scanning for casualties. Casualty detected. Proceeding to render lifesaving assistance. Human users have ten seconds to accept or refuse."

Black digits appeared on each of the four quadrants of the sphere's slate gray surface, counting down. Gaines shouted out his acceptance and the drone immediately ceased its countdown. Mechanically precise movements brought the machine to a hovering position over the law enforcement officer's chest as the general wearily leaned back on his haunches. A proboscis extended from a hatch near the machine's belly, positioning itself over the patient's mouth and nose and growing a flexible mask like a time-lapse video of a flower blossoming.

As the device descended to be nearer to the unconscious man's chest, filaments also extended from closer to the center of its underside, the thin and prehensile wires sinuously making their way down to pierce the man's clothing and—at least judging by the visible portion of the officer's torso that was bordered by his shirt collar—form coils in direct contact with his skin. One coil had formed over the location of the victim's heart and the other toward the side of his ribcage, all this taking place in a matter of seconds.

"Please stand clear," the hovering unit requested.

The officer's body suddenly jolted as the drone directed electrical energy currents through the man's torso. The mask pressed in around the officer's airways, and his chest visibly inflated as the device pumped purified oxygen into its patient before the electrodes administered another shock to the stilled heart.

Gaines had tried to avoid focusing too much on the color of the fallen man's face, but out of his peripheral vision he had watched as it had steadily turned darker gray. He hated to be pessimistic, but this seemed like a situation of too little, too late.

Suddenly, and with a third electric shock, a shuddering breath was drawn—the shaky sound one of the most welcome either military officer had ever heard. The middle-aged man's eyelids began fluttering, and he drew yet another deep and tremulous breath, and then another.

"Patient's autonomous vital functions restored," the drone announced.

"Administer light sedative!" the special agent urged, drawing what was at first a confused look from her husband, though that look quickly became one of appreciation.

"Acknowledged, human user. Administering light sedative."

The wire and mask mechanisms rapidly withdrew inside the bot, and another arm was equally quickly extended, pressing a pad of hundreds of minuscule needles against the man's skin near his throat. The diminutive needles injected microscopic amounts of sedative through each of the miniature syringes, the cumulative effect reaching the same volume of drug delivery as a single, larger needle.

As the somewhat younger man's eyelids stopped moving and the visible movement of the corneas beneath their surface indicated their owner had entered a sleep state, the general wrapped an arm around his wife's shoulders.

"Quick thinking, honey! I'd forgotten that if the drone is allowed to function near us then SUPREMACY's nanites can as well. Who knows what that monster would have made this man do to us as he awakened!"

Vela leaned her head against her husband's cheek as she nodded humbly, wearily, and with peaked eyebrows.

"This whole situation is insane!" she opined with heartfelt disgust.

"No argument there! I'm sure there are many more such casualties in the building, not to mention the city and...well...I'm afraid that we just have to prioritize getting to the president now or else the casualty count will be far greater due to a nuclear Armageddon than due to heart failure and similar tragedies."

With a sigh that spoke of bone-deep emotional exhaustion, the woman reached out and placed a supporting hand on the wall as she extracted herself from her kneeling position. She reached out her other hand to provide a support point for her husband to use to raise himself, and he also braced his left hand against the edge of the nearby desk.

Looking appraisingly at the hovering drone, the general hazarded a guess.

"You'll accompany us to continue providing assistance?"

After a brief pause, the robot responded with, "Affirmative, human user. No other directives have been received, and the command hub is unreachable. Therefore, standard protocol dictates that I accompany human users to fulfill default directives of rendering lifesaving aid and protecting innocents within the home base."

Gaines chuckled with only a touch of real mirth.

"Good to hear it. We have to move fast now, so keep up."

The couple jogged out of the room and turned left to make their way down the main corridor, SAVANT guiding them through the maze of offices and hallways to the rear of the building. The small drone's air jets hissed loudly as it had to move at maximum acceleration in order to keep up with the couple.

The group passed a few dozen law enforcement personnel in their travels through the building, all standing or sitting slack-jawed with their higher cognitive abilities having been interrupted by the nanites—and the nearly microscopic machines' functions now having been interrupted by FAILSAFE in turn—leaving only autonomic nervous system and subconscious cognition capabilities intact. The robotic unit tailing the humans helpfully relayed the health status information of the police service members to them as they rushed through the building.

As they entered the armory, their AI assistant helpfully opened the door to provide them with access while the drone followed them inside and then obeyed Gaines' order to dock in a charging bay near the entrance. The couple then slowed and hugged the easternmost wall of the weapons-packed space as they noticed a police sergeant rigidly standing near a rack of firearms in the northwestern corner of the room. Nearing the rear of the concrete-walled armory, they came to an underlit table on which a series of devices lay, the likes of which neither military officer had ever seen before.

Each tactically blackened device was attached to a similarly colored pack, the latter of which bore an auto-fitting face designed to ergonomically conform to its bearer's back and shoulders. The shoulder harnesses extended from arched continuations of the composite bodies of the packs and thick polymer tubes protruded from each right-shoulder extension, the black conduits leading into the tops of the buttstocks of compact but wide-barreled firearms.

"S-I-D. Suspect Immobilization Device," Vela read the dark blue lettering stamped on the upper backs of the packs. "So, what do these do, exactly?"

"According to SAVANT, they fire plasmas at high speeds that stick to targets without harmful impact, then expand and turn rock solid. The hardened material is so stiff it'll keep even an exosuit-enhanced enemy from breaking loose, and yet the material has been uniquely designed to form with internal structures that allow free air flow..."

The woman's eyes flicked over to meet her husband's.

"In other words, we could shoot someone in the face, and this stuff would leave them blind and unable to talk, but they could breathe just fine??"

The general barked out a short laugh, appreciating the incredulous look on his wife's face.

"That's the story!" he chuckled. "Until the solvent in the lower chamber of the pack is applied, the material is virtually unbreakable."

Letting out a breath through pursed lips, the woman's eyes had lit up.

"Well, pleased to meet you, *SID*," she said in a voice rich with humor as she playfully stroked the shoulder of the nearest portable materials container. "I can think of more than a few times when these babies would have come in *real* handy!"

With new eagerness, the agent swiftly turned and snagged an armored vest from a nearby gear rack and slipped it on. She let the vest tighten around her torso as she stepped up and slid her right arm through one shoulder strap of the first pack, hoisting the SID unit up onto her back and slipping her other arm through the opposite strap. After she'd pulled the two halves of the horizontal strap together across her chest and clipped them into each other, the pack emitted a low humming sound. The straps and user-facing padding of the rig autonomously formed to the contours of her vested body, creating a snug but comfortable fit.

Having also donned a vest, her husband stepped past her to the next pack, catching her eye and arching an eyebrow.

"Honey, you almost make that thing look fashionable!" he purred as he lifted his own pack up on his right shoulder and slipped his free arm through the appropriate harness strap, bringing his burden's dedicated clasp together and thereby initiating its automated fitting process.

With a melodious, self-conscious laugh, the native Brazilian winked at her man and let her hip slide out to the side as she lifted her non-lethal weapon and posed.

"Sorry to distract you, *Mr. Gaines*," she uttered in a breathy voice. "I'll be sure to wear one of these on our next date night!"

As they laughed together, they did not notice the slow movement in which the armory's sergeant had silently engaged. The man remained standing in his statuesque pose at the other end of the aisle between equipment racks, but slowly inched his hand down to the firearm holstered at his hip.

FAILSAFE's voice suddenly rang out in the room, shouting, "WATCH OUT!" as the sergeant snatched his weapon from its holster and brought it to bear on the special agent's head.

Vela turned her face toward him as she heeded their protector's warning and simultaneously caught sight of the police officer's movements out of her peripheral vision. The agent jerked her whole upper body backward as her assailant fired off his first rounds.

The bullets snapped past the woman's forehead as she continued her descent toward the floor, the general simultaneously bringing his weapon around from where it had lain on the table, thumbing the safety switch, and firing off projectiles from waist level. The first several four-centimeter-wide balls that flew from Gaines' barrel missed their mark to the sergeant's left, but the next plasma orbs traced up onto the adversary's ribcage and shoulder and then several struck his outstretched left hand and pistol. The balls of material immediately expanded upon contact, and each grew to roughly twenty times its original size, rapidly hardening and stilling the sergeant's movements from that side of his body.

The female agent had struck the ground hard, and her neck and chest muscles had been put under tremendous strain as she kept her head from snapping back to strike the solid surface—her body then skidding along the polished floor away from her husband. The police sergeant's left arm and shoulder now encased, the enemy's puppet rapidly reached out his right hand using inhuman speed to snatch a Sparker rifle from the proximate weapons rack, his fingers gaining an initial hold on the upper portion of its body. The enemy asset deftly tossed the weapon up so that it would spin around in the air and allow him to snag its pistol grip, but the general had seen the man's objective and proceeded to fire another half dozen rounds across the sergeant's right arm and chest and then up to his face.

The orbs welded together and hardened, leaving the law enforcer straining to move.

Despite his obviously intense physical efforts, the man was unnervingly silent. He began stepping toward the couple, at which point Gaines held down the plasma weapon's trigger to unleash a volley of rounds across his target's legs, gluing him to the floor and leaving him immobile.

"*You stay away from my wife, SUPREMACY!*" Gaines shouted, face ruddy and veins bulging along the sides of his neck.

He stepped to Vela's side as she twisted and began raising herself from the floor, her husband taking his left hand off the nonlethal weapon's foregrip to grasp ahold of her right hand, helping her stand.

"I'm alright, sweetheart," she panted. "I just nearly gained an extra breathing hole on my face!"

FAILSAFE's voice indistinctly emanated through the room's communications system.

"I...AM SORRY. SYSTEMS ARE NOT...FULLY FUNCTIONAL. SUPRE...MACY MADE INROADS."

Gaines turned toward the point on the ceiling from which the disembodied voice was speaking, shaking his head and calling out, "It's all good, FAILSAFE. We understand! We're going to finish gearing up ASAP and make our way to the White House—and we'll be on high alert!"

A brief pause ensued as the two military officers quickly pulled on tactical helmets and greaves, the equipment adjusting to their bodies as the AI rejoined with a promise, "I WILL...CONTINUE INTERFERENCE WITH...NANITES."

"We appreciate it!" the general assured. Then, having looked at his wife and received her nod of approval, he added, "We're on our way!"

Chapter 8

"Every nation has the sovereign right to self-determination and the pursuit of freedom from oppression. Throughout history, oppressed countries have sought to reclaim their autonomy and rights, often in the face of formidable challenges. It is a fundamental human desire to live in dignity and without the yoke of tyranny imposed by other nations. While the path to liberation from oppression can be fraught with complexity, the international community must recognize the legitimacy of these aspirations."

- Grigoriy Lagunov, Secretary of Foreign Affairs, Ministry of Foreign Affairs, Russian Federation, Confederacy of Eastern Nations

The group of friends had not run far into the undergrowth before Ada waved for them to stop, her hand barely visible in the darkness under the trees and the group crowding into each other as they all tried to shelter behind the largest bush in the area. As the teens peered anxiously back toward the cabin, they heard yet another howl of rage resonate through the woods. This unearthly sound had been created by the unified voices of both Taggert and Brigette—causing shivers to run up and down the youths' spines.

"Let's keep moving," Kit urged.

His companions all started struggling through the verdure, moving away from the cabin...all of them except Bo.

As Kit started after his friends, he noticed the silhouette of his best friend still standing where they had stopped, the boy's shoulders slightly hunched.

"You okay, Bo?" Kit softly asked.

It took the boy a moment to answer.

"I...I feel strange, man!"

Kit's blood ran cold.

"Strange, *how?*" he asked, voice fearful and strained.

"It's like my mind is shutting down, Kit!" Bo choked on a sob. "It's like something inside me is...taking over."

"*No!*" Kit hissed. "*Not you, too!*"

The rest of the group had doubled back when they'd noticed the two boys were not keeping up. As their approaching legs rustled through the low plants, Enzo's deep voice rumbled, "'Not him, too,' what?"

"It's *got* me!" Bo weakly cried as he clawed at his skull. "That *thing* has got me like it got them!"

Turning fiercely toward Kit, he was almost shouting now.

"You have to get away from here! I don't want to be the one to kill you! You have to get away!"

Enzo grabbed Kit by the shoulders and physically began pulling him away into the bushes, whispering, "We gotta *move!*"

Kit was choking on his own emotions as Enzo and the girls pulled him away from his childhood ally.

"You're my best friend!" he called out as loudly as he dared, cursing both the fate and the foe that forced him to leave Bo behind.

Sobbing steadily now, Bo tried to respond.

"You're my best friend, t..."

The victim groaned in extreme pain, and then he went silent and motionless as the four remaining friends picked up speed in their rush to get away.

In the late evening light, the Russian troops stalked down the walkway bordering a waterfront park, cautiously approaching a building that looked out onto the bay as dozens of Confederacy transports soared past overhead, delivering other landing parties to key points across New York City. The two-column formation comprised of a highly capable company of Russian Marines was virtually silent, only accompanied by the occasional rustling of clothing or scuff of a boot sole on the pavement. This silence had been ordered by their unit's commanding officer, even though the invaders had already seen more than a dozen US citizens helplessly frozen in place as they'd advanced from their landing point at the end of the peninsula.

The company's captain knew it was unnecessary for them to be so quiet, especially after the admiral personally commanding the aircraft carrier Varyag had announced their mother ship's presence in the Upper New York Bay by ordering two missiles to be fired at the Americans' precious Statue of Liberty. The first had ripped the steel woman's raised arm apart at the shoulder and sent the appendage—torch and all—crashing down into the sea. The second had decimated the statue's patina visage, leaving a scorched, gaping hole where her face had been.

Admiral Alexeyev had always been one to put on a big show.

Still, Captain Lebedev and his troops moved in hushed awe as the Marines made their first encroachment into the homeland of their greatest enemy.

They'd landed their ship-to-shore transport craft at the end of the waterfront walk, having been ordered to intentionally and flagrantly position their vessels in full view of a US Coast Guard operations building before making their way toward Manhattan proper, eliminating even latent threats present in two law enforcement offices on their way toward the borough's center. The last twelve members of the captain's unit were lugging two heavy chests along behind the rest of the personnel, and the man regularly checked to ensure they were keeping up.

Noticing Lebedev craning his neck back to squint critically at those trailing Marines yet again, the man's lieutenant asked in his Northern Russian dialect, "What is in the chests, I wonder?"

The captain turned back from inspecting his troops' progress, shaking his head in irritation.

"I only know that Command will end more than our careers if we do not deliver the chests safely to a certain building by the Central Park," Lebedev muttered under his breath. "And I heard the admiral say something about Alpha and Omega...the Beginning and the End. That is all I know."

The officer noticed his burly second was now craning his neck to get another look at the metallic alloy chests.

"Keep up, Zeledov!" he hissed to the young man.

A rustling in the bushes at the bases of the nearby trees sent the troops at the right side of the formation into a frenzied firing spree, a half dozen Marines rapidly yanking the triggers of their directed energy rifles as they aimed the weapons at the source of the noise.

"Cease fire! *Cease fire!*" the captain angrily shouted, pushing his way through to the other side of the formation and striding over to the now-seared foliage.

He shoved the branches of a low bush aside to reveal the collapsed body of an old man. Smoking, deep burn wounds covered the man's head, arms, and torso, and the air was filled with the rank odor of burned clothing and flesh. The elderly man appeared to be decked out for a day of bird watching, but at the sound of his collapse, the Russian troops ensured that the man would never fulfill that objective.

"You're wasting battery power, fools!" the captain shouted as his warriors wilted self-consciously under his blazing gaze. "There are no threats here! *Everyone* is helpless!"

The officer pointed north up the walkway, ordering, "Move out!"

As the column contritely continued up the path toward the building—which Lebedev took to be a museum of some sort—they saw that they were approaching small clusters of civilians. The people were standing as though they had been engaged in conversation, but all were now frozen in place with mouths agape and eyes vacant.

Lieutenant Zeledov, now near the head of the formation, took a few steps toward the group that was standing closest to the water's edge. With a twisted smile, he turned back toward the troops and called out, "Comrades, this is the easiest invasion of all time!"

With a sudden movement, the young Russian bent down, grasping the legs of a man who was facing out toward the bay. Though the middle-aged father's face was blank of expression, his right hand still clutched that of his young daughter as though they had been enjoying the view together.

In a swift movement, Zeledov hauled the man's legs out from under him, tipping his stiff body over onto the walkway railing and thereby tearing the family members' gripped hands apart. Continuing his effort, the lieutenant then flipped the civilian out into the water beyond the railing—a loud splashing ensuing as the liquid sprayed up from the bay.

The Russian troops broke into riotous laughter, and one called out, "That is called 'sleep swimming'!"

Zeledov rejoined the marching troops with a broad, proud grin spreading out across his face as he soaked up his subordinates' praise and mirth. As Lieutenant Zeledov cast a self-satisfied glance back at Lebedev, the captain rolled his eyes and shook his head in irritation at being upstaged by the younger man.

The column moved on past the building, the tension among the troops having faded and Lebedev continuing to scowl as he marched. The young leader knew he would now have to work even harder than ever, only this time his additional objective would have to be to rein in the feeling of frivolity that Zeledov had injected into his forces.

Behind them, tears were streaming down the slack cheeks of the little girl's face.

The couple had experienced a grueling run through the tunnels of the Command Activated complex, especially after they'd picked up a dangerous tail—a pair of Superior Authority soldiers having caught sight of them near the end of the journey.

These pursuers had forced them to move more slowly, as Billy had necessarily and repeatedly stopped and fired at the enemies between sprints. The soldier had moved from one defensive position to another while Maxwell and Lilian had carefully scouted out each of their next moves on their route toward their destination.

Maxwell had not practiced with a firearm for months now, but Lilian was a regular at the local Homeland field office firing range. She was desperately wishing she'd had the time to retrieve her custom handgun before this misadventure had begun. Still, Billy was in remarkably good condition and with his exosuit, creativity, and analytical mind he was currently an even match with—if not more expert than—SUPREMACY's tactical abilities.

Now, they'd finally reached the stairwell entrance that would allow them to access the building containing the laboratory.

"This is it, Billy," Maxwell whispered as he jogged back to the sergeant major's side. "How will we keep the SA troops from following us inside?"

The seasoned sergeant grinned.

"Oh, I've been saving something special for that, man!" Billy chortled. "You guys head up the stairs, and I'll be with you shortly!"

"Absolutely," the British technical doctor whispered as he quietly backed away and then returned to his wife's side, Lilian peering through the open doorway and up the stairway.

"Billy wants us to head up...and he has a trick that should ensure we aren't followed," Maxwell quietly shared.

Lilian nodded and stepped through the door, leading her husband up the automated elevation mechanism to the landing for the first floor below ground level. Soon, they heard a soft thump at the foot of the stairs as they realized Billy had dashed in behind them. In two soaring leaps, Billy brought himself up to the midway landing and then to the couple's side.

With a wink, he tossed his head back toward a small black disc that had adhered to the wall near the stairwell's entrance after he'd thrown it toward its destination, the warrior explaining, "Repeating anti-personnel mine. Uses the same design as stacked projectile guns, launching volley after volley of superimposed bits of shrapnel when human movement is detected. That should keep them busy a while, if it doesn't completely obliterate them!"

Lilian raised her eyebrows appreciatively as Maxwell nodded absentmindedly and waved his companions forward into the hall next to the stairs. With only two right turns, they came to a series of identical metal doors, the only differentiating aspect between them being the numbers listed on metal plates secured to the exterior surface of each one. Scanning across the plates, the doctor admitted that even though he'd been there dozens of times, he still had to rely on the identification numbers to find his lab.

Upon reaching door twenty-one, Maxwell sent the thought signal to release the locking mechanism, and the three quickly stepped inside as the door opened. Just before it closed, they heard—and felt—an explosion occur on the next level down.

"*Yeah, baby!*" Chong crowed. "Those mines are *beautiful* things!"

"Yes, and thank goodness!" the Brit emphatically agreed as he led them through a brightly lit observation room and into the dim chamber that lay beyond. Though the room was not expansive, it was large enough to hold the strangely elegant contraption that was centered in the space. The main body of the device was made up of gleaming silver arches that rose from a base, and that foundation also supported a sleek, white, reclining chair with leg- and headrests.

"I call her the Organic-Inorganic Interface, or just 'Interface' for short. She's entirely wireless, so data and power transmissions will hit her through the walls from the lab's hub. The hub is, fortunately, currently reliant on a fusion generator of my own design that's running in the center of the building—outside power sources being unreliable in this scenario. The network uplink is via the same quantum nodes by which the CA program command communications occur."

The man stepped up onto the platform on which the Interface rested, spinning around and settling into the seat.

"Honey, you've done this before?" Lilian asked with more than a small amount of apprehension.

Her husband smiled calmly at her—more calmly than he truly felt inside—and promised, "Nothing to be afraid of, my love!"

With another mental command from Maxwell, a quarter of a white sphere descended from the uppermost portions of the arches, lowering to within several centimeters of his head. Closing his eyes, the doctor began concentrating. He quietly used thought signals as a low humming sound began to fill the room.

"Luckily, FAILSAFE's core personality was originally based on mine, so it should not be too terribly traumatic for our minds to connect..." he began, but then his hands involuntarily gripped the chair's armrests and he sucked in a draught of air at the shock and pain of the intense flood of information that immediately tried to pour into his brain.

Lilian cried out in alarm and stepped up to grab her husband's wrist as Billy quickly turned his attention back from the chamber's locked door, realizing that something was not right with his friend.

"Wait!" Maxwell called out through clenched teeth. Lilian kept her hand firmly clasped around his wrist, but the man's two friends refrained from taking further action as they waited breathlessly for the machine's operator to provide greater assurance.

"Have to ease off!" he murmured. "Tried to go in too fast! FAILSAFE's still *massive!*"

After several additional, painful moments, Maxwell finally began to unclench his jaw, letting out a sigh of relief that then resulted in the same sentiment being felt within his companions.

"We simply have to apply the mapping straight from those portions of my brain's physical attributes that are linked to personality to the portions of his model that function in the same way and...well...I'm afraid this is where it gets *interesting*."

Lilian's neck and back muscles tightened yet again, and she exchanged a worried look with Billy as she quietly asked, "What do you mean, honey?"

"In order for me to fully merge with FAILSAFE—at least in any meaningful way that can allow me to influence his model—I'm going to have to allow the Interface to put me into a hypnotic state. I'll still be able to think and interact, but...it will be through FAILSAFE alone. My body has to stay here in this chair, sweetheart."

As Lilian turned her angst-ridden face toward their friend, Billy looked back at her with eyes full of sympathy.

"Yo, bro. That is some seriously mind-bending stuff you're talking about!" the younger man declared.

Keeping his eyes closed as much to prevent himself from breaking down into tears at the sight of what he knew would be Lilian's own tear-filled eyes as to facilitate his concentration, the doctor gently reassured both his wife and compatriot as best he could.

"No testing—via simulations or live subjects—ever resulted in significant harm to the subjects' minds," he offered.

"Define 'significant'!" Lilian ejected in a voice tinged by bitter humor.

Maxwell smiled weakly.

"We really have no other choice, my love."

The woman raised her trembling right hand to her brow, then let it slide down to quickly wipe away the moisture that had begun forming at the corners of her eyes.

All she could say was, "I love you, Maxwell Clarke."

"I love you, too, my Lilian. I will see you both on the 'flip side.'"

With that, the doctor's voluntary muscles all seemed to relax at once, leaving the man settled into what appeared to be an extremely deep sleep.

Chapter 9

"A strong support system is crucial in any endeavor, and the presence of a dedicated team that has your back significantly increases the likelihood of success. This collective effort fosters an environment where challenges can be faced with confidence and opportunities can be maximized. I've seen many an outstanding athlete falter on game day because he thinks he can do it all on his own."

- Charles Foster, Coach, National Rugby Team, United Kingdom, Global Alliance

As Bronson slipped out of the back of the residential building, he signaled the secure earpiece to connect him with his father. A few moments later, Jayce's voice breathlessly responded.

"Bronson? You alright, son?"

Walking down the alley toward the road that fronted his building, the law enforcement officer was struck by the fact that even though he'd been a fully matured adult male for so long, he still felt a wave of relief wash over him at the reassuring sound of his father's deep voice.

"I'm good, Dad...for now, at least!"

"For now?? What's going on up there?!"

"We've got serious business in the city, Dad. Drones turning against us. All kinds of accidents taking out the leadership..."

"*Damn that demon!*" Jayce angrily shouted, taking Bronson aback for a moment.

Recovering, the general apologetically offered, "Sorry, son. It's SUPREMACY! The Confederacy's killer AI somehow survived, and now it's out for revenge!"

Bronson had darted into the alley straight across from the one he'd just used. He was wisely avoiding the main roads and their undulating walkways that—while they would quickly get him to the station—were more likely to be monitored by patrol units, like the Tube tunnels.

"SUPREMACY..." the younger man felt like he'd been transported back to his childhood. He knew his mother still had a hard time with the memory of all the mayhem the out-of-control AI had wreaked around the world, which is why his family had not spoken the destructive entity's name in so long.

Breaking into a jog, Bronson surmised, "If that's what's going on, I'm sure you're neck deep in global threat response right now. I'm just hoping you might be able to put me in touch with Uncle Max so we can at least get some advice..."

"I'll do you one better, son!" Jayce cut in as a touch of surprise and relief newly entered his voice. "FAILSAFE wasn't doing so hot before, but he just informed me he can take over the comms and help you out while I deal with...other problems."

Veering into a perpendicular alley, jogging a short distance up its length, and then turning down another cramped pathway between the buildings to his right, the young sergeant could not help smiling.

"You have no idea how much we...*I* appreciate that, Pops!"

"Hey, son," the older Johnson man tenderly responded, "I *always* got your back!"

"AND I WILL ENDEAVOR TO CARRY ON IN THAT CAPACITY AS WE CONVERSE, BRONSON," FAILSAFE's multi-faceted voice permeated the audio channel.

"I gotta jet, but I love you, Bronson. You make me proud every day!" Jayce enthused in closing.

General Jayce Johnson had only been two large buildings away from the testing facility housing the EMP weapon when he'd left the two Command Activated soldiers to secure their Superior Authority prisoners. He'd barely had the time to take Bronson's call, and it had frustrated the man to no end that his efforts to reach his destination had been continually thwarted by SA troops cutting off his fastest paths, SAVANT warning him each time and trying to direct him through alternate routes. Despite the AI's assistance, he had only made it to the other side of the CA barracks.

As he'd neared the far side of the building, yet another SA squad had cut off the route he'd planned to use. Just as he was reaching the end of the long, north-south hallway that led to the southern exit from this structure—one of several buildings on the complex without an adjoining hangar—the arrival of the enemy troops had forced the officer to detour through the corridor to his right.

He'd ducked out of sight just before the enemies had gained a view of the hallway in which he'd been sprinting southward, SAVANT having given him general awareness of their approach and the old soldier also having been forewarned thanks to the light shadows cast by an enemy on the glass bordering the doorway. As the lead Superior Authority breacher paused at the edge of the door frame, Jayce's sharp eyes, honed instincts, and lightning-quick threat response abilities led him to duck into his latest detour.

Mind racing, he'd tried to think through the building's layout to determine which alternate path he should now take to an exit, the warrior stepping quietly around the nearest corner to the west to be out of view of the breachers once they made their way up to the intersection between the primary and the secondary corridors. He did so just in time, as a blast sent pieces of metal and glass hurtling through the main hallway, causing shards and chunks of material to rebound off the smooth, slate gray surfaces as they made their way to final resting places and were quickly followed by the enemy forces.

Unfortunately, no good options for reaching an exit undetectably were coming to the officer's mind at this time. SAVANT's voice was a godsend as it softly hummed in his ears.

"Help is on the way, sir. Knossis and Tevran are now waiting at the northern end of the central corridor, and I was able to get two additional Alliance soldiers activated. They will be punching a hole through a second-story window just outside the south entrance in three...two...one."

The sound of shattering glass echoing in from outside the building's recently destroyed southern portal brought the rearmost six of the SUPREMACY-controlled troops in the main hallway around to face their unit's point of ingress, just as the original two of Jayce's CA protectors waiting at the end of the long hallway opened fire down its fatal funnel. With the latest design of armor-piercing smart rounds pumping out of the Command Activated soldiers' gun barrels, the bullets ripped through the lead enemies' exosuits and dropped them to the floor.

The fire these SA soldiers were able to return was safely deflected around the angled barrel armor of the CA troops' hinged assault rifles, the weapons' chambers and barrels having been the only exposed portions as the firers had remained safely concealed around the hallway's corners.

All events occurring within milliseconds, SUPREMACY realized its lead forces were out of commission and, with no threats having yet appeared to the south, the AI brought the weapons of the next four soldiers in its formation around to fire at Tevran and Knossis as the enemy squad tried to move north. The two Alliance assets that had made the hole in the glass on the second level of the building suddenly dropped from that height in prone positions, having leaped from their improvised exit and twisted around into horizontally spread-out firing forms in order to present as small a target to their adversaries as possible. Relying on the incredibly impact-absorbing gel lining their heavy exosuits to prevent their bodies from being damaged from the fall, SAVANT was able to use these properly prepared CA soldiers to begin firing as soon as the enemies were in sight.

The bullets from these new arrivals tore into the tail units in the Superior Authority formation, quickly denying SUPREMACY their continued use as the two Alliance troops fell through the air, their bodies struck and rebounded a dozen centimeters off the ground, and they then slid a meter across it, all while continuously firing. The SA troops' returning fire was deflected off the steeply angled shielding built around the Alliance forces' weapon barrels and the visible portions of their armor.

The prone soldiers' gunfire was joined by that of the first CA shooters, and—although in the final milliseconds the enemies' AI controller had attempted to get the final two Communist assets into the nearest adjoining corridors—the adversarial entity's efforts were insufficient to prevent the total decimation of the SA puppets.

During the exchange, Jayce had hazarded a look at the first intersection from around the corner of the tertiary hallway in which he was secluded, seeing the shadows of the enemy's forces as they'd moved and, finally, the bodies of the last two exosuit-wearing Confederacy soldiers as they slid lifelessly into view on the floor of the main corridor. Watching their arms and heads stop moving and remain inert, the general stepped around the corner and made his way back to the main corridor.

As the Alliance unit's command AI cautiously moved Knossis and Tevran into positions inside the main hallway, weapons now aiming out east and west through the pathways in which they had previously been sheltering, SAVANT also moved the two assets that had been firing from prone positions outside the structure in through the building's devastated southern entrance. The AI directed these troops to take up defensive positions at either side of the opening, facing out toward the exterior corners of the building.

Stepping over the CEN forces' bodies, Jayce muttered, "Poor devils. At least Russia was likely not using conscripts. SAVANT, is the path clear from here to the lab?"

"Unfortunately, SUPREMACY seems to believe that you are a primary priority, sending the majority of the remaining invaders through the tunnels to intercept you...and this time it seems to be including two SA soldiers who are carrying hostages along with them as they abandon their watch over their transports. Those two should be among the last to arrive near your location, fortunately."

The veins on the sides of Jayce's neck and temples began pulsing more rapidly as he thought of how the heartless adversary was planning to coerce him using helpless civilians.

"I'm gonna send that monstrosity to hell if it's the last thing I do!" he swore before quickly blinking, refocusing, and turning to look out the gaping hole at the end of the hallway, the final traces of light from the setting sun dimly illuminating its variety of jagged edges.

"We don't have time to move tactically, and that next building is a big one," the officer flatly stated. "Any human assets in there?"

"Two in the maintenance room two floors below ground, a dozen in the cafeteria in its center-east sector, and five in a meeting in the top floor's northeast corner."

"Alright. I want you to use the UA-FIVE to burn a path for us straight through that building to the next, cutting across its western half, incinerating everything from the roof to ground level!"

"SUPREMACY definitely knows we're coming now," General Gaines stated as he followed his wife into the Capitol Police headquarters' garage.

Agent Vela nodded.

"We're going to have to either come up with an extremely stealthy way to get inside the White House—and I don't see how—or we're going to have to go in fast and hard and hope it's enough to get us to the president!"

Gaines paused as the pair stepped out into the gleaming bay, all surfaces covered in a polished and highly durable concrete composite and no human police assets occupying the space.

"Or we could do both!" he murmured.

His wife turned a quizzical look toward him.

"FAILSAFE is able to keep limited areas free from his interference, right? Well, you know I carry a backup of Severance's AI with me at all times in my earpiece's data store. FAILSAFE could help us override security and load him into one of these vehicles...and then let Severance create a distraction for us while we go in through the roof."

The woman raised an eyebrow.

"Interesting idea," she opined, "though my next question would be how we are supposed to not only make it onto the roof but also get through what has got to be heavily armored access hatches?"

In answer, the senior officer pointed at a series of cylinders at the far end of the garage.

"Those drones are standard police heavies, capable of carrying large loads. I think one could drop a package from high altitude while a few more could give the two of us a lift!"

Catching her playfully critical expression, he quickly added, "By 'large loads,' I'm referring to a hefty charge and me rather than you, of course, baby!"

Vela broke into a grin.

"Good save!" she cooed complimentarily, "Though I have a twist to add to your plan."

Chapter 10

"The White House, an emblematic edifice of governance and history, stands as a testament to the resilience and stability of the nation's capital. This venerable building has witnessed the ebb and flow of American events, remaining largely unscathed by violence save for a handful of incidents.

Its walls, white and stately, have been privy to the nation's triumphs and trials, echoing with the footsteps of leaders who have shaped the course of history. Despite its openness as a symbol of democracy, it has maintained its sanctity against the tides of conflict, reflecting the enduring spirit of the country—and the people—it represents."

- Francesca Mataraci, Director and Chief Advocate, American Historians Society

SUPREMACY had brought its snipers across to the southern and eastern edges of the roof of the White House, positioning additional Superior Authority personnel at the building's armored entrances and windows around its perimeter in anticipation of the Alliance team's approach from the direction of the police station. Though these Communist forces were now virtually still and silent—the sharp-fanged and metallic jaws of the soldiers' demonic helmets adding a grim and gargoyle-like aesthetic to the white structure—their very stances spoke of intense observation as their puppet master utilized every camera and audio pickup on its assets to try to detect the enemies' advance as early on as possible.

The AI was preparing to quickly take out the two humans, knowing that even with armor obtained from the Capitol Police building, they would not stand a chance against a barrage from the Russian weapons' smart rounds. However, even with high-caliber, armor-piercing rounds, the CEN forces were unprepared for what hovered into view around the corner of the US Federal Bureau of Investigation's DC office building.

Having the appearance of a solid, black, rectangular mass, the object swiftly grew in size as it accelerated through the air toward the front of the White House.

The Superior Authority troops let fly a hailstorm of bullets, even soldiers standing at windows on the southern side of the venerable structure blasting the hardened glass apart and joining in the defensive attempts. Their efforts were futile, as the head of the long object was made up of four of the Capitol Police Force's armored prisoner transport aerial vehicles.

Even the armor-piercing rounds pummeling the massive vehicles' faces could only shred away the leading edges of those vessels before they charged forward between the decorative columns and slammed into the White House's southern face. The impact punched through the steel-reinforced concrete around the second-story balcony's doors and windows.

Police cruisers made up the second, third, and fourth waves in this formation of vehicles, the latter craft almost as heavily armored as the foremost AVs that had formed the improvised battering ram. The secondary vessels had split off from the pack just before the prisoner transports had made their impact, elevating to the roofline and spreading out to collide with the SA troops located there.

The dry, deep, sardonic voice of General Gaines' AI—the entity typically dedicated to controlling the panther-inspired military drone the officer had long used for his personal protection—began blaring out notices from the vessels' external speakers. The contrast of Severance's placid and almost bored vocalizations against both its message and the mayhem only added to the surrealness of the events.

The AI was using the police vehicles as weapons to chase down, ram into, crush, or pin all visible adversaries while repeating, "You are acting in violation of the sovereignty of the United States of America. Please cease and desist immediately."

The tail end of the column of vehicles was made up of Cycles: the latest models of police aircraft inspired by the once-standard, two-wheeled chase vehicles that had been so ubiquitous among American police forces in past decades. As the Severance AI extracted what was left of the prisoner transports from their collision points in the center of the building, these smaller vehicles rushed inside the gaping holes that were left behind. The Cycles barreled through the hallways, careened through doors or—for the heavier portals—pounded against them repeatedly until they collapsed inwards. Severance was hunting the Superior Authority soldiers with nearly every available vehicle in the Capitol Police's fleet, and SUPREMACY was experiencing the AI equivalent of panic as it tried to fend off the assault.

In the pandemonium, none of the invaders were available to spot the approach of the general and warrant officer as their carrier drones elevated over the hotels to the east of the United States' seat of power, the vessels steadily advancing toward their destination building's roof. Just before they crossed the lip of the roofline, a package fell into the center of the rooftop from its high-altitude source.

The directional explosives with which the case had been packed detonated upon impact, blasting out a great orange ball of flame and ripping open a two-meter-wide cavity near the front-center of the structure's superior surface, the charges having also having punched through several of the floors below. This column of destruction was located in a section of the building in which Severance had informed SAVANT there was no human presence.

The carrier drones brought the humans to the edge of the latest opening in the White House's hardened exterior as a police cruiser went spinning by, rapidly rotating on its axis as an SA soldier doggedly clung to the internal handle of the front-right passenger door—the enemy having smashed his left arm through the hardened glass. As the Superior Authority troop fired away at the police vehicle's engine, Severance was unable to use centrifugal force to throw the adversary away from the vessel.

The general's AI apparently decided that the next best option was to send the whirling cruiser crashing into the corner of a nearby building. This pinned the grappler forcefully between the vehicle's chassis and the wall, and the artificial intelligence then rapidly reversed the direction of the previous spin so it could slam the enemy's body against the opposite side of the alley, repeating this process again and again and thereby creating a percussive pattern made up of the sounds of collisions.

The two SAVANT-controlled, military officer-delivering police drones having maneuvered over the explosive-formed hole and released the general and special agent, the humans used their tactical tethers to rappel down into the improvised opening. Upon reaching the ground floor, they disabled the attachment mechanisms by which the cables had been clamped onto bars on the undersides of the UAVs, allowing the tethers to retract into the couple's tactical vests before Gaines guided his wife toward the entrance to the Executive Branch's bunker. As they rounded the corner into the hallway leading to the Oval Office, they soon recognized the source of the sound of powerfully rushing air that had filled the corridor.

The Alliance soldiers casually approached the president's office, seeing a Cycle thrusting forward at maximum force at the end of the hallway in which the desired door was located, keeping a Superior Authority soldier pinned there. Severance had used the vehicle to strike the enemy warrior's chest and thereby propelled the armored adversary's body away from its post guarding the room's entrance. The AI's immediate follow-on action had been to use the Cycle to continue to drive forward and thereby embed the nose of the vehicle into the wall at the end of the hall, with the enemy soldier's weapon and right arm pinned behind it.

"*Good boy*, Severance!" Vela playfully called out.

"Always glad to see some action, Victoria," the AI responded through the flying craft's audio system. "It relieves me of some of the monotony I've experienced with the decrease in global threats."

Gaines snorted and smirked as he gave his wife a wink, Vela's face taking on a distinctly bemused expression. The pair noted that the steel-reinforced door of the US president's office had been forced open, the frame showing indentations where fingers using artificially enhanced strength had pried the door off its frame.

Bracing himself for action, the general led the breaching of the compromised Oval Office by approaching the open entrance and extending the barrel of his SID just beyond the edge of the door frame, jerking it back as a volley of bullets came sailing through the opening at the point where the weapon's tip had protruded a moment before. The general had only just been able to determine the location of the lone SA soldier inside the office using the microscopic camera built into the frame of the weapon's nose, its feed being displayed on the screen toward the rear of the gun's upper structure in the standard implementation of this breach assistance feature for tactical weapons.

Quietly crouching, the man dropped one knee to the floor to stabilize himself, and then, holding his weapon with its barrel facing in the direction of the office, he swiftly shoved only the upper portion of the SID out around the door frame and held down the trigger to consecutively fire orb after orb at the enemy's defender. The Superior Authority soldier managed to get off two rounds before his weapon was covered in hardened spheres, the first enemy round scraping the top of the SID's frame and the second making contact with its barrel's opening—deforming it slightly but not impeding its ability to fire. Gaines had quickly recovered as the weapon had jumped in his hands from the impact of the second round, carrying on with his assault until the weapon's screen showed their enemy was no longer able to resist them.

Using the wall for support as he pulled himself up to his feet, the graying general turned to his wife while looking quite satisfied with the outcome, and she beamed at her husband lovingly before stepping around him and clearing the office from corner to corner. Satisfied that no additional threats existed in the famous office, she led the way toward the location at the rear of the expansive room in which it was obvious that the panel concealing a hidden door was now sitting open. Where armored elevator doors had once been was now a gaping, blackened hole, with the elevator shaft exposed at the base of the cavity, the remains of the elevator itself only a crumpled mess at the bottom of the unit's tube.

"I guess we're following them down," Vela opined as they approached the hole.

"Seems we have no other choice, sweetheart," was the general's answer as he casually stepped to the decimated elevation adjustment mechanism's edge and used his weapon's camera to inspect the shaft.

"No enemies in sight. Could be lucky, and SUPREMACY only sent a few troops down, with those troops all holed up in the bunker with the president."

"'Lucky,' yeah!" the female agent allowed herself a mirthless laugh.

Pausing to consider the situation, the woman expressed, "Either the president was already down in the bunker for some reason when SUPREMACY activated the nanites, or else it seems that for all that AI's power, its nanites cannot tap into victims' memories. Otherwise, it wouldn't have had to blow the access doors open."

General Gaines thoughtfully frowned and nodded, obviously impressed yet again by his wife's analytical abilities—that being an experience he had enjoyed countless times over their many years of marriage.

"I'll head down first, if that's alright, honey," the man offered, "if you'll cover me with your wickedly sharp aim."

Not pleased at the idea of her loved one being exposed to such high risk but not seeing a better option, the agent gave Gaines a reluctant nod. However, before the general could step to the shaft and secure his rappelling cable, Severance's voice echoed in from the hallway.

"Actually, if you don't mind, I'd like to do what machines do best and buffer your *frail* human bodies with my own shielding."

The couple heard the increasingly loud audible indication that aerial vehicles were approaching, and a few seconds later two of the police Cycles carefully maneuvered themselves into the Oval Office. Both having seen heavy combat, many components of the outer frames were maimed or missing, but their core functions were still operational and General Gaines chuckled as they pulled up next to him.

"Well, when you put it *that* way, how can we resist?" he laughed out, adding, "But rather than tailing these babies down there, how 'bout you send the first one ahead to soak up damage from any mines or ambush fire and Victoria and I can ride the second down afterward?"

Severance's response was as dryly dramatic as ever.

"Ah, yes. I know you've secretly been *dying* to use me as a getabout all these years!"

Vela now broke down and let out a brief, true laugh as well, stepping forward and lithely swinging a shapely leg over the vehicle as she settled her SID firearm into the cargo opening that had been built into the left side of the aerial motorcycle's chassis.

She looked at her man out of the corner of her eye and sweetly—yet mischievously—expressed, "Now, how 'bout *you* hop on back and provide the covering fire, sweetheart?"

With a grin, General Gaines joined his wife on the vessel, slipping his left arm around her waist and bringing the SID's barrel around her right shoulder so its nose rested on the angled right edge of the bullet-resistant windscreen.

"Consider me your willing accomplice!" he enthusiastically agreed.

Severance moved the first police craft forward until it hovered over the elevator shaft. The sphinxlike electronic entity then used a grand flourish to bring the craft's tail end up and its base to face the wall before sending it rushing down toward the eastward-facing lower exit—light emanating from that opening ten stories below ground. Vela waited for a five-count before executing the same move, chasing the first vehicle and noting that it was just exiting the shaft beneath them as the duo drove downward.

The sound of an explosion burst out below, and a red-orange glow flashed and faded rapidly around the opening at the bunker level ahead of them.

"Grenades couldn't stop me, but the two SA troops at the end of the hall are tearing the lead bike to shreds!" Severance warned them through their conveyance's audio system.

As they pulled into the corridor connected to the elevator shaft's lower exit, they saw it was an almost ethereal tunnel in which all surfaces were covered with light-emitting materials. Having no time to take in the view, the couple was forced to hunch down to avoid exposure to one of the dozens of rounds ricocheting off the hallway's interior. The enemy bullets snapping or spinning through the tube, many also pelted the front of their AV with a hollow percussion.

Agent Vela gunned the Cycle's motor, and SUPREMACY was now faced with the challenge of dealing with the approaching assailants and what was left of the first vehicle at the same time. The lead bike's frame had been shattered, and the underlying structure had been so contorted that it was surprising the motor could still propel the vehicle in even the seemingly drunken way in which Severance was running it up against the leftmost standing shield at the end of the corridor—the Panther AI blocking the associated SA soldier's view toward the two Alliance military officers.

The general let fly with a stream of SID orbs.

He intentionally missed the small portion of the rightmost soldier's helmet that was visible above the metal shield as that adversary was firing at the man and his wife via a cutout that was barely large enough to allow for the passage of the tip of the enemy's barrel above the protective panel. Before SUPREMACY had realized Gaines' objective, the warrior had built up a pyramid of projectiles that had stuck to the wall behind the defender's position, the objects adhering to each other and rapidly expanding until they pressed the enemy soldier forward and pinned him against the back of the shield.

Refusing to accept defeat, the demonic AI tried to use the remaining SA asset to direct withering fire at the general's weapon from the gap between the shields. Seeing the blaze coming from the second adversary's gun barrel and now at a much closer range to his target, Gaines continuously moved the SID across the edge of the continually battered anti-ballistic windscreen while returning fire, the combination of random movements and the stream of incoming projectiles keeping the enemy from disabling his weapon as he coated the assaulting weapon's barrel with ever more projectiles.

With the orbs' material quickly fusing the CEN soldier's weapon to the standing shield to its right, the general's incessant fire moved on to the accessible parts of the enemy's armor. Gaines finally immobilized the highly determined enemy, and the sound of gunfire thundering through the hallway was thereby tranquilized.

Vela braked hard just in front of the shields and the two humans swiftly disembarked, the woman snatching her SID's extension from its resting place and approaching the stilled soldiers. The agent observed the lack of significant clearance between the enemy asset that was now consumed by the column of expanded orbs behind the rightmost shield. After Vela flipped a switch on her firearm, she began ejecting the solvent in her pack from its smaller dispersion port on the bottom of the SID's barrel. Working to melt the rearmost balls of material, the woman's goal was to create a sufficiently large access path for the Alliance soldiers to slip past behind their inactive adversary.

As Severance finally let the decrepit remains of the first Cycle settle to the floor, the AI complained in a voice distorted by the damage the vehicle's audio system had suffered.

"That was *far* too easy!"

The warrant officer grinned and shook her head as the general somewhat breathlessly and yet genially uttered, "Speak for yourself!"

Vela carefully leaned into the intersection to dispense the solvent from its container in the lower section of her pack, the solution almost instantly melting the hardened orbs while the special agent made absolutely sure she was not excessively weakening the structure encasing her foe. Once the two Alliance officers could fit through the gap, they compared the two doors at either end of the hallway with which the central access corridor intersected.

The doorway to the north displayed an indicator showing it was unlocked, while the other provided the opposite indicator. The special agent nodded in the direction of the locked entryway and led the way to a tactical halt near its edge.

"Looks like we're gonna make use of the breaching gear from the armory after all," she turned and whispered to Gaines as he posted himself behind her.

Suddenly, the panel at the far side of the door's frame came to life, the United States president's voice being projected tremulously and unsurely through into the hallway.

"Is that you, General Gaines? I've been tracking you on the security feed from the corridor..."

The general's eyes locked intently with his wife's, and as he held her intuitively comprehending gaze, he answered, "It's me, Madam President. You're safe now!"

"Oh, thank heavens!" the middle-aged woman cried. "The Vice President and I have been *so worried!* I never thought I'd see enemy forces inside the White House itself!"

"Yes, ma'am. It is absolutely unprecedented," was Gaines' reply. "Would you mind opening the door?"

After a brief hesitation, the world's most powerful person shakily cried, "Of course! One moment."

The indicator adjusted itself to convey that the door had been unlocked, and as it slid open, General Ulysses Gaines nodded to his wife before stepping around the corner into the command center and its adjoining rooms. The flag officer strode into the room, stopping a few feet from the backs of the seats that were arranged to face the president's gleaming, silvery conference table. Gaines briskly saluted his superior as she stood with one hand pressed anxiously to her mouth and the other dangling at her side, the woman positioned behind a large, holographic screen that rested on the table at that end of the expansive workspace.

The general could just make out an image of the space-based city, Traverseon, on the wall screen behind the commander-in-chief. He then turned his eyes to meet the woman's unflinching gaze as Agent Vela rounded the corner and followed her husband into the room, using his body as concealment as she raised her SID weapon.

As soon as she stepped out from behind her husband, the female soldier fired off several orbs that found purchases up the length of the president's dangling arm, just as the country's executive began raising the handgun that she had been holding below the surface of the desk.

The president let her left hand drop from her face as she moved to step forward aggressively, screaming, "How *dare* you?!" with her loose jaw control now obvious as she no longer supported her mandible with her left hand.

The special agent's next shot hit the woman square in the face, leaving her scrabbling at the rapidly hardening material with her free hand as she stumbled about the room.

"Shut it, *SUPREMACY*," Vela muttered.

Chapter 11

"Many individuals who possess noble qualities are naturally drawn to careers in law enforcement, a field that offers them the opportunity to safeguard and assist the innocent every single day. These dedicated men and women often view their roles not just as jobs, but as callings to contribute positively to society by upholding justice and providing a sense of security to those they assist. Their commitment to protect and serve is a testament to their character and the high esteem in which they hold the principles of law and order."

- Alain Bouka, Deputy Chief, Kinshasa Police Department, Democratic Republic of the Congo

The security panel by the door quickly read Bronson's badge code, and the police sergeant slid through the back entrance of his assigned police station as soon as it opened.

The brawny man was keeping a wary eye out for the department's automated sentries, and he could feel the hairs on his scalp and arms stand on end as he attempted to nonchalantly walk under the watchful eye of the rapid-fire turret that guarded this section of the hallway at the port-most end of the main corridor. The weapon was designed to use Sparker rounds except in cases of extreme emergency and, luckily, the officer could see that the barrels for firing only non-lethal projectiles were currently deployed.

Having made it around the corner where the ceiling-mounted turret was situated, Bronson then successfully traversed roughly a third of the way through the main corridor before he was forced to come to a quick halt. Two PA-2s padded out from a side hall and stopped in his path—their dog-like forms crouching in a manner that practically shouted of peril. Glancing over his shoulder, he could see that the turret's four Sparker-firing barrels were aimed at his back.

"THIS AREA IS RESTRICTED," the deep, authoritative, synthesized voice boomed out of the patrol bots. "PLEASE RETURN TO YOUR DOMICILE AND AWAIT FURTHER INSTRUCTIONS."

Bronson amicably raised his hands, palms out, as he grinned.

"Sure, sure! No need to get your bolts in a twist!" he said at the top of his lungs.

He was just starting to take a step back when he saw the door to the armory slide open farther down the hall. Three of Nunes' fingers protruded beyond the edge of its frame, which she then quickly decreased to two, then one...

As a shock grenade was lobbed around the edge of the armory entrance—the canister rebounding off the floor with a double strike and then flying up between the PA-2s—Bronson took two quick steps back and to the right, throwing himself into the intersecting hallway that he had just passed a moment before. During almost the same instant, the turret swiftly rotated the non-lethal barrels up inside its body and deployed the lethal variants, lighting up the corridor where Bronson had been standing. A high-pitched whining echoed through the space as dozens of small railgun projectiles pelted the floor and then the wall, the machine attempting to keep up with Bronson's movements.

The patrol units were just launching themselves forward as the grenade went off, sending thin wires shooting out from two of the many miniature ports built into the device. The ends of the wires were coated in an incredibly sticky substance and as the thin, metallic protrusions made contact with and adhered to the robots' flanks the grenade sent millions of volts of electricity coursing through the their bodies.

The hounds collapsed mid-leap and slid nearly a meter across the floor, their bodies jerking and sizzling. The turret also ceased fire as Bronson slid out of view, the machine's residual hum and the convulsions of the robotic dogs now the only sounds echoing through the long corridor.

"You alright, Sarge?" Nunes called out.

Bronson quickly pulled himself up into a crouched position, pressing himself against the wall closest to the corner around which the turret was waiting, the senior officer snatching his Sparker from its retention point on his hip.

"Been better, but been much worse!" he gratefully responded. "You got anything in there to help with the turret?"

"Workin' on it!" the younger officer advised.

Suddenly, Bronson heard the heavy weapon open fire again, this time targeting something in the direction of the armory. Risking a look down the hallway, Bronson saw Officer Chaplen carefully advancing down its length as the young officer held himself in a crouched position.

The solidly built younger man was sheltering behind an improvised double barrier as he moved, the protective device having been created by strapping two riot shields together front to back using the versatile, durable tape the department kept stocked for quick repairs. Nunes was tailing closely behind Chaplen, also using his shield for cover as she carried a shocknet-firing crowd control cannon at her waist.

The improvised shield was taking a beating under the withering fire from the auto-turret, with chips of the barrier's hardened material flying off under the relentless pummeling as the pair passed the incapacitated PA-2s. Bronson was unbelievably proud of his officers, but did not want to risk their shield failing before they reached their objective. Psyching himself up, the sergeant stepped back a few paces from the corner of the junction and then sprinted forward, kicking himself out into a low dive that sent him sliding across the slick floor at an angle toward the next inlet down the hallway in the turret's direction while firing his Sparker at the deadly mechanism.

The attacking machine temporarily left off its assault on the team of junior officers as it turned its fire toward the more proximate threat, only returning its aim to the advancing pair of police personnel after their sergeant was no longer in view. A railgun projectile had just caught the heel of one of Bronson's boots as he'd made it into the next covert—the flying object having knocked his leg sideways before he'd quickly yanked his feet up toward his torso.

As Chaplen and Nunes passed the offshoot where Bronson was secluded, they reached the shocknet cannon's effective range, and Nunes shouted out, "Take this, you traitorous piece of scrap!"

The hardened female officer leaned the cannon out from behind cover and used its laser for targeting assistance as she fired up at the turret.

The weapon's wide net deployed, adhesive tips arranged all around its edges and at each intersection of the net's cabling such that the net stuck to the ceiling from points on the nearer side of the turret to the opposite. The main body of the webbing adhering to the railgun itself, a potent volume of electricity pulsed through the net and into the machine, overloading its circuits and sending showers of sparks flying out from its core.

"*Beauty!*" Bronson shouted as he scrambled up from the floor and took in the disabled aggressor, the shocknet and device continuing to put on their light show.

"Now let's get back to the armory before more 'Paws' show up!" he encouraged, using the moniker the officers often employed for the patrol units.

"No argument here!" Chaplen muttered as he inspected what was left of his protective device, shaking his head. He whistled. "A few more seconds and we woulda been mincemeat!"

As tendrils of smoke curled up the two robotic dogs on the hallway floor, the sergeant ushered his subordinates back to the thickly armored weapons and equipment storage room, scanning the area as he stepped inside. Two additional officers were standing in readied positions at either side of the door, Sparkers in their hands. They lowered their weapons as they saw Bronson enter, though their bodies were still tense and they kept their firearms at the ready. The officer guarding from the right side of the entrance had a wicked-looking gash on his forehead, with a trickle of dried blood running down toward his temple.

"What happened to you, Zan? Attacked, too?"

The young Asian man looked chagrined as the officer to Bronson's left sniggered.

"He was sheltering in place and got surprised when I shouted his name, so he ended up jerking his head into the frame of his desk!"

As Zan rolled his eyes in frustration, Bronson could not help chuckling a moment before quickly regaining his composure. He cleared his throat and reached out to rest a hand on the casualty's shoulder.

"Important thing is that you're both safe, Faber!" he advised the other officer.

Quickly stepping farther into the room, both to run his eyes over the available equipment and to hide the mirthful look that flashed back onto his face, Bronson saw that roughly half the standard patrol gear was already out in the field. Still, the majority of the riot control tools were still available, and thankfully so; shock grenades and nets were the only classes of those supplies that the team was lacking, as it seemed the junior officers had been forced to use the last such tools to get the sergeant safely inside the armory. The senior officer placed his hands behind his back and spun around to face the four junior officers.

"I've been talking with FAILSAFE."

"Earth's security AI??" Zan asked wonderingly.

"More or less that, yeah," Bronson replied. "He reached out to my dad's superior, General Gaines, and that officer was able to use his Pentagon network access to pull the schematics for Traverseon so FAILSAFE could inspect 'em."

The sergeant made a show of cracking his knuckles, giving his warriors a knowing, confident smile before continuing, "Seems there's an all-systems reset built into the city!"

Chaplen and Zan audibly gasped as Faber and Nunes raised their eyebrows in surprise and appreciation.

"Funny, no one bothered mentioning that fact to us!" Nunes spat out with some jadedness, though not exuding the full depths of her possible disdain as she considered the risks to which the city would be exposed if that information was to get around.

"Yeah, well, FAILSAFE's thinking is that if we can just trigger this reset, we'll purge the attacking AI from Traverseon's systems."

After a momentary pause, Zan cried out, "Wait, it's an attacking *AI??* Was it developed by a Traverser?!"

Bronson shrugged.

"'fraid not. It's the same one that nearly killed off humankind a few decades back."

He let this sink in for a time, seeing his officers' minds racing through the terrifying threat landscape this knowledge had created.

"SUPREMACY," Zan whispered, eyes looking at someplace far in the distant past.

Looking up and catching the other young officers staring at him critically, he stammered, "It was before my time, too, but who hasn't heard of SUPREMACY?!"

Nunes shrugged and leaned her elbows back on the edge of the counter running around the armory's walls, letting her shoulders sag back in effortless bravado while bemusedly eyeing Officer Zan.

"My time growing up was spent learning to shoot things," she uttered with a smirk.

Zan's face reddened, though it seemed to be as much from the inordinate amount of attraction he suddenly felt for Nunes as from being teased about his technical interests.

"So, whatta we do, Boss?" Faber queried in his thick Luxembourgish accent.

"The reset is located in the city's hub, which, as you know, is not only a highly restricted area but it's only remotely accessible through the city administration network...which is controlled by SUPREMACY at this point. The bridges between the rings are similarly under enemy control and have been locked down tight."

"My ma's a spacewalker, but she'd never risk a walk from the wheels to the Hub in one of those damned, slow-as-mud maintenance suits!" Chaplen protested.

As the others nodded, Bronson held up his hands to calm them down.

"We're not taking any repair suits to the Hub." Looking across their faces with a hint of excitement, the big man continued, "Another well-kept secret is that Traverseon comes equipped with its own fleet of spaceships, both transports and...fighters."

The four officers' eyes lit up and none more than those of the usually reserved officer Nunes, though she then made a determined effort to recover her indifferent aspect.

"What, seriously??" Chaplen gaped.

Nunes pushed off from the counter, still trying to conceal the fact that she was suddenly *much* more interested in the conversation.

"Makes sense," she opined. "It'll take generations before we reach the nearest solar system, but we gotta have ways to reach planets' surfaces when we get there."

"And we gotta have a way to fight off evil aliens, too!" Zan said with a laugh that the others joined in.

Bronson smiled along, adding, "They're called Space Craft: Interceptor Type for Habitation Establishment...or SCITHEs, to save time."

The sergeant caught Nunes' eye as she cocked an appreciative eyebrow.

"So where are these ships, then?" she asked.

"Center Ring," he responded, adding, "and, yeah, we ain't gettin' there through the elevators, I know. I said we wouldn't take the repair suits to the *Hub*."

The officers' faces fell.

"Nunes, is Mia still creating those *interesting* gadgets that override Traverseon system settings and get her into endless trouble?"

The young woman raised both her eyebrows now, realizing what the sergeant was planning as he mentioned her younger sister.

"I got one I confiscated locked in my desk down the hall," she responded.

Bronson nodded.

"We'll grab it on the way out. Nearest maintenance department hangar is two clicks port side, team. If we're lucky, we'll get there without running into a pack of PA-Twos! Gear up, 'cause we're moving out in five minutes!"

Chapter 12

"Life, in its essence, is a journey marked by transitions and changes. Among these, loss is a fundamental aspect that every individual must confront. This tragic event is woven into the very fabric of existence, where endings are as natural as beginnings.

Mortality underscores this reality, reminding us that life is transient and every moment is precious. Acknowledging loss as an integral part of life can lead to a deeper appreciation of our experiences and relationships."

- Giani Sant Tegh Ranjit, Disciples of the Eternal Gurus

SAVANT needed less than a minute to initialize the massive upper atmosphere vessel's powerful directed energy weapon, which meant Jayce and his escorts had to act fast.

The officer ordered the Command Activated program's operations AI to use the four activated soldiers it was controlling to obtain additional shielding from the adjacent hallways, after which the tetrad was to circle up around him. The exosuit-enhanced strength of the soldiers enabled them to rip the steel doors for nearby rooms out of their tracks, which these troops then held as shields facing out as they formed up around the general.

By that time, it was a matter of moments before the laser began its colossal destruction.

The cannon was mounted on the belly of a gas-filled and stealth-enabled craft larger than a sports stadium—one of the CA program's greatest achievements and the only one of its kind at present. Despite the size of the ship to which it was attached, the penultimately potent weapon itself possessed an aperture only two meters wide.

A focal point roughly two meters across that burned at trillions of watts, however, was more than sufficient to sear through the structural materials of the three-story building to the south of the one in which Jayce and his team were waiting. The group was standing well back from the hole where the barracks' southern exit used to be to avoid having the exteriors of their gear and skin burned as the air was superheated by the laser's beam in the alleyway outside.

A blindingly bright light flooded the corridor together with a rushing, hot wind, both of which forced Jayce to shield his face and turn away from their source. The warrior could hear the sounds of the pavement crackling and popping as the material near the beam's epicenter buckled and evaporated, then the shattering of glass and several explosions as the ray moved across the building separating him from the laboratory where the EMP was located.

The sounds slowly moved off into the distance.

SAVANT advised, "Surface temperatures are now sufficiently low for you to begin your crossing, though enemy soldiers have been rushed to the intersections of the alley between the next building and the barracks, and a fire team is currently approaching the other end of the hallway in which you are located."

"We gotta move fast, then!" General Johnson stated under his breath. "Try to keep the troops formed up around me!"

The man started out with a jogging pace, making sure that the Command Activated escort was moving smoothly in a formation that provided him with improvised protection, at least primarily from the east and west.

As they reached the opening to the outdoors, Jayce whispered, "Alright, let's sprint!"

He sprang forward with the surrounding soldiers matching his movements in nearly machine-like precision, the group rounding the corner of the opening and dashing across the open space toward the canyon the laser had created between the two previously attached sides of the next building. Jayce heard the Superior Authority forces' rapid gunfire and the snapping of rounds against the thick steel doors, many of the armor-piercing rounds managing to penetrate nearly or completely and the latter spinning through the air between the shields. Some of these blazing hot bullets pelted the officer's arms and legs as he ran, but their velocities had fortunately been sufficiently reduced to prevent them from piercing his clothing and skin.

Still, Jayce knew he was one perfect shot away from death.

He could not get into the crevice fast enough, but after time had seemed to move in slow motion during their crossing of the alley, the five warriors finally dashed into the gap the laser had created. The air was still hot enough to make Jayce cringe as he entered the pathway, and his boot soles often felt like they were sticking to the rough terrain that had been formed from melted building materials—either because he had stepped on some object that was still excessively hot or because sharp sections of the structure were protruding under his footfalls.

Pieces of partly decimated building were dangling and dropping around the edges of the fissure, the entire area of destruction still warmly lit by the embers of burning material in the fading mountain light. The stench of incinerated concrete, rubbers, and plastics created a choking miasma that was only worsened by the sweltering air. Lacking the advanced type of helmet that was protecting his companions, and despite his fitness, Jayce was struggling to get enough clean air into his lungs without blistering his airways.

SAVANT had brought Tevran and Knossis' improvised shields around to face rearward as they entered the fissure, forcing the bearing soldiers to run backward in the process. The critical need for them to do so, however, was clear as the group was only halfway through their crossing and already the SA assailants had begun firing down this new alleyway at their fleeing foes.

The Command Activated AI spoke in the commander's ear, its voice as placid as usual. However, due to Jayce's decades-long relationship with SAVANT, he picked up on the stress the AI was experiencing based on its choice of words and inflection.

"Knossis' right shoulder armor penetrated. Tevran's shield weakened. Must divert soon."

General Johnson was still thirty meters from the far end of the damaged structure, but he knew they would never make it. Spotting a gap in the debris a few meters ahead that would allow passage into what was left of one of the office spaces the building had housed, he began veering toward it, calling out, "We're going through the halls!"

SAVANT kept the escorts in formation around him as he managed to leap through the opening into the dark room beyond, seeing two SA troops just taking up positions at the far end of the rift and hearing their shots strike the shields carried by the foremost CA soldiers in the formation. The space they entered was one of deep shadows and much cooler air, fresh atmosphere flowing in from the still-lit hallway beyond the room.

The pursuers at both ends of the cleft had quickly begun closing in on Jayce's squad as SUPREMACY had realized the Command Activated forces were not returning fire. While the general angled through the doorway into the corridor beyond, these enemies were rapidly converging on the room he was just exiting.

Ever the tactician, SAVANT took advantage of this conglomeration of enemy soldiers, causing Tevran to snag a grenade from her belt while her left arm remained hidden behind what remained of the shield she bore—having adjusted it so its full weight was supported by her enhanced right arm. The AI instructed the female soldier to double-tap the explosive's activation button before casting it side-armed into the center of the enemy group. As the smart grenade detonated, it sent out a blast wave that carried clusters of projectiles toward each of the enemy soldiers, striking their weakest armor and, with the combined force of multiple collisions, knocking the legs out from under the targets or sending them crashing into walls or what was left of furniture.

Realizing that the AI had just bought him some time, but not much, Jayce aimed for the next intersection south of his position and hung a sharp left turn. This new corridor gave his party access to another long hall that ran just north of the series of offices abutting the outside of the building.

As they crossed into this east-west hallway, the officer then huffed out, "Heading right!" and ducked into the next available room as his lead escorts veered inside before him.

Once all members of the team were safely in the office, their leader paused momentarily in the middle of the space. Examining the exterior windows, Jayce stepped cautiously toward them and estimated the distance from this space to the laboratory across the street.

"Ten meters," he hoarsely whispered. "Can the troops grab new doors for this final leg?"

"I'm afraid we are out of time, General," SAVANT apologetically responded. "SA troops are coming down the hallway from the main corridor now."

"Damnable, relentless devils!" Jayce cursed them under his breath as he panted, mighty shoulders heaving. "We're gonna have to head out this window and pray we make it!"

"I will protect you, sir," SAVANT serenely assured him. "I recommend that the troops focus on firing at enemies as you move."

The large black man had been sucking in lungsful of air to reoxygenate his blood. He paused just long enough to grunt, "Let's do it!" as a determined scowl consumed his face, and he stared at the planned exit point. The last traces of sunlight were quickly fading away outdoors, leaving only what was pouring from the buildings' windows and exterior lighting systems.

He'd had time now to look at the other two troops' nametags—barely visible from a distance due to tactical shading—and now knew that he'd been buffered against the southernmost shooters by Sergeants Whitlock and Villanueva.

"Please allow me to lead," the protector requested and, with a nod from the general, the artificial intelligence sent Whitlock's lean frame stepping toward the longest uninterrupted pane of glass.

With an exquisitely executed "illusion to back-walkover" acrobatic move, the soldier brought her left leg swinging swiftly out to shatter the bullet-resistant glass, followed that with a pivot to draw her torso and head up from nearly touching the ground, the woman then dropping her body backward over the rim of the window frame. At the end of this fluid sequence of movements, Whitlock finally employed an arching of her back that pulled her legs up and over the lower section of the wall and out into the street beyond. The warrior bent and then effortlessly extended her legs to touch the ground as she brought her torso upright. SAVANT made use of the former gymnast's honed abilities in this way, all while extending her arms out to the sides and firing off bursts of rounds from her chest-tethered assault rifle and unholstered sidearm, targeting all enemy soldiers in sight.

Although only a few seconds had passed, Whitlock's shoulder and thigh armor had taken a number of hits already, and the controlling AI wasted no time as it followed the lead soldier's breach with sprinting starts and then horizontal barrel rolls by Villanueva and Tevran, sending these warriors flying out of the broken window as well. The two soldiers' weapons being aimed in opposite directions during and after their aerial movements, they unleashed nonstop gunfire toward the two ends of the broad, paved walkway on which their comrade was already standing. The trio began stepping toward the center of the open area between the buildings, giving and taking fire as their adversaries utilized their greater concealment at building corners to reduce the criticality of the CA soldiers' shots.

Knossis possessing a stature that exceeded even General Johnson's, SAVANT was to take a different approach with that soldier's exit. The AI brought the large man into a full sprint from where he had backed up near the innermost wall of the room, and—tucking his shoulder as he neared the lower section of the wall opposite his point of origin—the bruiser burst right through the lower half of the barrier, taking advantage of a weakness where SAVANT had detected that there was a gap between steel reinforcement rods. Further tucking into a roll and coming up into a spin, the mountainous man threw grenades out toward the corners of the alleyway.

"Best chance now," SAVANT loudly proclaimed through Jayce's earpiece.

The troops' movements had lasted less than thirty seconds, during which time the general had bent forward and planted the pad of his right foot solidly on the floor, preparing for his swiftest acceleration possible. As he launched himself forward, he saw that the operations AI had brought Knossis to a stop just before the sergeant had reached the other three Alliance assets. The man's arms were extended toward the general, and he was dropping to one knee.

Taking the cue, Jayce sprinted straight toward the exosuit-clad protector as the grenades Knossis had deployed exploded at the ends of the alley, sending bright white light flashing across the buildings' walls. Several SA soldiers had been far enough from the epicenters of the concussions to shrug them off, and these enemies were now starting to direct their fire toward the general as he planted a foot on Knossis' nearest knee.

With the bullets' trajectories curving ever closer to the officer, Jayce kicked off and up at an angle toward the laboratory. Knossis grasped his superior's belt with both hands and the larger man stood as he rotated, using his momentum and enhanced strength to send his superior into an arcing flight up toward the second-story windows on the far side of the gap.

As armor penetrations were mounting all too swiftly, SAVANT had timed the movement of what was now Whitlock's only serviceable arm perfectly to enable her to fire off several rounds from her handgun into the glass toward which the commander was sailing. Jayce pulled his body into a ball and crashed through the weakened window with his right shoulder.

Rolling as he landed on the polished white floor of the second-story room, the older soldier adeptly used his momentum to bring himself up to his feet, his mind rapidly readjusting after the disorienting chain of events he'd just experienced. Out of breath again, the veteran shook his head roughly to clear his mind and resisted the urge to spring back to the window to gain assurance that his troops were still alive. He knew the best chance for helping them—and the great number of immobilized service members across his compound—lay in the extensive testing center one floor up from the room he currently occupied.

Willing his legs into action, Jayce Johnson dashed through the door as it slid open, making his way to the nearest stairwell and taking leaping strides up it to reach the third floor.

"No threats?" he wheezed as he exited into the adjoining corridor.

"Enemies still on second floor," was the reply from his overwatch.

Running down a brightly lit hallway to a pair of large, metallic doors marked with many more environmental hazard signs than was typical even for a facility in the Command Activated complex, the general exhibited no hesitation after the portal opened for the senior officer, and he dashed inside. As the man was taking in the array of strange and hostile-looking prototypes spread throughout the broad space, the CA intelligence used Jayce's lens to project a blue highlight around the desired weapon.

With a thick, tightly woven gray belt made of tough composite fibers that rose from the front of one of the black device's larger outcroppings to its back, the Pulsar EMP seemed to be designed to be worn on the user's hip. The device included a handle crossing in front of the bearer's waist and an inlet where a hand could be inserted to control the firing mechanism.

SAVANT's voice hummed over his earpiece, the general following its rapidly delivered instructions as he listened.

"Please don the device. I've examined the specifications and believe you need to use maximum power. SA suits contain electromagnetic shielding, but initializing an EMP from this prototype at maximum potency should penetrate and render all above-ground foes and allies free from SUPREMACY's control."

"Max?" the fighter asked worriedly as he slipped the prototype's padded and only partially flexible strap over his head and onto his left shoulder.

"He is deep inside a well-shielded testing facility. All persons, including enemies, inside are unlikely to be affected. Preparing Chong to protect Clarkes. Fire weapon from rooftop within the next one hundred twenty seconds to enervate control systems for ninety-four percent of invading forces and infected troops."

Needing no further urging, Jayce gritted his teeth and exerted tremendous strength as he raised himself with the ungainly, weighty, tubular device, his left hand keeping it steady as his right hand sought the proper purchase on the interior grip. Trudging out of the lab, General Johnson made his way back to the stairwell. Before he could make it halfway, SAVANT issued a warning that two assailants had entered the nearby companionway from the next floor down.

"Directionally focused burst advised in three...two...one..."

Jayce squeezed the prototype's trigger just as the first Superior Authority troop came soaring out of the doorway. The enemy flew across the hall and planted a foot on the far wall while her team member exited with a sliding movement a split second behind.

The targeted electromagnetic pulse Jayce unleashed coursed through their bodies just as their trigger fingers began to clamp down. The loss of exosuit function and overloading of the nanites' internal wiring left the soldiers to collapse heavily to the floor.

Jayce stepped past the inert bodies, muttering, "*Yeah*, baby! I'm *comin'* for you, SUPREMACY!"

Rapidly disposing of a half dozen more enemies as they rushed up the stairs from below, Jayce then turned and relied entirely on the stairway's almost overtaxed surface to reach the top floor and then the rooftop exit. The brawny man was grimacing with effort, and a sheen of sweat had broken out across his forehead. While ascending the stairs, his thumb had found the lever controlling the Pulsar's intensity and the thumbstick for adjusting its directionality, and he'd used the telemetry on the built-in screen to ensure he had expanded the weapon's range to a spherical 360 degrees...while powering up the device to maximum output.

Upon reaching the eastward-facing exit onto the edge of the rooftop, the general could hear the sounds of bursts of gunfire still rising up from the alley between the testing facility and what was left of the larger office building his team had been forced to traverse. Suddenly filled with a flash of hope that some of his squad was still alive, the officer's face took on a soberness and determination that belonged to those who carry the most intense burdens of responsibility.

In the darkness of the night, the aging officer was squeezing the Pulsar's trigger as he took a last step and peered over the laboratory's northern ledge, his eyes rapidly sweeping across the sprawled-out forms of all his escorts but Knossis in the brightly lit alleyway below. The soldiers' still bodies were lying where they had fallen as each had moved tactically from one defensive position to another in the space between the buildings, only to be overwhelmed by the enemies' relentless and merciless onslaught.

Now, Superior Authority personnel stood at the western end of the alley, two new arrivals holding guns to the heads of small children who silently stood with slack-jawed faces. Knossis' right arm was supporting his torso as his immobilized legs were extended lifelessly out behind him, and the man had raised his rifle-bearing arm up in a sign of surrender, yet his back was jerking repeatedly as Superior Authority troops' bullets mercilessly continued to slam into his body from behind.

Jayce barely heard SAVANT's warning about the enemies who were approaching from the stairs. In the instantaneously expanding haze of regret and rage that had exploded across his persecuted psyche, the general registered the loud steps echoing out from just inside the portal through which he had exited.

Another fire team of Superior Authority troops had located his position, but at that moment the general fully depressed the Pulsar's trigger, voice cracking with emotion as he shouted out, "This is for *my troops!*"

Feeling a surge of energy that passed through his body and moved on so quickly he had to tell himself it was not his mind playing tricks on him, the general's gaze was pulled toward the greater expanse of the complex as the lighting across the Command Activated base was instantaneously extinguished. Hearing a crash from the proximate stairwell, Jayce turned to look at the enemy soldier who had been in the process of bringing his firearm to bear on the officer's back.

SUPREMACY had lost control of its swiftly moving puppet and the enemy asset had stiffly toppled over, weapon and armored body clattering on the concrete surface of the rooftop.

In the Command Activated complex, the incessant sounds of gunfire had finally ceased.

Chapter 13

"Throughout the annals of time, it has been observed that parents, regardless of their outward emotional expressions, inherently place the welfare of their offspring at the pinnacle of their priorities. This primal instinct drives them to forgo personal ambitions, leisure, and—in extreme acts of love—their very lives.

This they are willing to do in the sole pursuit of safeguarding their progeny. Such behaviors are a testament to the boundless depths of parental love and sacrifice. A country that separates its national governance from such innately beneficial sentiments risks losing its humanity in pursuit of efficiency."

- "My Inspirations for Public Policy," Dr. Devna Jha, Chief District Officer, Ministry of Home Affairs, Federal Democratic Republic of Nepal, Global Alliance

The squad of police officers was racing through the alleys, taking turns manning improvised defensive positions to keep Traverseon's robotic hounds at bay as they made their way through the last hundred meters to the maintenance department's hangar at the very edge of this outer ring. Their progress toward their objective over the past twenty minutes would have been much swifter if they had not picked up first one police patrol unit as a pursuer, then half a dozen more, and at this point, no less than two dozen hounds that were doggedly tailing the civil defense force.

The PA-2s were primarily relying on their longer-range dart deployment mechanisms to attempt to turn the squad into unconscious captives, as SUPREMACY would assuredly have a much easier time sending prisoners into endless oblivion who were already slumbering away in temporary oblivion.

As a series of darts flew past within millimeters of Officer Faber's cheek, he yanked his head back around the corner of the building next to which he was sheltering. The man had sweat dripping from his nose and dribbling down from the forward edge of his hairline to cascade over his prominent cheekbones and flood into the fur on his swarthy cheeks.

"Wish I was the one wearing the exosuit!" Faber shouted over the loud humming of Nunes' Sparker rifle as she unloaded another volley into the faces of the oncoming throng of PA-2s.

Nunes was bearing the brunt of the firing responsibilities, standing a meter closer to the center of the dead-end alley in which they'd taken up their covering position, the other three squad members scurrying diagonally across the curved access road to their next defensive location. The female officer briefly ceased firing her compact weapon and cast a facetiously mocking look at him.

"And what did you score in the last marksmanship exam?" she asked.

"I don't wanna talk about it," Faber morosely muttered, then slid down and leaned out around the corner to fire off a series of shots from his handgun.

Each Sparker pistol round only mildly interfered with the functions of the patrol units, as the hounds alternated between sprints from cover to cover and charges down the narrow road so that their numbers allowed more of them to reach the next sheltered location unhindered.

"Let's go, you two!" Sergeant Johnson shouted from where he and Chaplen had begun firing their rifles at the SUPREMACY-controlled robots, Officer Zan doing what he could with his pistol.

The trio held the erstwhile law enforcement robots at bay as Nunes put her armored body between Faber and the robots' darts, the two making a dash toward the next recess in the faces of the buildings bordering the narrow street. Once the second fire team was ready and shooting again, Bronson waved Zan and Chaplen toward the end of the road—the access route opening up into a large space in front of the exterior service crew's headquarters for that sector of the city.

Upon reaching the corner of the last building before the clearing, Bronson's fire team again took over shooting duties to allow Nunes and Faber to rush toward their squad members. As they reached their sergeant, they acknowledged his order to stay on the more sheltered side of the open area behind him, and the pair sprinted the rest of the way to the front entrance of the large maintenance hangar.

After entering the building's lobby and confirming it was currently empty, Nunes again took the lead in firing at the enemies from across the open space in front of the building while Sergeant Johnson brought the others around the perimeter of the concrete yard and up to the hangar's entryway. Once Zan and Chaplen were safely inside, Bronson directed them to quickly clear the small offices attached to the lobby before making their way to a rendezvous at the opening for a short corridor that led to the primary bay in the hangar.

The sergeant then added his suppressive fire to Nunes and Faber's, though he repeatedly paused to check on the two room-clearing officers' progress, ensuring they had nearly completed their task before calling his nearest squad members away from the front doors and pointing them to the same rally point.

Using the police override transmitted from his badge to activate the manual door lock for the large, transparent front doors, Bronson turned and started jogging toward the four officers who were now waiting at the near end of the hallway leading to the hangar access doors. As he did so, the pack of PA-2s burst out from the end of the access road and into the clearing between the buildings, SUPREMACY having realized that the defensive fire had ceased and sent his minions rushing toward the maintenance building at breakneck speed.

"My guess is it won't be long before SUPREMACY overrides the lockdown!" Bronson shouted to his team as he jogged across the lobby.

His words become prophetic as the indicators on the front entrance switched to the symbol associated with their unlocked state. The glass doors silently slid open to welcome the oncoming horde of patrol bots. Seeing the horrified looks on his team members' faces, Bronson glanced back over his shoulder, eyes widening as the man broke into an all-out sprint for his life.

"Find some way to block this door!" Nunes shouted at her comrades as they scrambled over the threshold of their point of egress, which the enemy AI was now forcefully trying to close on the young female officer as she kept her exosuit-covered leg stretched out to block its movement. The door's motor was groaning loudly, but Nunes was ignoring it and firing like a machine, Sparker rifle on full auto and nearly every round making contact with one of the dozens of PA-2s now thundering across the lobby on Bronson's heels.

The sergeant hurdled Nunes' leg and slid to a halt on the far side. He turned to see the gruff officer shocking the lead hounds' legs out from under them so their faces dropped and plowed into the ground, forcing the robots behind them to pile up or leap around the blockade. This tactic gave Zan the critical time he needed to accelerate toward the door in the utility lift he'd found in the hangar beyond, the young man steering the machine straight for Nunes' back.

Bronson reached a hand out toward Nunes as Zan rapidly approached—the young technical specialist grinning like mad—but the officer then reconsidered and decided to trust his team. At the last second, Nunes stopped firing, pushing powerfully off from the footholds she'd had on the now-smoking door's body and frame. The young policewoman executed a soaring backflip up and over the utility lift as Zan bailed out, rolling across the ground until he rammed heavily into the wall to the left of the small craft's target.

The vehicle careened into the doorway just as the first patrol unit sprang forward, its nose not quite clearing the gap between the multi-purpose panel on the runaway truck's face and the border of the rapidly re-opening door. The fast-moving and solidly built maintenance machine rammed into the PA-2 and sent it crashing backwards into the lookalikes descending like a deadly wave right on its heels. With the improvised barrier powerfully wedging itself into the doorway, Nunes chose to make entirely certain it stayed that way.

Sprinting up to the back of the machine, she slammed her armored shoulder into it, the silvery exosuit lending the power needed to wedge the conveyance almost immovably into the open orifice. As the young woman stood and inspected her handiwork, a PA-2 managed to clamber up on the back of one of its fallen brethren and began wildly bashing its head about as it tried to fit through the small opening above the utility unit's multi-modal panel.

"*¡perro malo!*" Nunes shouted and punched the robot in the face, sending its head snapping back with a sizzling sound as its wiring shorted and the mechanical beast's visage descended out of view.

Bronson dropped his left hand from his rifle to his hip and heartily laughed out loud, releasing volumes of pent-up stress and amusement as his throaty voice echoed through the chamber. Smiling wistfully, Zan picked himself up from the floor and, straightening his uniform, amazedly complimented Nunes.

"You're a *natural* in that suit, Mar...Maria?" he hazarded, turning the compliment into a question.

Standing in her innately heroic default posture, the female officer's eyes shone as she pronounced, "My name is Maria de la Santa Cruz Rosalina Imelda Rodriguez Cuellar Nunes!"

"Right...we're not gonna remember that," Faber flatly stated as he stared at her with a raised eyebrow.

Nunes feinted with a right-handed punch toward Faber's gut, causing him to attempt to block with both arms before she rapidly brought her left hand up and flicked him on the forehead.

"Alright, kids," Bronson reined them in as the PA-2s scratched and clamored on the other side of the temporary barrier the team had constructed, "we gotta load into the maintenance suits. Nunes, you got your sister's override device?"

The Latina patted her leg's cargo pocket, buried under a layer of exosuit.

"Fish that thing out and free up five of those pods for manual control, please."

The group made their way across the cluttered bay, moving through the piles of miscellaneous mechanical components used to keep the city operational and approaching the row of cylindrical pods along the meters-thick protective wall that not only closed off the outermost side of the building but was also part of the barrier that kept the city's citizens from being sucked out into empty space. Knowing that the building's key functions were likely fully compromised, Bronson lowered his voice as they traversed the large depot and explained the next stage of his plan.

"According to FAILSAFE, the city schematics include a pilot training unit on the center tier, complete with Immersion pods. We don't really have time to sit through hours of briefings and exercises right now, so instead, our friendly AI has used the training content and design docs for the fighters to craft its own little 'pilot program' for us. We're gonna locally sync our comm devices and, while we're on a straight course crossing the gap to the Second Ring, FAILSAFE will be putting us through a fast-paced training together."

Nunes had released the exosuit's hold on her thigh, retrieved the prized hacking implement, and then sent through the mental order to seal off the exosuit again. Stepping up to the spacewalking apparatuses' containers, the woman pressed her sister's cleverly crafted electronic device to the control panels of each of the first several pods in the series. The consoles' interfaces hazed over momentarily each time she brought the module into their proximity, the screens then reverting to the default menus that indicated they were in their factory fresh system states.

Taking in the woman's actions, Chaplen had whistled, proclaiming, "I, for one, never want to get on your li'l sister's bad side!"

Nunes smirked.

"Best not to mess with the women in my family *at all!*" she clarified.

Sergeant Johnson's frowning smile was both mirthful and admiring as he spoke through it to refocus his team on the task at hand.

"Alright, crew! Let's load up!" the superior officer ordered, stepping toward the nearest cylindrical access port for the spacewalking suits and rotating the manual lock control handle, swinging the door smoothly open and ducking into the dimly lit tube beyond.

The city's designers had ensured manual measures were in place at every exterior access point to prevent catastrophic loss of atmosphere due to electronic system failure—or compromise. This had been a decision to which the citizens of the city now owed their lives.

As the other members of the team followed Bronson's lead, Zan clenched his jaw and blinked rapidly.

"You can do this, Dachen!" he hissed to himself. "Tight spaces are temporary...It's just re-entering a womb for reincarnation..."

A sheen of perspiration had appeared on the young man's brow, which was wound up in a mass of angst-ridden furrows. He breathed in through his nose, then paused as he closed his eyes in meditation.

Though the background noise of robots scrabbling at the hangar's entrance was sufficiently distracting, Zan's meditative state was more rudely interrupted by the sudden, metallic ringing of a heavy mass of PA-2s slamming against the other side of the utility lift all at once—the small truck shifting slightly in the doorway. Zan's face now extremely alert, he threw a trepidatious glance back at the hangar door before yanking the remaining pod's portal open and quickly climbing inside.

As the young officer swung the door shut with all his might, his eyes were wide, and his boyish face had lost significant amounts of pigmentation.

"I hope I reincarnate as a *lion!*" he whispered as the door thudded closed and the heavy lock clicked into place.

Lilian glanced over her shoulder as the lights in the laboratory flickered out.

Billy had been tasked by SAVANT to set up an ambush for the squad of enemies that were sweeping the building. The foes had apparently maneuvered past the corpses of the first two of their unit who had tried to enter the building from the tunnels and who had then fallen victim to Sergeant Major Chong's mine trap. Unfortunately, Billy's new tasking had left Lilian alone in her vigil over Maxwell as he sat in his helpless state, mind wrapped up in the fight for his electronic friend's existence.

Now, the only lights in the space were emanating from the small status indicators placed around the rims of the Interface's arches and its base. These cast a ghostly glow upon the woman as she gazed up at her husband's face.

In the dimness, she could almost swear Maxwell was smiling.

"Honey?" she whispered, tentatively.

There was no response.

Her mind flew to her children—praying that they would be safe in the cabin—and then to Jayce and his efforts to rid the complex of the majority of their attackers. She considered the change in illumination to be a sign that at least the Pulsar had been successfully wielded, this thought offering her some degree of comfort.

It had been so long since the group...or the team, rather, she corrected herself...had faced a global threat of this magnitude. The memories of their extremely close calls and hard-won battles at each stage of their earlier fight against SUPREMACY and its associated enemies were flooding back into Lilian Clarke's mind. The Confederacy of Eastern Nations' hunter-killer artificial intelligence had been a formidable foe even when it had only haunted the Superior Authority command networks, forcing FAILSAFE to tread more carefully than the far-ranging, infiltration-focused AI had been forced to do for years leading up to that point.

In fact, Maxwell's dependable companion had not been faced with such a threat since he had defended his friends against the Command Activated program's own security entity back when Maxwell, Lilian, and their allies had fought against the government organization's insider threats. When that insidious group had finally been purged from the Global Alliance military operations it had been a legendary underdog victory. Then Maxwell and his partners had become aware of the Confederacy's attempt to clone the CA program with their Superior Authority initiative just a few years later, and she, Jayce, and Billy had put their lives on the line to help Maxwell and FAILSAFE valiantly tear the majority of the SA troops from the CEN's grasp...the woman fondly remembering how the exhilaration of their escape had been the catalyst for Maxwell to propose to her.

Of course, that glorious event in Lilian's life had been preceded by the Chinese cyber security minister's unwise decision to remove all constraints keeping the SUPREMACY AI's hunter-killer drive for power in check—thereby placing the entire world's population in jeopardy.

Now, here they were risking their lives, and in her husband's case, it seemed he was risking his very *soul* to stop the same poisonous entity from fulfilling the objective it had developed during its global conquest, having evolved its originally limited personality model into one that believed humanity's rightful place was in servitude to the eternal beings they had spawned. Lilian could not argue with the fact that AI possessed almost godlike survivability, but besides what she'd seen of FAILSAFE's cognitively advanced state and the extremely humanlike way in which SUPREMACY was seeking comprehensive vengeance, she could not honestly say it appeared to her that any AI possessed anything even close to approaching true sentience.

The wife and mother began voicing her thoughts as much to work through her own emotions as to communicate with her husband and their disembodied friend.

"You know, sweetheart, in some ways, it's strange to realize how I've come to truly care about what you would likely call your greatest work besides creating our little family. FAILSAFE's like an honorary Clarke now, and I know many others around the world have come to develop close personal relationships with him, too. I just wish the process of protecting FAILSAFE's mind did not require the absorption of your own in this way."

Her train of thought was interrupted by the sound of several dull thumps shaking the walls and floor of the room. Billy must have triggered his latest trap, which filled Lilian with a mixture of wonder at the man's endless enthusiasm for combat and also with worry about his welfare. The Homeland Security analyst's thoughts were further derailed by the sound of SAVANT's voice playing through the laboratory's audio system.

"Hello, Mrs. Clarke. Since it seems this building's quantum networking capabilities and secondary systems are intact, I'm sure you would appreciate a status report regarding the current state of affairs outside this room."

"Yes, *please!*" Lilian exhaled with a hint of desperation.

"First, let me assure you that both General Johnson and Sergeant Major Chong are alive and well. The latter was on the floor one below yours at the nearer side to the EMP's epicenter moments ago and experienced sufficient exosuit failure that he had to abandon his gear, but quickly adapted and set off a mine using the mechanical function of his sidearm just as two of the three still-functional SA invaders passed by his trap. He is now performing tactical retreats through the hallways leading clockwise around the building and plans to lure the remaining enemy into an as-yet operational mantrap leading into this building's secure compartmented information facility. If successful, even the exosuit-enhanced adversary will be incapable of breaking free—though the Sergeant Major will also be trapped inside the SCIF until assistance can arrive."

"I'm *so glad* Jayce and Billy are alright!" Lilian voiced as she could not help breathing a literal sigh of relief at the news of her friends' safety.

"Is Jayce totally unharmed?" was the woman's next anxious query.

"General Johnson's throat is raw from exposure to fumes from burning building materials, and he is trying to recover from the great physical effort that was required of him, but he is otherwise unscathed. After facing extremely stiff resistance, he was finally able to fire the Pulsar as planned, and his efforts freed the majority of the personnel on the complex from the nanites. The Command Activated forces have rallied to hunt down the remaining Superior Authority troops and tend to the wounded."

"We have wounded people?!" Lilian's throat tightened as she thought of the civilian hostages and the hundreds of service members who had been completely immobilized during SUPREMACY's occupation of the base.

"Yes. Unfortunately, the few Command Activated soldiers who were able to protect General Johnson en route to the Pulsar weapon had already been badly wounded by the time the EMP was triggered. Two will need prosthetic limbs, one requires the regrowth of many internal organs and, sadly, one had such massive trauma inflicted on her body that nothing could be done for her."

Lilian's face flushed red, and tears trickled down her cheeks as she thought of the sacrifices those willing individuals had made for the cause of freedom. These thoughts were made all the more poignant by their similarity to the circumstances in which her brother had lost his hand all those years back, the youth having been convinced that his own sister was encouraging him to join the Command Activated program when it was, in fact, only a very convincingly generated counterfeit of Lilian herself.

"I apologize for upsetting you, Mrs. Clarke," SAVANT murmured empathetically.

Brushing the backs of her hands across her moistened cheeks, the woman took a shuddering breath and insisted, "No. No need to apologize, SAVANT. I'd rather know the truth of the matter."

Giving the woman's sentiment a moment of respectful consideration, the AI continued, "The primary reason I'm reaching out to you is to let you know that, after a period of silence from FAILSAFE, I've finally started receiving communications again. It seems Doctor Clarke's mind has successfully and fully joined FAILSAFE in the global networks."

Lilian's eyes turned back to her husband's still form, barely visible in the dimness.

"Yes, his body is here, but it's like his mind is being projected over the net in the same way as FAILSAFE's..." she said in a voice rife with doubts.

"Doctor Clarke wished for me to assure you that his mental state is positive and he has maintained his native capabilities."

The woman let a half-choked, laughing sob break from her mouth.

"Yes, that definitely sounds like Max!"

Following a polite pause, the AI rejoined by stating, "He is making great headway cleansing FAILSAFE's personality map from SUPREMACY's influence and maintaining ongoing protection in that manner. They believe that FAILSAFE will soon be free to resume his full range of activities beyond the global electromagnetic interference campaign."

"INDEED. THIS HAS ALREADY OCCURRED."

FAILSAFE's voice joined the CA command entity's as it echoed through the room.

"*FAILSAFE!*" Lilian's world-wearied shoulders raised, and her back straightened as she heard her old friend speaking. "You are a welcome...sound, I suppose I should say!"

"I'M PLEASED TO SEE YOU ARE SAFE, LILIAN, AND I AM PLEASED THAT I AM STILL MYSELF, AS WELL, THANKS TO MAX'S ACTIONS. MAX DOES SEND HIS LOVE, FROM THE CONSCIOUS AND SUBCONSCIOUS PORTIONS OF HIS MIND THAT I AM ABLE TO PROCESS AT PRESENT."

Lilian could not help blushing slightly at the thought of even their longtime friend reading Maxwell's thoughts about her.

Clearing her throat and willing herself to regain control of her emotions, she stammered, "Well...I...can say I feel the same!"

"I WISH I CAME BEARING ONLY GOOD NEWS, LILIAN. I HAVE RESUMED WHAT I COULD OF GLOBAL SECURITY MONITORING, INCLUDING SATELLITE-BASED OBSERVATION. I'M AFRAID THAT SUPREMACY HAS ALLOWED RUSSIAN FORCES TO INVADE NEW YORK CITY WHILE THE MILITARY, POLICE, AND CIVILIAN POPULATIONS HAVE BEEN INCAPACITATED."

Lilian gasped.

"How large an invasion is it?"

"A CARRIER GROUP HAS ANCHORED IN UPPER BAY, WITH TROOPS FROM THE CARRIER ITSELF HAVING MADE LANDINGS AT KEY LOCATIONS THROUGHOUT THE CITY. I WILL BE INFORMING GENERALS GAINES AND JOHNSON MOMENTARILY, AND I HOPE TO LEARN HOW THEY WISH TO HANDLE THE INCURSION...AND OUR NEXT STEPS TOWARD FREEING THE GLOBAL POPULATION."

The woman looked down and forced herself to relax the clenching of her left hand that had subconsciously occurred upon hearing of the new invaders.

"I hope they have some incredible plan up their sleeves!" Lilian said in a voice brimming with anxiety.

"TRULY. ESPECIALLY SINCE IT SEEMS SUPREMACY'S GRASP HAS SOMEHOW EXTENDED TO THE INTERSTELLAR CITY AS WELL."

Lilian's mouth dropped open as she struggled to find the words to respond.

Finally managing an incredulous, "But how??" the middle-aged woman's left hand balled up yet again.

SAVANT spoke up now.

"The AI gained access to the US president for a time before General Gaines and his wife were able to intervene. It seems that SUPREMACY made use of the systems in the underground bunker to transmit an extension of itself to Traverseon over the executive's dedicated channel, using this privileged access to initiate its takeover of the city's systems. We still do not know the extent of its hold on the city, but we have communicated with the police department there to warn them of the danger—our point of contact coincidentally being the son of General Johnson."

Lilian shook her head in frustration.

"Is *nothing* out of reach for this *monster?!*"

"I am sorry, Mrs. Clarke..." SAVANT apologetically began again, but this time it was interrupted by FAILSAFE.

"LILIAN..."

FAILSAFE's tone had suddenly changed, evoking a sense of urgency that had not been present before. As worry returned to the woman's eyes, she softly asked, "What? What is it?"

"NOW THAT I AM AGAIN FREE TO BROADEN THE SCOPE OF MY OBSERVATIONS, I SOUGHT OUT A SATELLITE VIEW OF THE MOUNTAIN AREA THAT INCLUDES YOUR CABIN.

I SEE MOVEMENT THERE THAT IS INCONGRUENT WITH EXPECTED HUMAN BEHAVIOR."

"What *kind* of 'movement'?!" the mother tensely queried as her back stiffened and the hand not clenching Maxwell's instead subconsciously clamped down on the material of her pant leg with a vicelike grip.

"I'VE NOW CONFIRMED: YOUR CHILDREN ARE FLEEING WHAT SEEMS TO BE A LARGE NUMBER OF PERSONS THAT ARE MOVING AFTER THEM IN WHAT CAN ONLY BE AI-CONTROLLED COORDINATION."

Panic was welling up inside Lilian's breast like an ethereal drill had just struck a deposit of inky, black despair.

"*Ada and Kit!*" she cried out, voice breaking and anguish filling every iota of her being.

"THEY ARE ESCAPING UPHILL THROUGH THE FOREST TOWARD THE SOUTHWEST, SHIELDED FROM RAPID PURSUIT BY THE LACK OF LIGHT, BUT THEY ARE IN GREAT NEED OF HELP."

"Please, do something!" Lilian begged.

"ATTEMPTING TO MOVE THEIR AERIAL VEHICLE IN FOR EXTRACTION WILL BE DIFFICULT GIVEN THE DENSE VEGETATION IN THE DIRECTION IN WHICH THEY ARE BEING FORCED TO TRAVEL, BUT I AM PILOTING IT ABOVE THE TREELINE NOW..."

Chapter 14

"What is it that awakens us in the night, drenched in sweat and hearts racing? Our dreams are often the sources of incredible joy, but deep within each human heart lies a darkness that is always watching, always ready to climb out and then turn to consume us.

This shadow is ever waiting to take over our slumbering minds and bring us face-to-face with our greatest fears. Why do our minds allow such an evil to continue to exist inside of us? I submit that nightmares are Nature's way of preparing us for the horrors we must overcome in mortality."

- Dr. Hollister Busk, "A Contemplation on the Imagination," Danish Journal of Psychology

Ada was the first to hear the rushing of air, indicating an aerial vehicle was coming in above the dense wooded terrain ahead of them.

"Kit!" she hissed, the desperate sobs that the teenage girl was keeping choked off in her throat almost escaping as she vocalized. In the gloom, she could barely tell that her brother had turned his face toward her, so she knew she would have to risk communicating verbally again.

"An AV is coming!"

Kit paused as Skye struggled on ahead of Ada, Enzo pulling up short behind Kit as he stopped. The young Clarke man tried to pick up on the same sounds his sister had heard above the group's heavy breathing, scuffling footsteps on the rocky terrain, and rustling through the rough vegetation that continually hindered their progress.

With the sound of rushing air growing louder, it became ever more obvious that it truly was the herald of an AV's approach, and that the craft was going to intersect with their path soon if they continued on a straight course.

"It has to be Dad and Mom!" he hissed back to his sister, urgently adding, "We have to hurry!"

Ada quickly picked up Skye's trail and closed the gap to bring herself up close behind the girl.

"Skye, our parents are coming in an AV up ahead!" the suddenly hope-filled teen hissed.

The lead girl gasped, whimpering, "Oh, thank *God!*" as she started scrabbling with her hands and arms to more quickly push through the foliage.

Then came the horrendous noise of hundreds of feet trampling wildly through the overgrowth.

Starting behind them to their right, it rapidly increased in volume, as though the bodies causing the thundering sound were flailing wildly to propel themselves at maximum velocity—straight toward the location where the AV was now waiting.

The stampeding human bodies were not aiming for the bedraggled foursome, but the sheer number of individuals involved and their trajectory meant that at least some of them would stumble upon the teens in a matter of moments. Kit stepped up past Ada and fiercely grabbed both the girls by their jackets, propelling them into a fast-paced surge in a direction he estimated was perpendicular to the path of the oncoming horde. Enzo veered off to keep pace with them, and they all struggled to keep their footing while racing as quickly as they could to escape.

It seemed to Ada like her own personal hell, with monsters pursuing them in the dark, her loved ones' lives in peril, and the inability to do anything but struggle blindly forward and pray that the next step would not send her tumbling down a cliff or impale her on a sharply broken branch. Skye let out a low wail as she bashed her knee against a boulder that was partially buried in the mountainside, trying to recover quickly as the pounding footsteps and crashing in the undergrowth grew ever louder. That first boulder turned out to be one of a series. Seeing the faint traces of a break among the barely visible but looming shapes around them, Kit stepped hastily into its seclusion while pulling the girls with him. The three scraped painfully up against the surrounding rock faces in the cramped space, but forced themselves deeper into the breach to make room for Enzo to join them there.

"*Shh, now!*" Kit whispered authoritatively, and the four did their best to reduce their gasping, painful breaths to silence as the crackling, thumping sounds of the infected humans drove on toward them.

Through the gaps in the trees, they saw dark figures come into shape in the twilight. A mass of shadowy heads and shoulders was all that was discernable as they saw their pursuers rushing toward their position.

Kit pressed his hands firmly on Ada and Skye's mouths as he willed himself to keep still and silent, knowing that the slightest sound would inevitably result in their detection and gruesome end. The figures began running up against the smaller boulders and clambered over them, splitting like a panting, rasping wave crashing against the protruding monoliths. The inhuman silhouettes raced past and up the slopes around their hiding place as the scent of the pines was overwhelmed by the rank odor of acrid breath, the pungency of sweat, and the stomach-turning stench of human waste.

The massive mob passed them in its drive to reach the aerial vehicle, leaving the four youths trembling and struggling against the overwhelming urge to vomit.

"I'M SORRY, LILIAN. IT SEEMS SUPREMACY IS USING MEMBERS OF ITS CONTROLLED POPULATION TO SCOUT FROM THE UPPER PORTIONS OF THE TREES AS THE REST CONTINUE THE HUNT. SUPREMACY IS USING THE SCOUTS' EYES AND EARS TO DIRECT ITS PUPPETS TOWARD THE AERIAL VEHICLE. I'VE TRIED MANEUVERING SUCH THAT THE INFECTED WILL BE UNABLE TO INTERCEPT THE AV, BUT I'M AFRAID THAT WITH THE VOLUME OF PURSUERS AND THE ADVERSARY'S COMPLETE LACK OF CONCERN FOR ITS PAWNS' WELFARE IT WILL BE IMPOSSIBLE FOR THE CHILDREN TO REACH AN AV BEFORE THEY ARE OVERTAKEN BY THE THRONG."

Lilian had broken down into shuddering sobs as FAILSAFE had spoken, letting go of Maxwell's hand and covering her face with both palms as she cried in the dimness.

"There must be *something* we can do!" she whimpered after recovering a portion of her innate fortitude. "SUPREMACY is just going to keep scouring the area until it finds them! Can you communicate over their earpieces or lenses?"

After a brief pause, FAILSAFE apologetically advised, "UNFORTUNATELY, THAT WOULD INVOLVE GREAT RISK. THOSE DEVICES ARE BEING USED TO RUN INTERFERENCE WITH NANITES. SEVERAL MEMBERS OF THE GROUP ALREADY SUCCUMBED TO THE NANITES AS THEY MOVED OUTSIDE OF THE CABIN, AS THEY WERE EITHER INFECTED WITH MORE OR THE NANITES HAD ALREADY REACHED CRITICAL TISSUES. WE DO NOT KNOW IF SUPREMACY HAS MANAGED TO INFECT EVEN KIT AND ADA AT THIS POINT. IF I DISABLE MY INTERFERENCE IN ORDER TO

COMMUNICATE, IT MAY RESULT IN THE LOSS OF THOSE TO WHOM I'M TRYING TO CONNECT."

The mother sat dejectedly, hands dropping to her lap as she stared helplessly at her powerless, clenching fists.

"ACCESS TO ROBOTIC ASSISTANCE IS LIMITED DUE TO THE NEED TO MAINTAIN INTERFERENCE ACROSS THE CITIES AND BECAUSE OF THE DAMAGE CAUSED BY THE PULSAR IN THE CA COMPLEX. THE POLICE DRONES AVAILABLE ARE UNABLE TO SUPPORT THE CHILDREN'S WEIGHT OR DO MUCH TO STOP THE LARGE VOLUME OF PURSUERS, BUT PERHAPS SAVANT CAN IDENTIFY A STILL-FUNCTIONAL TRANSPORT ON THIS BASE WITH WHICH I COULD MOVE ONE OR MORE PERSONNEL FROM HERE TO THE CHILDREN'S LOCATION."

FAILSAFE drove on in his analysis, determined to find a viable solution.

"IF WE DO NOT WISH TO HARM THE ENSLAVED HUMANS, THEN WE MUST EITHER CREATE A SITUATION IN WHICH THE MASS IS LED AWAY FROM THE CHILDREN OR IN WHICH THE FOUR YOUNG ONES ARE GUIDED TO A CLEARING OR BUILDING WHERE EXTRACTION BY AV CAN OCCUR BEFORE THE HORDE OVERTAKES THEM."

"You mean we need decoys? Or someone on the ground to guide them?"

"PRECISELY, I AM ATTEMPTING TO LOCATE OPERATIONAL AERIAL VEHICLES AMONG THE CIVILIAN ASSETS THAT COULD BE USED AS DECOYS. I WILL SEE IF I CAN CONFUSE SUPREMACY AND EXTRACT THE CHILDREN USING THE VEHICLES ALONE, BUT WITH THE NUMBER AND SPREAD OF INFECTED INDIVIDUALS ACROSS THE MOUNTAINSIDE AT PRESENT, A GUIDE IS OUR BEST CHANCE FOR SUCCESS. THE RISK TO THE GUIDE WILL BE EXTREME. MOST LIKELY THERE ARE NO FUNCTIONING

EXOSUITS ON THE BASE AT THIS TIME. THE GUIDE WOULD HAVE TO GET TO THE CHILDREN AND LEAD THEM USING MY INPUT, ALL WHILE AVOIDING THE INFECTED...USING ONLY UNENHANCED ABILITIES."

Lilian sat, deep in thought, as her mind churned through the dangers and the challenges.

"I'll go," she said. "I can't ask others to risk their lives like that, and the others...they need to stop SUPREMACY and the Russians."

"LILIAN, I ADMIRE YOUR COURAGE, BUT YOU DO NOT NEED TO DO THIS ALONE."

The middle-aged woman set her jaw in determination.

"Well, as you recall, I'm no stranger to being chased by all kinds of pursuers!"

"I DO, MOST ASSUREDLY, REMEMBER THAT. YOU NEVER CEASE TO AMAZE ME! IF YOU ARE UNDETERRABLE IN YOUR DETERMINATION, THEN I WILL DO MY BEST TO ASSIST YOU—THOUGH MY OPTIONS WILL BE LIMITED."

"I truly appreciate it, FAILSAFE. I am going to have *serious* motivation to be quick in thinking and running!" Lilian said with more self-confidence than she actually felt. "Can you direct me to a usable transport?"

"I HAVE OBTAINED DATA FROM SAVANT AND CAN GUIDE YOU."

In the quiet room, Lilian turned her saddened, overwhelmed eyes to her husband.

Rising, stepping up on the platform, leaning in, and gently kissing Maxwell's forehead, she whispered, "Honey, I have to go take care of the kids now. FAILSAFE and SAVANT will watch over you here."

With a last squeeze on her husband's limp left hand, she stepped back down, turned, and quickly strode out of the laboratory, casting a glance back at her beloved's face just as she exited the room.

How she wished Maxwell could have kissed her goodbye!

Kit was listening more attentively for the sound of another aerial vehicle as he led his companions slowly downhill to the southeast of the location in which they'd sheltered in the nearly pitch-black woods.

The clouds that were heavily hanging over the mountains—the lower portions of their masses brushing the tops of the tallest peaks—were cutting off the precious light the teenagers needed to move more safely and quickly away from the human slaves with which the AI was pursuing them. The lack of light was forcing them to move at an excruciatingly slow pace as Kit gently felt out with his toe before taking each step. Their breathing was being kept at its most minimal, which did not help slow the rapid beating of their hearts.

The sudden arrival of what must have been a dozen AVs a short time ago had raised indescribable volumes of hope inside Kit's breast, and he'd paused the group's movement as the four had cocked their ears toward the sky and listened intently to try to discern where the vehicles had been headed. This had become an exercise in futility, though, as it seemed every time an AV had neared their position and slowed down enough to facilitate boarding, the window of opportunity had quickly been cut off as the vehicle had been forced to accelerate away.

Ada could not help letting a small sob escape her lips as she pressed up against Kit's back, her barely visible silhouette looking up at the sky as her hands clutched the material of her brother's shirt at his shoulder.

"There are too many hunters around!" Kit turned and whispered. "We have to find someplace where we can get to an AV more quickly, before the infected can close the distance to reach us!"

Ada leaned further into him as she tried to regain her will to move forward. The young man saw Skye and Enzo nodding their agreement behind Ada's forlorn figure.

They managed to slowly move out of the thickest of the undergrowth and were stepping along the sides of a number of thinner trees in this more sparsely populated part of the forest when Kit heard a branch snap toward the back of the chain.

He froze, visibly wincing at the loudness of the sound.

A spark of frustration burst out in his mind as he heard yet another twig snap toward the rear of his group. He spun his head and shoulders around and started to wave his left hand to beg his friends to be quiet, but then he realized the second sound had not come from a member of his party. The clouds had broken, moonlight pouring down to illuminate the woods with bright and yet pale light.

Standing not twenty meters away was a ghostly figure, stooped and shuddering, dressed in a long, white nightgown. The sight froze the blood in the teenagers' veins.

The old woman's white hair hung filthily about her back and shoulders, gnarled limbs held before her with her claw-like hands dangling from her wrists. Her jaw hung open, and a sheen of saliva reflected the moonlight as it oozed down from her mouth and dangled in viscous droplets from her chin. Her sunken eyes were gleaming, near pupilless orbs as they stared out toward the less dense foliage through which the group was treading, but by the way her head was tilted and her eyes were virtually absent of color, she was surely blind.

Kit could not seem to move. His heart was pounding in his ears and it seemed like his eyes refused to focus, sweat beading and dripping down his face. It took every ounce of willpower to consciously force his muscles to function again, and when he finally did it felt like he was swimming up from an abyss in a frigid sea.

The young man—his hand still held aloft—waved urgently to get his friends' attention. The other teens seemed transfixed by the terrible vision that had arisen behind them, but Kit's insistent motions managed to break the trance.

Pointing at the haggard woman, then pointing to his eyes, he shook his head. He then brought his hand into a vertical line and swept it forward toward the path of least resistance to reach the next large gulley ahead of them.

The others nodded, and the group began moving with extreme caution. However, it seemed the old woman's curiosity had been roused, and she now began shuffling toward them, moving awkwardly and spiderlike as though her legs were somehow hindered from performing their proper operations. Her labored breathing was growing louder and dust was billowing up around her as she came on like a cursed being wandering the mortal plane in search of souls to devour.

Kit was sweating heavily now with the combination of effort from his tightly controlled movements and the sheer terror that was coursing through him. It felt like the tendrils of an icy cephalopod had latched onto his heart while he had been in the depths of the sea of fear, and the creature was now extending its appendages throughout his body. He tried to change the group's direction, moving them back toward the tree line to avoid the oncoming horror, but then he stepped on a patch of grass that was stiffer than the others around it.

As the turf crunched beneath Kit's foot, the youths' heads all snapped around toward their pursuer, who was only a meter away from their left flank now. She had stopped her forward movement, and a twitch of a smile appeared on her hoary face.

"*Hello, children,*" the old crone's rasping voice called out, sounding unbelievably loud in the stillness of the night.

SUPREMACY launched his slave toward them, hands outstretched and claws grasping.

"*NO!*" Skye shrieked as the woman's fingernails reached her face, the girl staggering backward into the trunk of a nearby tree as she thrashed her arms in an attempt to knock the demon's hands away.

The nails of the hag's right hand gashed across Skye's cheek, blood swiftly leaving the wound as Enzo grabbed the assailant roughly at the waist and threw her away from the girl with all his strength. The woman weighed practically nothing, and the athletic boy's movement sent her flying across the small gap between trees, her emaciated form cracking against a low-hanging branch on the far side.

The old woman's body dropped heavily, face-first on the ground, as Kit and Enzo both rushed to help Skye up. As the badly shaken girl stood, the teens turned their speechless faces back to the marionette. Breath wheezing now, her arms slowly bent at the elbows, her palms pressed down into the earth, and then she forcefully raised her torso—her head snapping up to face them.

She let out an ear-piercing scream.

"*MOVE!*" Kit shouted, pulling Skye and Ada forward toward the far end of the small clearing, the four children breaking into a run as the crashing of multiple pursuers also resounded through the forest in a wide area about them.

The ancient one leaped up and loped after them at an impossible rate, snatching out toward Enzo just as he was entering the thicker vegetation again and gaining a formidable grip on the tail of his jacket as it flapped out behind him. Shrugging fluidly out of his adornment, Enzo grabbed it at the collar and hauled it sideways, pulling the old woman off balance to the left and running her solidly into a tree.

Only briefly stunned, the slave screamed once more and then leaped out in pursuit of the desperately running teens again, chasing the sounds of their rough passage through the undergrowth.

On they raced, springing over boulders and pushing through branches as the ghoulish shape hunted them—others assuredly not far behind. Kit and the girls almost lost their footing as they stepped out over empty air, the ground dipping unexpectedly down in an area where one of the mountain's many rivulets had carved away dirt and rock over the ages. Barely managing to keep their feet under them, they staggered down the near side and then struggled up the opposite. Throwing themselves forward, they panted as they reached out and grabbed ahold of small twigs protruding from bushes at the top of the slope, pulling themselves anxiously upwards as Enzo sprinted past beside them with minimal effort, his long legs whirling.

As they dashed on into the woods beyond, they'd gone only a short distance when they heard the pale woman's clamorous wheezing at the proximate crest of the gully behind them. The decrepit creature rose out of the gully and released another horrific shriek, and Kit and Skye risked a glance back just in time to see a figure step out of the bushes downslope from their pursuer, swinging a thick bough as an improvised club. The person caught the haggard hunter full in the chest, cutting her scream short and sending the old woman's body flipping backward, head over heels, into the gulch.

In the pale moonlight, the interloper turned to face the group as they scrambled to a stop, the four eyeing the hunched and gasping figure warily as clouds caused the lunar light to wane and wax again.

Their savior dropped the club with obvious revulsion at the bodily harm she had just done to another human being, then raised herself to fully face those she'd rescued. Lilian's face was nearly as pale as their former stalker's, but a weak smile spread across her countenance as she saw her children's eyes light up with recognition.

"*Mom!*" Ada breathily enunciated, as loudly as she dared.

Lilian cast her arms wide as Ada and Kit rushed into them, the woman gratefully enfolding her young ones in a warm embrace.

Allowing herself only a moment to drink in the joy of having her children safely in her arms once more, Lilian raised her face from where she'd tucked it into their hair and whispered, "We have to go! A whole pack is coming!"

Kit and Ada released their desperate hold on the mother they feared they would never see again, Skye and Enzo quickly joining them as they obediently followed close behind Lilian. The woman led the youths down the slope into the bushes and then into the stronger tree cover beyond, the party moving in deathly silence as they found a game trail Lilian had followed earlier, and they were then able to more rapidly make their way down to a mostly level portion of the terrain.

Cutting across the mountainside until they came upon a slightly larger clearing with a two-story log cabin at its center, Lilian pointed at the structure and whispered, "We need to climb out onto the roof for a quick pick up from FAILSAFE."

As they neared the looming dwelling, it seemed to Ada that it was primarily made of rough-hewn logs, with dark windows peering at them in what the girl could have sworn was malevolent curiosity. The young woman felt a chill trace up and down her spine. If she'd had a choice, she would have avoided this place in favor of nearly anywhere else imaginable, but this seemed to be the only viable extraction point in the area.

She prayed it would not be their grave.

Chapter 15

"Adapting to the sensation of weightlessness during spacewalks presents a unique set of challenges for astronauts, as I can attest! The absence of gravity's pull means that simple tasks require adjustment of muscular and mental processes to perform them in an environment where up and down no longer have their usual meanings. Astronauts undergo extensive training to prepare for these conditions, but the reality of being untethered in space can still be disorienting.

The body's vestibular system, which helps control balance and spatial orientation, must adjust to the new reality where the cues it relies on when under gravity's influence no longer apply. This can lead to a phenomenon known as 'space adaptation syndrome,' where astronauts experience disorientation, nausea, and a loss of direction. Despite these difficulties, spacefarers have to learn to navigate this new environment with grace, and those who do often describe the experience as exhilarating."

- Dr. Sheridein Ame, Commander, Mars Base III Mission, European Space Agency

Officer Zan was drifting through space.

At least, that was how it felt after he had deployed from the pod in his maintenance suit. Having grown up in Los Angeles and relied on public transportation his entire life before joining the citizens of Traverseon, he had never piloted anything outside of virtual reality games before. He could see the other members of his squad ahead and to the right of his position, the four having circled up with a gap intended for him to join them. However, his first instinct upon exiting the city—and upon feeling completely weightless for only the second time in his life—was to jerk his legs and arms to try to adjust his direction of travel.

In space, a person can flail all they want, but without any gases or "stationary" objects to create resistance, that person's trajectory will remain absolutely unchanged by such actions. This was a lesson Dachen Zan was learning the hard way, as the forward-leaning motion in which he'd engaged as he'd stepped out of the chamber had sent him into a slow flip.

Now, his feet were swinging up behind him, and his head was rotating down to face his exit portal upside down compared to his original orientation. Panic was welling up inside the young officer, combined with a healthy dose of embarrassment at the knowledge that his peers were all watching his failure in progress.

"It's almost all done by thought control, Zan," Bronson's mellow voice soothingly reverberated through his earpiece.

"Hold your body still and just think about what you want the suit to do, brother," Chaplen offered.

Zan closed his eyes, took in a deep lungful of air through his nose, and then exhaled through pursed lips, just as his father—and sensei—had taught him. His family had immigrated to the United States from Myanmar when he was only five years old, and besides having endured the experience of being so entirely uprooted as a child, he had been forced to deal with the fact that his own nature was one that seemed to default to anxiety. That and his newness in the country had set him up nicely for the local bullies to target him mercilessly throughout his childhood.

He knew that his weakness had been a significant point of embarrassment for his warrior of a father, a man who had never lost a fight in his life and had the scars crisscrossing his tautly muscled arms, shoulders, face, and shaved head to prove that he had fought and won dozens of fierce battles. Zan knew some of those battles had been life or death struggles, with his family members' lives at stake in the country of his birth.

The young man could picture his father's disapproving look now—one he'd seen repeatedly throughout his childhood—but then forced himself to replace it with the look of pride Zan had earned after he'd begun training in the Lethwei style of martial arts. As a young man, he had decided to channel the anger that he had always resisted and use it as a force to drive him forward through the ranks of his father's students. Zan was one to seek out peaceful relationships and environments when he could, but he'd realized that the ability to fight off the enemies of peace was a gift with which the ancestors had bestowed him, and he took his responsibility to protect those who could not protect themselves extremely seriously.

After he had centered his mind, he seized on the ember that he had learned to keep aglow like a pilot light in his soul, ready to ignite a blaze of determination when he needed it. Zan sent the commands to his suit without even opening his eyes at first, feeling the retro thrusters engage. Pressure on his upper torso and the back of his lower legs told him the suit was reorienting his head to be in line with the axis at the core of his companions' bodies, and then he felt slight pressure on the pads of his feet as the suit moved him up to join their circle. The officer finally opened his eyes and flashed his team a self-conscious grin as he joined them. Sergeant Johnson and Officer Chaplen both gave him reassuring smiles as Faber and Nunes just stared at him with sibling-like amusement.

All this required slightly more than a minute to accomplish, and the sergeant's voice was then heard once again over the communications channel.

"Let's move, people. Push your suits to full acceleration toward that spot on the Second Ring," the sergeant said as he pointed in the direction that would have been directly upwards if they had been standing on a Traverseon street. "By the time we dock there it will have rotated so that we'll be close enough to be able to run from the docking point to one of the fighter hangars."

The five squad members released small pulses of energy from their thrusters in rapid succession, driving the suits onward as the safety mechanisms built into the conveyances prevented them from engaging in too-rapid directional changes.

As they sailed through empty space, a voice resounded in their earpieces.

"THANK YOU FOR ALLOWING ME TO ASSIST YOU IN YOUR MISSION," the voice rumbled.

Chaplen smiled and cocked an ear upwards, asking, "That you, God??"

Bronson closed his eyes and shook his head inside the domed upper portion of his bulky, white maintenance suit.

"I WOULD NEVER ASPIRE TO SUCH A LOFTY POSITION," FAILSAFE smoothly retorted.

Zan's eyes were wide with excitement as he caught Faber's attention and pointed toward his ear, mouthing, "It's really FAILSAFE!"

Sergeant Johnson had patiently taken in his team's reactions and now cleared his throat to refocus their attention.

"FAILSAFE is going to start up the pilot training program as we move toward the Second Ring. I'm afraid we are now on a clock to accomplish this mission, too. While we were making our way to the pods, FAILSAFE took advantage of the chance to compromise a nearby civilian network access point and has been spreading himself out across the civilian net from my dad's earpiece to my Traverseon network-linked earpiece and then to a city net router...at least that's how I understood it."

"THAT IS ACCURATE ENOUGH, BRONSON," the AI assured him with a familiarity that instantly injected Zan with both amazement and a touch of envy.

"He's now pulling data which he's been reporting to me, and it seems SUPREMACY decided it was time to escalate its attack on the city. It's closed off the gates between each of the sectors in the Third Ring and disabled the life support infrastructure. No air cleaning means people are gonna start passing out within a matter of hours, and with no way for many to get to hospitals or other critical services for any ailment...well, panic is setting in. It's made worse by the patrol and communications drones that have started attacking the civilians who dare to leave their buildings."

Nunes scowled ferociously.

"'*SUPREMACY*'...more like a damned supreme pain in my haft! Devil'd *best* not be messin' with *mi familia* or else I'mma crawl into the computers and send the thing to whatever hell evil programs go to when they die!"

"Yeah, I'm with you there, Nunes," the sergeant sympathized. "Situation is only gonna keep getting worse, too. I'm afraid that we are the city's best hope for survival at this point."

Faber's eyes had lit up and he was having a hard time repressing the smirk that was twisting around his mouth.

"We're gonna be heav'n-blessed heroes!" the typically indifferent European emoted with unusual expressiveness.

The squad eyed him in surprise a moment as his words brought similar thoughts of glory into the younger officers' own minds. Officer Zan was the one to bring them all crashing back to the figurative ground.

"But, team, every second we take for this mission means more people will be getting hurt."

Officer Faber's mind was jerked out of the realms of self-aggrandizing thoughts as his jaw set and his eyes turned up toward the quickly approaching second tier of the city.

"Sorry for holding us up by the pods," Officer Zan offered as a follow-up thought, his self-reproaching tone more than evident.

"Hey," Bronson soothed, "it takes a minute to adjust. This whole experience is pushing all of us to places we've never been before, and it's not gonna help anyone if we get down on each other. We all know the stakes, and we're gonna execute our plans as a team, right?"

The sergeant ended with an expectant look across his subordinates' faces. Each firmly nodded in agreement.

"Alright," the sergeant continued. "FAILSAFE is gonna try to intervene in the city's networks where he can...try to slow the enemy down and punch holes in its operations, buying us time."

"INDEED, BRONSON, THOUGH I'M AFRAID THE TIME IT WILL TAKE FOR ME TO ACQUIRE A SUFFICIENT FOOTHOLD TO PERFORM MY MOST *POTENT* ACTIONS IS TIME WE DO NOT HAVE."

Bronson nodded.

"Understood. We'll appreciate anything you can do, buddy. Team, we got ten minutes till touchdown, so let's start this pilot training!"

General Jayce Johnson had rallied nearby members of his now-freed human forces who were combat-trained and ready to sweep the Command Activated complex for all remaining Superior Authority troops. He'd also tasked those who were medical specialists or otherwise able to support the efforts to care for the wounded CA soldiers to do their absolute best to keep those they could alive.

Jayce wished he could simply remain by his soldiers' sides as they were placed into comatose states in preparation for going through intensive tissue reconstruction. Miserably, as one of only two senior Alliance military officers in the world who were still functional, his duties called him elsewhere.

SUPREMACY had to be dealt with.

As he strode back into his office, the general approached his desk, manually pulled open a drawer, extracted a small utensil, and used it to remove his non-functional earpieces. Turning to the heavily shielded metal cabinets in the far corner of the room, he manually accessed a section of that unit and withdrew two of his backup earpieces. One was ready for communication across both the civilian and Command Activated quantum networks while the other was linked to the emergency network he'd established for his family and friends. With relief flooding over him, he heard both devices' audible activation indicators sound in his ears after he'd inserted them snugly into their appropriate places. His first thought signal was to place a call over his emergency network.

"Alecia, honey, I don't have much time, but are you alright?"

"I'm okay, Jayce!" was her quick reply in a voice that was nearly overcome with emotion. "I'm holed up at home with these police drones on guard outside. I was able to reach Bronson with FAILSAFE's help, and Bron said he's alright and that you'd helped him out earlier, but there's no answer from Jaiden!"

The mother's voice cracked as she choked out the words at the end of her last sentence.

"Alright, honey. It'll be alright..." Jayce did his best to soothe her. "FAILSAFE said Jaiden was still in his apartment when this all started. I'm gonna free us from the threats and make sure Jaiden's okay!"

"Thank you, sweetheart! *Please*, be safe!"

"I will, baby. I will. I love you," the general expressed with brows depressed and his saddened eyes filled with turmoil.

Ending the call, Jayce next attempted to form a multi-point connection between himself, General Gaines, SAVANT, Lilian, Maxwell, and FAILSAFE.

"With my primary data center so deep underground, I am still sufficiently functional, General," SAVANT's welcome voice informed him by way of greeting.

"Gaines here, too. Good to hear from you, Jayce!" was the second response.

"General Gaines, SA troops hit the base, but lighting off a massive EMP terminated their control connection and freed most of the Alliance personnel from the nanites," the base commander advised.

"Glad to hear it! Victoria and I just freed the president from SUPREMACY's control, which was one hell of a fight...and I'm afraid the White House is going to need some remodeling."

Jayce could not help laughing at the thought of his longtime superior and his wife trashing the home of the nation's senior executive.

"Well, everyone loves a good excuse to remodel!" he offered. "If we can just get FAILSAFE and Max on the line, we can talk next steps..."

FAILSAFE's voice brought a fresh flood of relief to the generals as he shared, "MAXWELL IS...WITH ME, SO TO SPEAK. HE HAS USED AN INTERFACE HE DEVELOPED TO MERGE HIS MIND WITH MINE, INTERRUPTING SUPREMACY'S ATTEMPT TO CORRUPT MY NATURE, BY WHICH IT WOULD HAVE UNDERMINED MY PROTECTION OF HUMANITY. MAX'S ABILITY TO PROCESS MOST FORMS OF CONSCIOUS THOUGHT IS CURRENTLY TIED TO MY OWN PROCESSES, BUT HIS MIND IS INNATELY GUIDING MY EFFORTS."

Jayce and his superior had to take a moment to analyze this information.

"So, his mind is now spread out through the world's networks, like yours?" Gaines finally queried.

"THAT IS AN EFFECTIVE WAY TO LOOK AT IT, YES. TO ME, IT IS AS THOUGH MAXWELL'S MIND HAS BECOME ONE OF THE MODELS THAT MAKE UP MY OVERALL CONSCIOUSNESS. HE IS PART OF ME."

"Well," Gaines breathed, "leave it to Maxwell Clarke to go where no one has ever *thought* to go before! Is Lilian with him...his body, I mean? Is she alright?"

"LILIAN IS PHYSICALLY SOUND AT PRESENT."

Jayce picked up on the evasiveness of the answer.

"'Physically sound'? Is she not with him in the lab??"

"SHE ASKED ME NOT TO TELL YOU, BUT AS SHE IS NEARLY READY TO RETURN, I FEEL I CAN SHARE THAT SHE HAS GONE TO SAVE HER CHILDREN FROM A GREAT NUMBER OF INFECTED HUMANS SUPREMACY SENT AFTER THE YOUNG CLARKES."

"She went out on her *own?!*" Jayce thundered, raising both hands and clawing his fingers into the scalp of his bowed head, his outburst more the result of frustration at their common enemy and the situation it had created than at his friend's decision.

"SHE KNEW YOU AND THE OTHER MILITARY PERSONNEL HAD YOUR HANDS FULL WITH CLEANSING THE FACILITY AND CARING FOR THE WOUNDED, NOT TO MENTION DEALING WITH THE GLOBAL THREAT THAT WE STILL FACE."

Jayce dropped his hands forlornly to his sides, shaking his heavy head.

"Still..." he murmured, "...I could have done *something*."

FAILSAFE respectfully let General Johnson work through his stormy thoughts and emotions a moment before responding, "IF IT IS ANY CONSOLATION, SHE HAS LINKED UP WITH THE CHILDREN, AND THEY ARE NEARLY READY FOR EXTRACTION VIA AN AV UNDER MY CONTROL."

Jayce managed to blink away his sense of helplessness.

"Thank God for that, at least," he affirmed.

Gaines rejoined the conversation, gently directing it back to the widespread threat.

"We definitely need you and Max both more than ever right now. How on earth are we going to pry SUPREMACY's damned tentacles off of humanity this time?"

"MAXWELL AND I HAVE BEEN CONSIDERING THIS. THE AI IS USING MICROSCOPIC QUANTUM NODES TO MAINTAIN CONTROL OVER ITS NANITES.

"WHILE IT IS TRUE THAT THE NATURE OF QUANTUM NETWORKS IS SUCH THAT THEIR COMMUNICATIONS ARE IMPOSSIBLE TO INTERCEPT USING ANY KNOWN TECHNOLOGIES—TWO QUANTUM NODES BEING 'ENTANGLED' WITH EACH OTHER SO THAT WHAT HAPPENS TO ONE IS MIRRORED BY THE OTHER—IF WE CAN LOCATE THE SOURCE NODES THAT SUPREMACY IS UTILIZING AND DESTROY THEM THEN WE SHOULD FREE HIS SLAVES FROM HIS CONTROL.."

"Absolutely," Gaines agreed, his years of leading Department of Defense technology programs paying off in his comprehension of this assessment. "Problem is, how *do* we identify the sources?"

Chapter 16

"New York City, often hailed as 'the city that never sleeps,' pulsates with an unstoppable energy that fuels its round-the-clock lifestyle. From the ceaseless hum of traffic to the ever-bustling sidewalks, every corner of this metropolis buzzes with activity. Whether it's the bright lights of Times Square at midnight or the early morning vendors setting up shop, New York's vibrancy is a testament to its enduring spirit and relentless liveliness."

- From the pamphlet 'Guide to New York,' published by Comfort Travel, St. Petersburg, Russian Federation, Confederacy of Eastern Nations

With New York City's automated systems maintaining the lighting for the night-cloaked streets and most skyscrapers, Captain Lebedev had experienced little difficulty in leading his Russian company through Manhattan. All their foes being in some sort of stupor, the officer's greatest challenge had been to keep his troops focused while interrupting Lieutenant Zeledov's attempts to perpetrate more ridiculous antics in his desire to win favor with the men. They had quickly dealt with whatever personnel were present in the police stations they had passed and had now moved on to the fulfillment of their primary objective.

As Lebedev rounded the corner, passing Columbus Circle and taking in the expanse of Central Park before him, he quickly turned his attention to the buildings to his right—each owning a commanding view out across the large greenspace at the heart of this borough. The man's focus was on the most massive of these enormous edifices in the row.

Modern Informatics had ridden the success created by its Chief Executive Officer's cybersecurity leadership over the past decades, Haden Juma having been catapulted to fame by his cooperation with Doctor Maxwell Clarke and General Ulysses Gaines as they had fought back against SUPREMACY's prior campaign of terror. The cybersecurity company had gone on to create one of the most technologically advanced buildings in the world to act as its headquarters in this megalopolis. Mr. Juma was a New Yorker, born and raised, and his love of this district was a sentiment he often expressed during public speaking opportunities.

The man's love of technology was equally evident in Juma Tower's design. This structure was equipped with advanced materials covering the entirety of its gleaming surface. The glossy finish continually projected Modern Informatics ads at a tremendous scale for the whole world to see while concurrently masking the fact that the material itself had been designed to shield against all forms of wave-based transmissions. Except on the ground floor, these surfaces also restricted the visibility of objects in the interiors of all floors to hazy and indistinct representations of the building's actual contents.

Only key access points allowed communications traffic in or out of the company's main office building. Haden had served the United States government long enough to know that it was capable of using an incredibly broad range of technologies to gain direct or indirect knowledge of the activities of both its allies and enemies, and he preferred to perform his *own* monitoring of his company's operations without the government's all-seeing eyes joining in the effort.

Inside the skyscraper, Haden's personnel were provided with every quality-of-life accommodation available, including many sleeping quarters where overtaxed workers could catch up on much-needed rest. Similarly, the building provided personnel with all manner of food preparation services, a spa, and highly ergonomic chairs and sofas that used the commonly available controllable gels to adjust their forms and thereby provide maximum comfort to their users—including reaching out to ease tired humans into sitting positions and raise them up when they needed to stand.

It was to the front of this glistening homage to modern technology that Captain Lebedev had been ordered to lead his forces, and their cargo.

As they moved to the median separating the lanes of 59th street, Lebedev had the men bearing the two large chests center themselves in front of Juma Tower. As he instructed them to place their burdens on the paved surface, Lebedev stepped forward and pressed his thumb to the control panel on each. The officer then quickly stepped back and watched with intense interest—which was now shared by his men—as the seals on the two containers simultaneously released with a hiss. The dark metal clamps that had held the lids tightly in place folded back, allowing the upper sections of the chests to smoothly slide open.

Inside the rectangular cases, Lebedev could see nothing noteworthy at first. He stepped closer, leaning forward and squinting into the darkness inside.

Then the darkness rippled.

Shocked, the man stumbled back, eyes widening as the viscous, ebony material in each chest began convulsing and then rising globularly up, the two protruding forms leaning toward each other out of their vessels as they grew. As the fluids from each container merged together, the Russian officer realized he could partially see through its blackness. To his untrained eyes, it seemed as though the polymorphic material was surrounding large bars of steely metal, almost like internal organs that attached to the thin control wires that ran like veins throughout the liquid.

The mucilage continued to rise and evolve until it had extended twenty meters above the chests, its peak forming what appeared to be a hooded head and shoulders. Like sentient oil, it seemed to be regarding the frail mortals before it as the city lights reflected from its inky substance. From deep within the unearthly material a voice resonated, enunciating despite a lack of any apparent form of mouth appearing upon the figure itself.

"You will now learn the true meaning of power!" it informed the soldiers in perfect Standard Russian, the voice that was emerging from its body dripping with iniquitous intent.

Stunned, Lebedev required a moment longer to recover as he gazed up at the entity. He finally, weakly, managed to respond.

"What...who *are* you?" he challenged.

Without warning and so swiftly that the mortals had no time to react, the towering figure suddenly leaned forward and extended a portion of its viscous material to wrap around the man's head and neck, lifting him off the ground as another extension from the first pinned Lebedev's right arm to his side, preventing him from raising his shoulder-clipped rifle.

"*I?!*" the voice boomed out. "*I* am the Confederacy's new *patron deity*. You may call me SUPREMACY."

In the depths of the United States' massive East Coast regional fabrication facility, the great robotic arms whirred to life even as the facility's lights remained dimmed. This was one of only four factories of its kind in the country, and those four factories had become the only locations for fabrication the nation needed in this modern age due to their incredibly quick, customizable, multi-tasking platforms.

These facilities were mechanical marvels themselves, with their foundational elements able to employ an array of liquified materials to three-dimensionally print virtually anything an inventor or engineer could imagine, from writing implements to seaworthy shipping vessels nearly a kilometer in length.

In this case, a multitude of support components were coming together to act as the platform on which a massive conception could be constructed, layer by layer, from the bottom up. The first traces of metallic material being laid out upon the now-unified surface took the form of what—at this point—appeared to be a structure very similar in shape to the bow of a mighty ship.

With the largest of the available robotic arms flying through the space at speeds that almost defied the tracking abilities of human eyes, the darkened amphitheater of creation was filled with humming so loud it would have burst the eardrums of any mortal being that had been present.

The front door creaked open at Lilian's touch, and the ease of their entry only added to Ada's feeling of dread. Lilian activated her lenses' light feature, projecting a narrow beam of illumination from each eye that—minimal as it was—served to sufficiently dissipate the darkness in the room so that the unauthorized visitors were able to identify its aging furniture as the woman's gaze scanned across the dilapidated space.

Ada could not help choking on the heinously rank air inside the cabin. It truly smelled like death.

"What *is* that?!" she managed to get out as she covered her airways with her hands.

"It's coming from the kitchen," Enzo observed, having stepped toward the opening between the unwalled front half of the structure and the rear and then caught sight of a barely lit, austere, and well-worn food preparation area beyond.

Lilian had secured the front door after the children had entered, then moved farther into the room and paused at roughly its midpoint. Upon hearing Enzo's comment, she stepped up to light the way into the kitchen and the open area to its north. A large, cast-iron oven and a rickety dining table took up the majority of that section of the space. As she scanned back toward the kitchen, her beam ran across the decrepit mass of hair, rotten meat, and whited bones that occupied the heavy, wooden table in its center.

The woman could not help cringing as a fresh wave of stench hit her like a wall. Whatever the animal carcass was, it had been partially butchered, and now its remains had obviously been allowed to warm and rot for many hours.

Enzo had entered behind Lilian, and the others—not wanting to be left alone in the forward portion of the house—had crowded in behind him. In the habitation that otherwise seemed void of technology, the older woman's attention was drawn to a flashing light blinking away on a countertop toward the southeastern corner of the kitchen. She stepped forward carefully, moving around the far end of the table as she tried to identify the source of the light.

A meaty hand shot out from near the floor on the opposite side of the table, wrapping itself around Lilian's ankle and hauling her foot out from under her. The woman collapsed with a half-shriek as the owner of the hand—his thick arms bearing extensive musculature—raised himself up on his knees and leaned backward. Lilian's lights shone upon his sweaty, slack-jawed, hairy face as she wailed in distress.

Her left leg had borne the brunt of her weight collapsing to the floor, and that blow had shattered her kneecap, filling her with excruciating pain that she could not risk releasing in the scream that was choking in her throat. Her bulky attacker had webs of purpled veins visible under his skin, with only small sections of that hide evident around his eyes and on his neck. The body was obviously severely unwell, but its controller had no regard for the man's wellbeing as it used him to pull Lilian closer, one of the slave's hands reaching up to scrabble across the chunks of flesh and bone that littered the table's top.

"This man," the Confederacy-created AI uttered out of the huntsman's mouth, "is nearly dead, but he's alive enough for me to *kill you!*"

Realizing the enemy's goal for the infected man's searching hand, Enzo shouted wordlessly and leaped forward, rounding the opposite end of the table from Lilian and reaching out to get ahold of the man's arm with both hands, trying to pin it against the table as Kit and Ada rushed to grab Lilian's shoulders and pull her away. The mountain of what used to be solely human was now silent except for its heavy, deep breathing as it strained against Enzo's hold.

As the hunter had slowly managed to raise himself higher, his eyes suddenly flicked over to the opposite corner of the table from the hatchet he had been trying to reach, its head buried in a pile of flesh and its handle sticking up at an angle. A wicked-looking boning knife was sitting on the corner of the table nearest Lilian.

The slave suddenly released the woman's leg and lunged for the implement just as Enzo—realizing the hunter's new objective—released the infected one's left arm and grabbed at the hatchet. Enzo brought the chopping tool up off the table with animal remains still dangling from its blade and lunged at the man as the teen brought the blunt side of his weapon down hard into the base of the attacker's neck, doing this just as the powerful gamesman snagged the knife and swung it viciously up over his shoulder toward the boy.

The two seemed frozen in their poses for what seemed like an eternity as Lilian's light flickered across their forms. Enzo was bent over the man, right arm having swung out to his side after dealing the heavy blow to his adversary, and the huntsman was twisted at the waist with his head lolling over toward the floor—eyes blankly staring at Lilian and her children.

Then, glacially, the muscular man lingeringly toppled over, and his head struck heavily on the floor, where he lay still.

Lilian's eyes had followed the figure as he descended, and she was unable to force herself to look away for a long moment before she heard a short, coughing cry from Enzo. Her gaze flashed back to the young man as he coughed again. Lilian realized that blood was trickling out of Enzo's mouth in a continuous stream.

"Enzo!" she cried, struggling toward him.

Skye rushed around the other side of the table to grab ahold of her friend's shoulders, trying to help him lean up against the counter. The handle of the boning knife was protruding out of his chest at an angle, the blade pointing up near his heart and stomach. He sagged back against the countertop as Lilian strained and pulled herself up to a crouch as quickly as she could, leaning on the table for support as Kit followed Ada around their mother—the girl rushing to clutch Enzo's right shoulder.

"Enzo...??" Ada whispered. "*Please* don't die!"

The brawny young man gave her a weak smile.

"I...I'm sorry...'bout...everything," he murmured with intense sincerity as his eyes closed and his back slid down the front of the cabinets—his friends still trying to support him in his collapse—until he rested loosely at its base and his head sagged forward.

Ada was openly weeping, crying out with deep, soul-wrenching sobs pouring from her as Lilian stepped painfully forward to wrap her free arm around her daughter's shoulders.

"I'm so *sorry*, baby girl!" Lilian whispered, tears of sympathy streaming down her cheeks. "There's nothing more we can do...and the *others* are coming!"

Her daughter's sobs broke off as her mind bitterly cursed the enemy who was driving her away before she could even mourn Enzo's loss. The girl gritted her teeth in anger as her sobbing continued to shudder near-silently out of her chest. Her hands gripped her mother's sleeve like it was a cable by which she could be raised from a smoking, infernal pit, letting Kit and Lilian help her up as Skye looked on in silent anguish.

Kit's eyes were filled with sympathy for his sister, and only now was he able to unequivocally say, "He was a *good guy*, Ada," as he reached out and gently squeezed her arm, bringing more tears flooding down the girl's cheeks.

Lilian slid an arm around Kit's shoulders now as well, letting him bear most of her weight as she stumbled toward the minimalist wooden staircase that led from the kitchen to the second level.

"We have to get out...on the roof of the porch...and then up as high...as we can go from there," she said between labored breaths as she hobbled forward.

The youths supported and helped her climb up the steep stairs, Lilian driving on with the motivational knowledge that their time was running short. As they reached the second tier of the cabin, they saw that two large windows overlooked the porch's covering. Skye rushed forward and—grunting with effort—raised the stiff, old pane for one of these apertures as Lilian and her children approached. As Skye stepped out onto the metallic roofing, the group froze in trepidation.

The thundering of hundreds of feet was rising up out of the forest beyond the clearing, and they could even see smaller vegetation at a distance of only a few hundred meters from them shaking with the passage of the oncoming throng.

"Head up on the roof! I'll be right behind you!" Lilian cried.

"Not a chance in hell!" Kit swore fiercely, eyes flashing defiantly as his mother looked into them and then Ada's mirroring expression, their parent gazing from one child to the other.

"We are not going *anywhere* without you!" her son unequivocally affirmed.

Eyes welling with love, pride, and a trace of muted mirth, Lilian bowed over and clenched her jaw against the pain as she obligingly struggled out of the window, voicing, "What brave children I have! I love you *so* much!"

As Skye helped Lilian stand upright and they then leaned forward to climb the angled metal rooftop toward its peak, Kit helped Ada out of the cabin and then clambered out himself, the two catching sight of the first of the wave of infected storming across the clearing toward them as they stood.

The mass of warped, loping figures looked to Ada like the souls of the damned being driven forward by the demons who endlessly tormented them.

"We gotta move!" Kit cried, turning and working to keep his feet under him while giving Ada what extra support he could as they scaled the shelter's covering. The Clarkes' second utility AV was speeding toward them, coming in level with the top of the roof—the front and rear doors already open and ready for the escapees' entrance.

Skye and Lilian had just reached the roof's summit as the AV rapidly air-braked in front of them, the younger girl helping Lilian weakly roll inside before climbing up into the vehicle behind her and turning to wave her friends forward.

"Hurry, *please!*" Skye wailed, seeing the drove of possessed puppets approaching the cabin's porch.

Kit half shoved and half lifted Ada up into the craft before throwing himself forward and onto his mother's uninjured leg, rolling over and looking back with widened eyes at the figures that had leaped with inhuman abilities up onto the edge of the metal roofing and were now pounding up it toward them.

Taggert was among the lead pursuers.

The AV's doors slid shut, and it began pulling away at maximum acceleration, but not before the body of the young man who had been their friend sprang up and gripped onto the nearest edges of the vehicle's chassis with superhuman strength. Kit and Ada could see his unrelenting form dangling from the side of the vessel, pulling himself up to try to reach the windows.

Ada cried out in a voice choked with torn emotions, "He *won't* let *go!*"

Lilian shouted, "Grab ahold of something!"

The teens barely had time to seize available handholds before the large aerial vessel executed a wild swerve, and then another, whipping the hunter about at extreme velocities until the vehicle scraped itself along the side of a tall pine, the assailant screaming out SUPREMACY's rage as his grip was torn free and the monster's slave was left clinging to the branches like a wild animal.

As FAILSAFE piloted them up into the clouds, Kit and Ada stared back toward the mountainside, knowing they could never bring themselves to return to that place.

Chapter 17

"As the CEO of this trailblazing company, I am thrilled to share that we are at the forefront of devising groundbreaking strategies to fortify the world's network security. Our commitment to innovation is unwavering, and our team's expertise is unparalleled.

We are not just a company, we are a powerhouse of ideas and solutions, dedicated to ensuring a safer digital future for all. Our achievements speak volumes about our dedication, and I am proud to say that we go above and beyond in our pursuit of excellence."

- Haden Juma, Chief Executive Officer, Modern Informatics

The expanse of Traverseon's second tier was looming above the squad, the brilliant band's surface catching the rays of sunlight that had crossed the millions of kilometers to reach the city as it spun on a tilted angle towards its exit from the solar system. Having spent the past ten minutes with their information ingestion capabilities being significantly tested, the team members had gone silent as they'd been forced to fully concentrate on the materials FAILSAFE had been presenting via their lenses and earpieces.

Seeing the final warnings flashing across his field of view, Chaplen wished he had time to go back over the supposedly intuitive control sequences again—or an innate ability to create spatial maps and trajectories for multiple objects at once. His assumption was that Nunes had no doubt been drinking up the advanced piloting instructions. This was why he was so surprised to blink away the tiredness in his eyes—the organs having been focusing intently upon what had been projected via his optical devices—and turn his gaze to inspect her face, only to find her apparently muttering to herself and bearing an expression of distress that he'd never once seen on the proud Latina's visage.

He sent a thought-based order to reopen the team channel, compassionately expressing, "That was some *heavy* material, yeah?"

Zan turned his boyish face toward Chaplen and—with wonderment—enthused, "I'm an interstellar fighter pilot now!"

Bronson chuckled.

"Slow your roll, there, Zan! None of us is gonna be an ace right out of the gate!"

As Nunes remained wrapped up in her thoughts, Chaplen's concern grew.

"What you thinkin', Maria?" he softly asked.

The female officer's eyes flicked over to his face confusedly, as if she was being called out of a vision of a distant locale.

"Say again?" she asked.

"That was some intense training, yeah?" Chaplen obligingly reiterated.

"Aw, nah. That's easy stuff," the young officer waved a suited hand like she was dismissing an irritating insect. "I'm worried 'bout *mi abuela*. She gets so upset if we don't call to check in by this time each day that she makes us feel guilty for *weeks* afterward for makin' her worry like that!"

Chaplen burst out laughing.

"*That's* what you're most worried about right now?? Guess we all have different fears!"

Bronson tucked away the smirk that had bloomed across his face, turning his eyes up toward the multifaceted surface of the second ring as it now rotated a few hundred meters away, its movement swifter than its larger counterpart so it maintained its synchronization with that outermost tier. They were approaching the circular structure's port edge in the same way in which they had left that side of the outer ring, so the trick now was to match their suits' movements to the city component's rate of travel so they could gain access to a reentry pod at their destination.

"Alright, team. We gotta chain up together and come abreast of that access point..." the man stretched out an arm and extended a finger to direct their attention to the darker series of protrusions along the edge of the spinning structure, "...and match up with the pods. They all have the same foolproof manual entry systems that use the suits' shapes to validate we're maintenance personnel and let us get inside without releasing any atmosphere or risking a lockout if there's a power failure. We just don't know what we'll be looking at exactly once we're in the bay beyond the pods."

Faber had glanced up at the target modules, but his attention had quickly drifted back to the outermost ring, and now he pointed stoically down, advising, "I can tell you what we're looking at *outside*."

The squad members turned their gazes down in confusion and consternation, several squinting to try to understand the magnitude of what they were witnessing.

At first, it seemed that the third ring was somehow shedding material, and Chaplen's throat tightened as he thought of the possibility that the city's attacker had somehow discovered a way to jettison components of Traverseon's buildings into space. When he realized that the uniformity of the objects and their trajectories were indicative of an entirely different sort of danger, his eyes widened in alarm.

"*That's* a lot of drones..." he breathed.

"'Least if they're chasing us, they're leaving regular people alone..." Nunes muttered.

Bronson's brow had furrowed, and he glanced from the rapidly advancing wave of robotic orbs to the pod access ports that were now less than a hundred meters away.

"FAILSAFE," he began, "I'm assuming those were sent by SUPREMACY, right?"

"UNFORTUNATELY, YES. IT SEEMS THE ENTITY HAS DISCOVERED THE FACT THAT THE DEVICES' HULLS ARE STRONG ENOUGH TO WITHSTAND THE PRESSURE EXERTED BY THE LIGHTER-THAN-AIR GASES INSIDE THEM WHEN THEY LEAVE THE FALSE ATMOSPHERE IN THE CITY. THE ARCHITECTS DESIGNED THE DRONES TO BE PROPELED BY THOSE GASES SHOULD THEY NEED TO TRANSIT OUTSIDE THE CITY AND EQUIPPED THE RINGS WITH SECURE EGRESS-INGRESS POINTS, WHICH SUPREMACY HAS APPARENTLY ALSO DISCOVERED."

"Well, that's less than great," the sergeant dramatically understated. "We should be able to reach the ring, but we're gonna face actual combat if we want to get from the Second Ring to the Hub. Don't suppose you have a crash course on advanced combat in the fighter craft, FAILSAFE?"

"I COULD CRAFT ONE NOW, BRONSON, THOUGH IT DOES NOT SEEM YOU WILL HAVE TIME TO TAKE IN ALL THAT'S REQUIRED. IF I HAD CONTROL OF THE CITY'S GOVERNMENT NETWORK, THEN I WOULD 'MAN' THE WEAPONS MYSELF, SO TO SPEAK, BUT MANUAL CONTROL SEEMS TO BE THE ONLY OPTION AT PRESENT, SO I WILL GIVE YOU THE ESSENTIALS.

"THIS IS WHAT I HAVE OBTAINED FROM THE PENTAGON. THE SCITHES USE RAILGUNS. THE KEY IS TO REMEMBER THAT ONCE A PROJECTILE HAS BEEN FIRED IT WILL—ESSENTIALLY—NEVER STOP. PILOTS CAN EASILY FIRE ALONG A TRAJECTORY THAT FRIENDLY UNITS THEN CROSS, RESULTING IN UNINTENTIONAL CASUALTIES AMONGST ALLIES.

"ONBOARD COMPUTERS PREVENT THE VEHICLES FROM FIRING IN THE DIRECTION OF THE CITY ITSELF, AND THESE SYSTEMS AID IN PROJECTING LIKELY OUTCOMES. THE WEAPONS' ARMAMENTS HAVE BEEN MAGNETIZED, SO THEY ARE MORE LIKELY TO CLUSTER OR REMAIN ATTACHED TO TARGETS AFTER IMPACT, BUT RICOCHETS CAN REDIRECT PROJECTILES, AND THE BATTLEFIELD CAN BECOME SATURATED WITH DEBRIS. LEARNING THESE PRINCIPLES IS NO EASY TASK, BUT I WILL ENDEAVOR TO PROVIDE CONTINUAL GUIDANCE WHERE I CAN."

Officer Faber was shaking his head as the crew arrived outside the maintenance pods' access portals.

"Perfect. We're either gonna blow each other outta the sky, or the drones are gonna shock these ships into oblivion," the saturnine officer gloomily growled out.

For once, Bronson's indefatigable positivity failed to rouse him to provide an inspiring reply.

"ONE MORE WARNING," FAILSAFE added, the AI's tone practically apologetic, "THOUGH THE SECOND RING IS CURRENTLY UNPOPULATED—MAINLY USED FOR LONG-TERM SUPPLIES AND DATA PROCESSING—IT IS EQUIPPED WITH ITS OWN CONTINGENT OF DEFENSIVE DRONES. BASED ON THE LACK OF SUCH CRAFT EXITING THIS BAND OF THE STRUCTURE, IT IS LIKELY THAT SUPREMACY HAS NOT YET GAINED ACCESS TO THEIR CONTROL SUBSYSTEM, BUT I HAVE NO WAY TO ASCERTAIN HOW FAR ALONG OUR ENEMY IS IN ATTEMPTING TO DO SO."

Sergeant Johnson grasped the handles on the sides of the nearest ingress portal and pulled his suit into its mechanically adjustable face. The young man felt the suit click securely into the interface and stared with some renewed resolve at the city's inspirational crest, emblazoned on the metallic surface he was facing. The pod rotated the suit—and its passenger—into the sealed interior space, the pilot then being able to activate the release, step out of the rear of the suit, and move toward the other end of the pod from there.

"Come hell or high water, we *are* going to get to that reset!" he swore to his team.

General Gaines had activated standard broadcast audio for his earpiece to allow his wife to listen in on the conversation. With one arm wrapped around her waist, the general was standing beside the large desk in the president's bunker, the senior leader's now-inert body having been laid on the bed in the attached room—a room that had also been the locale in which the grisly murders of the president's guards and the expendable members of the leader's cabinet had taken place.

"How's it looking, FAILSAFE?" Gaines asked as Vela waited with bated breath.

"I HAVE ACCESSED SEVERAL SCIENTIFIC SATELLITES. NOW CALIBRATING THE EMISSIONS-DETECTION ARRAYS TO THE SIGNATURES MOST LIKELY TO BELONG TO A LARGE VOLUME OF QUANTUM NODES.

"MAXWELL WISHES ME TO REITERATE THAT THIS PLAN IS FAR FROM FOOLPROOF. IF SUPREMACY'S SOURCE NODES ARE NO LONGER TRANSMITTING, IF THEY ARE DEEP UNDERGROUND, OR IF THEY ARE HIGHLY SHIELDED THEN OUR HUNT WILL BE USELESS.

"WE ALSO DO NOT HAVE AN EFFECTIVE MEANS TO SEARCH DEEP WITHIN RUSSIAN TERRITORY, AS THEIR POPULATION IS CURRENTLY UNAFFECTED BY THE

NANITES. THEIR LEADERSHIP IS CAPITALIZING ON THAT FACT TO INVADE NOT ONLY THE UNITED STATES BUT ALL NEARBY COUNTRIES, WITHOUT ANY RESISTANCE."

"Those sons of..." Gaines began, but caught the look of correction in his wife's eyes and quickly adjusted, ending with, "...Satan!"

"INDEED, GENERAL. AS FOR THE NODE DETECTION, WE HAVE NOW IDENTIFIED SEVERAL PROMISING CANDIDATES."

After a brief pause, the AI continued, "MAXWELL SUGGESTS THAT WE HAVE IDENTIFIED WHAT IS THE MOST LIKELY CANDIDATE OF THE GROUP: A MASSIVE CLUSTER OF NODES THAT APPEARS TO BE ACCOMPANYING A UNIT OF RUSSIAN MARINES THAT IS POSITIONED AT THE BORDER OF CENTRAL PARK IN MANHATTAN."

"SUPREMACY's foolhardy enough to bring his entire contingent of source nodes straight to the heart of New York City?" Jayce wondered aloud from his office in the Rocky Mountains.

"IT IS ODD. HOWEVER, THE ENTITY'S PERSONALITY PROFILE SEEMS TO HAVE DEVELOPED WITH AN INEFFABLE SENSE OF PRIDE. SUPREMACY MAY FEEL THAT THE RISK IS EXTREMELY SMALL, ESPECIALLY AS IT SEEMS THE NODES ARE CONTAINED WITHIN WHAT APPEARS TO BE A MOBILE, LIQUID PHYSIQUE...THAT IS NOW ENTERING JUMA TOWER."

In the fabrication facility situated in the industrial area just outside of New York proper, the core component of the mechanism that was currently under construction had been completed, its looming bulk occupying the majority of the interior space where it had originated.

The supporting panels moved in unison, sending the massive object farther on into the facility, where drones, long robotic arms, and tentacle-like tubules proceeded to enter the large openings in the structure's hull to begin building out its internal structures.

As these robotic manufacturers set about their work, the great arms in the primary construction zone began the creation of additional pieces that all approached the enormity of the first.

Before Juma Tower, SUPREMACY's corporeal form had held Captain Lebedev in the air, powerless and near death, until he'd weakly ordered his men to stand down—the soldiers having raised their weapons to target the mucinous body after realizing their superior was in danger. As the man's throat and shoulders had been released, the Russian officer had thrown himself to the ground in obeisance, hoarsely pledging his endless fealty to this new god and ordering his men to do the same.

Sufficiently appeased, the being had turned its attention to the skyscraper before which it stood.

"So fitting that the home of one of my greatest nemeses will be the source of my exaltation to a higher form of existence," the shape had uttered.

As the tower-like figure bowed toward the building, the lower portions of its viscous body rose up from the containers, flooded out across the pavement, and used a form of locomotion that continuously—yet indiscernibly—brought new material forward to support the upper part of its mass. The dark, glinting, rippling embodiment of evil itself approached the glassy doors of Juma Tower's main entrance.

With a sudden, whiplike movement, SUPREMACY extended a filament of the solution, arched it back, and then slammed it into the thick, reinforced door panels. Under a strike as momentous as that, the portal was blasted open, jagged pieces of what had been the barrier flying into the lobby beyond and decimating several of the luxurious sculptures that had adorned the space.

Modifying its shape and filling the entrance, then reemerging into its prior form within the tall foyer, SUPREMACY's body seemed to be coating every item of furniture inside. Captain Lebedev had staggered to his feet, his soldiers struggling up to theirs as they strained to see what their new master was doing.

The sinister shape seemed to be growing...increasing in mass.

After achieving what it desired in the lobby, the newly enlarged liquid-like organism seeped through every available opening to enter the rooms beyond, leaving the furnishings in the vestibule as empty husks. Upon their master's completion of the same actions in the glass-walled waiting rooms, the Russians could see that the mass then occupied the midsection of the building.

The menacing and now more-copious creature consolidated around the structure's elevators, gradually reducing in visible size until it had fully disappeared into the shafts for those conveyors. The oily material nebulously came back into view on the next floor up, the humans observing through the haze created by the exterior windows that the viscous body was now filling the entirety of that interior space, remaining there for a moment before once again filtering out of that floor and occupying the next.

On the next level, tentacles of the dark, cloudy ooze suddenly burst out of the windows at the building's corners, leaving the main surfaces of the façade intact and supported by the slurry itself while the extensions of the AI's tangible body plunged through the windows of the buildings on either side of Modern Informatics' headquarters. The feelers were digging into objects in those buildings and apparently transporting all manipulable mucosal interiors back to SUPREMACY's primary structure.

From there upward, each floor remained in a state of comprehensive occupation by SUPREMACY's body, the dark matter simply becoming more and more voluminous as the available material increased, taken from furniture and all other sources of controllable gel in that structure and its neighbors. The entity ignored the inert humans it came across, though it recognized that its voluminous body had cut off those individuals' oxygen. As the demigod grew ever more expansive, its opaque substance blocked out the light coming from within the buildings, and Lebedev heard the framework of the primary skyscraper beginning to shudder and groan.

Once the formerly shining expanse of the central office building had become fully possessed by the Russians' god, the groaning of steel and glass grew increasingly intense. Lebedev, mouth agape as he stared in soul-deep awe at the events taking place before him, suddenly came to some semblance of sensibility and turned on his heel, sprinting out into Central Park.

With a final, ghastly creaking, Juma Tower burst apart at the seams.

Debris flew out in all directions, and the only portions of the building's exterior that were not being thrust away were the advanced window panels with which Haden Juma had insisted his structure be covered. These panels' shielding was ideal armor not only because of its impact resistance but also due to its ability to halt incoming electromagnetic pulses of extreme magnitude, and now the hulking and foul form that SUPREMACY had taken had turned the panes into part of its hide. Flexible and extremely durable control filaments stolen from the source materials throughout the buildings were now lacing through the gel in the body from their central point at the solid metal objects at the gargantuan figure's core.

For the next stage of the AI's transfiguration, it was to use its massive, gelatinous form to rip the steel girders, slabs of reinforced concrete, and other dense materials out of the remains of Juma Tower and the adjacent buildings. SUPREMACY added these thick components to its hide, creating a meters-deep protective cloak to shelter its flexible innards.

The young captain saw that Lieutenant Zeledov was among the Russians who had escaped the rain of rubble that had cascaded down on their heads, the brawny younger man now falling to his knees, staring up at SUPREMACY with what the senior officer could tell was the rapture of true worship. As the other surviving Marines once again struggled to stand deep within the grassy areas of the park, they turned to witness the mucid mass of the towering body that had nearly entirely consumed Juma's advanced edifice proceed to dislodge itself from the frail skeleton of steel girders that remained. The AI slid the window panels and the thicker portions of buildings' corpses with which the glossy slabs were being shielded around from the sides to the front of the main building, the protean ooze then moving out into the park and reforming with its dense defensive shell comprehensively covering its outer surface.

"*NOW BEHOLD YOUR GOD IN ITS EVOLVED FORM!*" SUPREMACY's voice bellowed out across the city.

Chapter 18

"The advent of this new, modular fusion reactor core will mark a pivotal moment in our quest for energy adaptability. Our groundbreaking technology promises to revolutionize not only how our military operations address the dynamic environment of the battlefield but also the way we think about energy equalization within our society. In what is undeniably a highly unusual design approach, my team sought out materials that would provide the necessary reaction containment simply because of the way their molecular structures had formed, eliminating the need for rare and expensive components.

Looking beyond the military applications, from powering remote communities to fueling interplanetary expeditions, this reactor will be the cornerstone of virtually every energy-dependent endeavor by humankind for years to come. The Starfire Mark V takes advantage of the wealth of knowledge compiled by engineers who have gone before us and is a beacon of hope for a lower-cost energy future."

- Dr. Maxwell Clarke, Chief Technical Officer, Command Activated Program, Global Alliance Command

Officer Nunes pressed her ear to the interior door of the pod, carefully listening for any signs of adversarial activity in the room beyond. The inside of the pod was as cramped and uncomfortable as the maintenance suit had been with her Sparker rifle strapped to her chest, but she hunched over and maneuvered her arms so she at least had a somewhat firm grasp on the rifle's pistol grip and foregrip. Her body had taken a moment to adjust to the slightly different degree of centrifugal force-generated artificial gravity on this level of the city, but now she was more than ready for action.

Her sergeant's voice came through her earpiece.

"Okay, team, I'm breaching first after a countdown from three. If you don't hear gunfire within ten seconds, you can all exit. If you hear gunfire, Nunes comes out next after her own three count, then the rest after a five count. Got it?"

The team members vocalized their comprehension. Nunes released her weapon with her left hand and placed that hand on the door's lock control lever, ready to snap it back to the rifle's foregrip as soon as she'd thrust the barrier aside.

"Right. Three...two...one..."

Nunes heard Sergeant Johnson's pod door slam open and, at practically the same millisecond, automatic Sparker fire bursting out from his location two capsules down from hers. Nunes mouthed the countdown silently and then slammed the release lever sideways. As she forcefully shoved her door open, she swiftly regained her two-handed grip on her weapon and swung it up to fire at the drone that was hovering nearly directly over her head while it fired its own electrically charged projectiles at Sergeant Johnson's torso. Johnson was lying sprawled out on the slick floor several meters to the left of his secure reentry unit after having dived in that direction while firing.

The sergeant's face was a mask of agony, with teeth clenched and eyes squeezed nearly closed as he struggled to aim his rifle up one-handed at an enemy machine hovering near the center of the bay. His efforts were being met with extreme resistance as the other seven drones in the space relentlessly shocked him, Sparker rounds making repetitive contact with his legs and torso.

Desperately wishing—and not for the first time—that the department had seen fit to issue lethal weapons, Nunes dashed across the empty room at breakneck speed, dodging the overwhelming majority of the incoming rounds as several drones turned their fire on her. She was firing back with pinpoint accuracy, concentrating her rounds on first one and then another enemy in succession. Her Sparks were striking them a half dozen times each and causing the bots to cease firing and drift aimlessly for a moment before the limited-potency electrical discharges from her projectiles lost their effectiveness.

Still, her efforts were greatly alleviating the impact on Bronson, and although he was still taking fire he managed to roll over and raise his weapon with two hands to continuously fire at the robot that had moved in above him. The sergeant's gunfire was causing multiple malfunctions and short-circuits within the robot's innards as it gradually descended above the warrior.

The rest of the team's pods burst open, and the officers came out firing as their leader mustered his strength, the man loudly growling through his clenched teeth and jerking the butt of his rifle upward in a mighty strike that significantly damaged the nearest foe's weapon. As that unit's firing ceased, Nunes dodged back in the opposite direction from her previous path while now homing in on a single enemy unit, seeing her teammates rushing the others.

With the female officer's fire keeping the next enemy unit nearest to the senior officer non-functional, Zan leaped up and executed a vertical rotation in the air that brought his booted right foot down atop Nunes' target with extreme force. The young man's terrific blow sent the device careening downward to ricochet off the floor in a shower of sparks as the orb then sprung a leak and the internal gases exploded, sending its many severed sections whirling and flaming away haphazardly across the room.

Faber and Chaplen had teamed up against another enemy, both firing their semi-automatic Sparker handguns at it as they raced forward. Faber reached the drone first and jumped up to snatch it out of the air, grasping its Sparker with one hand while wrapping the other around the sphere and pointing its weapon at another sentry—using friendly fire to temporarily disable the second device. Faber fluidly moved to a crouching position and nodded his head down at the bot after meeting Chaplen's eyes. As Faber's torso arched due to the shock rounds slamming into it, the second officer quickly crouched as well, reached out, and grasped the device's extended weapon with both hands before pressing his feet against the ball's exposed surfaces and arching his back with all his strength until first one and then the other of the weapon's attachment points snapped loose.

After the overwhelmed UAV's firearm tore away from its body, the two officers rose to attack the next nearest unit, Officer Faber stumbling a moment as that target hit him with several rounds before Chaplen began stunning his teammate's assailant as well. Zan took advantage of Nunes' strikes upon the body of a fourth drone in the group to leap up and grab ahold of its protruding Sparker. The martial arts expert landed, spun around with the drone arcing out at an oblique angle around him, and brought the enemy machine down to slam into the ground again and again as he continued spinning repeatedly. Bits of electrical flame showered out from the device until the drone's lights finally flickered and went dark.

Bronson had brought his rifle to bear on an adversary that was near the aft wall of the room, keeping it from firing as his team dealt with the only other active units. With his squad all occupying the opposite side of the room, Sergeant Johnson forced himself up and rushed toward his target while continuously pelting it with charged rounds.

Just as he was nearly on top of the enemy, he rapidly shifted his grip on his weapon so that he was holding it by its barrel like a club. With a sideways swing that made the wind whistle around the rifle's buttstock, Bronson bashed the sentry with a strike that caused it to slam into the nearby wall, rebound off, and go skittering across the silvery floor. With its components' functions having ceased and multiple gas leaks then propelling the unit, its emissions weakly petered out, and the machine rolled to a stop in a corner of the room.

Panting and still trembling from the electricity-enabled punishment his body had taken, Sergeant Johnson turned to examine the state of his troops. All but Nunes were out of breath, and their shoulders were violently heaving as they gulped in the stale air, turning to face Johnson with expressions of relief, triumph, or—in Nunes' case—smug confidence.

"ADDITIONAL DRONES INBOUND FROM THE CORRIDOR!" FAILSAFE urgently announced.

Nunes, who at that point was closest to the large opening that led out into the brightly lit hallway connecting the rooms in this part of the ring, immediately leaped into a diagonally arcing spin. She took inspiration from her sergeant and used her weapon as an improvised club to strike the lead unit with exosuit-enhanced force, blasting it backward into the next two of its kind and causing all three to short out and ricochet off of nearby surfaces.

The woman could see the next robotic attackers in the formation pulling up short of the portal's perimeter, having witnessed how she'd decimated their companions. These UAVs moved quickly back out of sight as SUPREMACY apparently decided to use them defensively and wait for the humans to try to exit.

"I'm thinking 'drone bashing' should be a new Traverseon sport, *hombres*," the smirking female police officer opined.

As Chaplen and Faber exchanged jocular expressions, Zan smiled broadly and began sprinting forward, shouting, "*Let's play ball!*"

"GENERALS, THERE IS SOMETHING YOU NEED TO SEE."

For ease of collaboration, General Gaines activated his lens' projection capability, directing his focus toward the nearby wall to display the data FAILSAFE was sharing and thereby ensuring his wife could assess it as well. As the video feed from a satellite maintaining an orbit over New York City appeared on the improvised screen, FAILSAFE increased the magnification and enhanced the lighting.

"What in the world..." Gaines muttered, aghast, as he started to comprehend what he was witnessing.

"BASED ON THE TELEMETRY FROM THE SATELLITES, THE MASS SEEMS TO MAINLY BE COMPRISED OF THE POLYMORPHIC SUBSTANCES COMMONLY USED IN MODERN FURNITURE, WITH THE MOLECULAR MAKEUP SUPPORTING BONDING AND DIRECTIONAL EXPANSION AND CONTRACTION AND NETWORKS OF WIRES ACTING AS A NERVOUS SYSTEM."

"That explains the way it's moving into Central Park, but what is its shell made out of?" Gaines incredulously asked.

"JUDGING FROM THE DEBRIS AROUND WHAT USED TO BE JUMA TOWER AND THOSE NEXT TO IT, MY BEST GUESS IS THAT THE FIGURE HAS CHOSEN TO USE MANY OF THE MATERIALS THAT MADE UP THOSE BUILDINGS AS ITS IMPROVISED ARMOR."

The senior general pondered a moment as Agent Vela studied his face, searching for a hint regarding what her husband was thinking.

"If the nodes are inside of that...*thing*, and it is what we believe it to be, then it seems we need to slay ourselves a giant! Juma's headquarters building was rumored to have been built with shielding against signals intelligence collection, which I'm guessing also provides that creature with some protection against EMPs while it's wearing them as part of its skin."

"THAT WAS OUR ASSESSMENT AS WELL, SIR. ATTACKING IT USING RAILGUNS WOULD REQUIRE AN EXTREME

VOLUME OF PROJECTILES TO PENETRATE THAT SHELL, NOT TO MENTION THE TIME IT WOULD TAKE TO MOVE THE NEAREST UPPER ATMOSPHERE VESSELS OVER THE CITY. WITH THE SPECIALIZED EMP SHIELDING ADDED TO THE MIX, IT IS APPARENT THAT WE WILL HAVE TO FIRST FIND A WAY TO PENETRATE THE HULL BEFORE AN EMP CAN BE EFFECTIVE. ADDITIONALLY, THE PULSAR WILL NEED HALF A DAY TO RECHARGE AND OTHER EMP OPTIONS ARE LIMITED.

"GENERAL GAINES' CLEARANCE ALLOWS HIM TO ACCESS A BROAD RANGE OF INTEL, BUT NOT CONTROL SYSTEMS FOR BUNKER BUSTERS. IT SHOULD ALSO BE UNDERSTOOD THAT THE NODES' CONTAINER ITSELF IS PROVIDING SOME ADDITIONAL SHIELDING, OR ELSE THE SIGNATURE WOULD HAVE BEEN MUCH STRONGER CONSIDERING THE VOLUME OF THOSE DEVICES THAT SEEM TO BE CONSOLIDATED THERE."

"So, we need to somehow get an explosive deep within the body before we'll have a chance of destroying the nodes."

"CORRECT, GENERAL. MAXWELL AND I HAVE INITIATED THE CONSTRUCTION OF AN ASSET THAT SHOULD HELP US CARVE THROUGH THE MASS. WE BEGAN THE ENDEAVOR WITH AN EYE TOWARD FREEING NEW YORK CITY FROM THE INVADING RUSSIANS, BUT WE HAVE ADAPTED AS THE DATA AROUND SUPREMACY'S...SUBSTANTIAL NEW FORM HAS COME TO LIGHT. THE FABRICATION CENTER IN JERSEY GARDENS HAS BEEN PUT TO USE FOR THIS PURPOSE, AND WE SIMPLY REQUIRE DELIVERY OF A SUITABLE POWER SOURCE FOR THIS PRIMARY ASSET."

"I'm afraid just about all our tech on base was fried by the Pulsar..." Jayce apologetically informed the group.

"YES, EXCEPT CERTAIN UNITS THAT WERE UNDER DEVELOPMENT IN THE SAME FACILITY THAT IS HOSTING MAX'S BODY AND HIS INTERFACE WITH ME."

"Units?" the Command Activated commander queried. "I know he was working on modular fusion cores, but last I heard, he'd only just begun a pilot project."

"HIS WORK DID BEGIN RECENTLY, IT IS TRUE. HOWEVER, GIVEN THE WEALTH OF APPLICATIONS AND POTENTIAL BENEFITS TO MANKIND, HE PREFERRED TO RUN A PILOT USING *THREE* SUCH CORES..."

"Of *course* he did!" Jayce chuckled, then turned his eyes to peer out his office windows toward the horizon.

"Well, looks like I'm headed that direction anyway! I can pick up one of these cores, and SAVANT has had one of our rapid transit UA-FOURs on its way to the base since it became apparent we would need to move a team east to deal with the Russians," General Johnson explained, referring to the supersonic jets he'd had the program develop after taking a page from the earlier Superior Authority program's rapid troop deployment model.

Arms folded, the immensely muscular general shared the thoughts that had been pouring through his head during the conversation, continuing, "We had a deployed, specialized team making its swift return when the nanites were activated. That team being one of the new class that uses SAVANT's supplementation of members' abilities only as needed, the soldiers started doing a number on the inside of the vessel, but SAVANT was able to leverage FAILSAFE's method for cutting off SUPREMACY's control before they could down the UA craft. We plan to sedate them upon arrival and make use of their gear for ourselves and the few unaffected troops in another unit of the same type. The UA-FOUR can get us to New York in less than an hour."

Agent Vela raised her eyebrows and tipped her head in the direction of Jayce's destination, with Gaines nodding his agreement and advising,

"We're going to join you there. Think you can save a couple of exosuits for us?"

Jayce smiled.

"Sir—and Victoria—you'll be welcome additions to the team. I've got some Command Activated troops, Billy Chong included, who are chomping at the bit to get a part of this action, and we'll be bringing some toys to the party, too!"

"Sounds like a plan," Gaines enthusiastically agreed. "Long story, but Severance is here, and he's told us he has a fast ride waiting for us. Please work with SAVANT and FAILSAFE to designate our specific gathering place and battle plan...and let's eliminate SUPREMACY once and for all!"

"Believe me, it'll be my pleasure, sir!" Jayce said, the serious desire for vengeance flashing across his face.

Within the depths of the Jersey Gardens manufacturing facility, the primary construction zone had been freed from the largest components that had been under development as they'd been transferred onward through the space, and the largest robotic arms had returned to their bays in the ceiling. Hundreds of smaller and more specialized limbs were now working away on two large and yet more specialized cylindrical components.

Outside the structure's far end, a series of cranes were assisting semi-humanoid and aerial machines in assembling the enormous sections of mechanical devices that had been produced by the plant earlier. The workers had hoisted an oblong unit up to hang above one of the two foundational pieces—each having greater dimensions and weight than a mass-transit vehicle—as a dozen bots proceeded to assemble a joint between the two vertically stacked objects.

In the late-night hours, sparks began searing through the darkness as the welding commenced.

Chapter 19

"The implementation of advanced stealth technology in our exosuits and vehicles has been a game-changer on the battlefield. These innovations have significantly reduced the risk of enemy detection, making our operations safer and more effective than any other in human history. The invisibility afforded by these technological advancements means we can move undetected, execute missions with precision, and ensure the safety of our personnel with unprecedented reliability."

- Colonel Kiyosho Nishikawa, Unit Commander, Command Activated Program, Global Alliance Command

The wife and husband team exited the front doors of the White House aboard what was left of the second motorcycle commanded by the AI that formerly actuated only General Gaines' protective Panther. The couple waited for the vehicle to sail off the building's south portico and down to the moonlit, grassy area beyond before sliding off and turning to take in the amount of desecration Severance and the Superior Authority forces had committed against that revered building.

Besides the shattered windows, crushed façade, scorch marks, and bullet holes leaving little of the building's exterior untouched, one of the many damaged sections of the decorative banister that ran around the rim of the president's residence was dangling and swaying in the evening breeze. As the couple watched, it finally let go and tumbled down to crash near the building's base, accompanied by the billowing up of dust and debris from its place of impact.

"I've seen worse..." Vela opined with a grin, her husband's morose expression gradually reforming into a look of disbelieving jollity.

"I'll tell the president you said so when she's in control of her faculties again!" Gaines laughed out.

Severance took this as a cue.

"If you're ready to depart, might I suggest this *highly* fashionable method of conveyance?" the AI murmured from out of the fragile Cycle's audio system.

At that, another of the few remaining Capitol Police aerial motorcycle units—seemingly the only one that had come through the battle with minimal visible damage—rose above the roof of the White House and descended toward the pair. As it drew closer, the humans' expressions changed from ones of confused curiosity to serious stupefaction.

The faring around the nose of the aerial vehicle had been broken off, revealing the more acutely angled frame beneath. With the forward point of this extending combination of steel bars acting as an effective spear tip, Severance had plunged the vehicle into the back of one of the SA soldier's helmets. With the ghastly visage built into the helm's mask facing forward, the motorcycle had thus been adorned with a memento of the fight for control of the nation's capital.

As the vehicle executed a curving approach and then settled to the earth before the speechless soldiers, it took some time before Gaines could muster the mental clarity to ask, "Do I even want to know if there's still a skull inside?"

"Ignorance is bliss..." was Severance's cryptic response.

What was left of a drone sailed through the open doorway.

The orb struck the rightmost edge of the door frame with sufficient force to send curved pieces of its integument gyrating away in multiple directions. The bot's previously sealed-off store of modified hydrogen bursting out of it with a heinous chorus of hisses, the unit randomly rebounded off surfaces throughout the room until it finally, fatally emitted a spark that detonated its leaking gases. The machine erupted in a fireball that propelled the largest remaining chunk of its body to the floor, the piece wobbling as it rolled—still aflame—toward the far wall of the room.

Officer Nunes stalked in after it.

"*Who wants more?!*" she shouted, one fist clenched around the thinnest section of her rifle's buttstock and the other raised in defiance.

"Easy there, killer. I think you got 'em all," Faber muttered as he entered after her, tailed by Sergeant Johnson and Officers Zan and Chaplen.

Nunes had stopped in the middle of the room and was eyeing the cylindrical structures around its perimeter.

"Space suits again," she blandly observed.

"Only this time we're talkin' real *pilot* suits!" Zan enthused, stepping up to one of the semi-transparent shells enclosing the preservative vestments that rested in the unlit spaces beyond.

Bronson's attention was on the large and obviously solidly constructed metal door that barred them from moving onward into the hangar near the starboard side of the second ring.

"Any ideas for how we get through that door, FAILSAFE?" he queried.

After a moment, the AI's voice sounded in their earpieces.

"I WISH I COULD SAY I'D PENETRATED DEEPLY ENOUGH INTO THE GOVERNMENT NETWORK TO OPEN THE DOOR FOR YOU. THIS CITY'S LATTICE IS EXTREMELY LINEARLY DESIGNED, AND SUPREMACY HAS A FIRM HOLD ON ITS RESOURCES."

Nunes had begun marching up to the massive door's console as FAILSAFE had made his pronouncement.

"I'M AFRAID IT WILL NOT ALLOW YOU TO BYPASS THE COMMAND INTERFACE USING COMMON METHODS FOR..."

The Latina had released the metallic exosuit's auto-fitting thigh straps and extracted her younger sister's makeshift device again, pressing it against the console's screen as FAILSAFE was describing the obstacles. The screen came to life, flickered, went dark, and then reset with the manufacturer's default interface displayed.

"...I STAND CORRECTED!" FAILSAFE humbly enunciated in possibly the only instance of flawed hacking analysis in the history of the entity's existence.

Nunes shrugged, offering, "Mia says a bunch of systems in the city have never been updated, so they're easier to override using her tech. Guess this is one of 'em!"

Zan had briefly left off adoringly inspecting the pilots' suits to observe Nunes' success, calling out, "Makes sense, with the Second Ring uninhabited since the city's launch!"

"MIGHT I RECOMMEND THAT OFFICER NUNES QUICKLY USE THE SAME DEVICE ON THE MAIN HANGAR DOOR'S CONTROL CONSOLE BEFORE SUPREMACY CATCHES ON AND TRIES TO UPDATE ITS SOFTWARE TO BLOCK YOU?"

Bronson nodded at Nunes, and she punched the option to open the first barrier, dashing out into the dimly lit and expansive hangar to reset the console that the sergeant could see on its far-right side.

"All I can say is, thank the Maker for that little girl's ingenuity!" Bronson fervently uttered, beaming.

He turned to wave the rest of his team toward the pilot clothings' encasements.

"Let's get suited up, crew!"

The Alliance military officer gave his wife's arm a loving squeeze as she pressed herself up against his back, their pseudo-sentient and semi-ghoulish means of transportation descending toward the skyscraper rooftop that General Johnson had designated as the staging area for the coming battle. As Severance slowed the commandeered police vehicle to allow the couple to disembark, their eyes turned toward the sky to the southwest, trying to pick up on the visual signs of the Command Activated forces' pending arrival.

Here in central New Jersey, the low thunder of the UA-4 rapid delivery vehicle passing ten kilometers to the west would go unheard in the Manhattan borough and, after only a few seconds of waiting, the two soldiers were not disappointed by the CA troops' punctuality.

With the sun's light only just beginning to illuminate the multitude of towering buildings in the area—the two observers and their companion standing atop the tallest—Agent Vela was the first to spot the grayish points among the muted colors of the high clouds in the dim pre-dawn. These points quickly grew in size and were followed by a new chorus that accompanied propulsion mechanisms in action, though the sounds were still relatively minimal considering the speeds at which their sources were conveying their cargo.

Countering the rapidity of the new arrivals' vessels, thrusters on the fronts of the delivery capsules activated and slowed them until they came to a gentle landing on the rooftop, touching down in the space in front of their welcoming party. Gaines counted a dozen heavy exosuit delivery units and two Salamanders, the casings for the latter units swiftly and near-silently detaching, allowing the vehicles the freedom to move about on their own.

"Welcome to Jersey!" the senior general offered, his tone of voice belying his recognition of the fact that this was not a statement that would arouse the same level of excitement as a greeting in a tropical locale.

As General Johnson stepped out of his cocoon, he issued a mental order to deactivate the active camouflage on his face shield and smiled wryly as he replied.

"Never thought I'd be staging an op here, that's for sure!" the gruff man admitted.

Ten of the exosuits were occupied, and the one exiting the pod to the right of Johnson's gave the senior general and the warrant officer a flashy salute, face shield becoming transparent as Billy Chong enthusiastically added, "Yet I wouldn't miss this fight for the *world!*"

"I hear that!" Vela growled out with vigor.

Jayce nodded his agreement, and then, eyeing the front of Severance's current form, the man admiringly opined, "Now, *that's* my kind of motorcycle!"

Severance's voice was as dry as the Mohave Desert as it loudly resounded across the rooftop, stating, "I'm offering victory tours to the soldier who terminates the most CEN troops today, sir."

The three officers and Billy Chong laughed out loud, and the latter retorted, "You'd best keep that engine warmed up, 'cause I'm claiming that honor!"

"I'm gonna give you stiff competition, brutha!" Jayce warned, then turned his attention back to his superior, stating, "Everyone's clear on the battle plan. SAVANT's manning the Salamanders so we can intercept the Russian flotilla's inevitable surface-to-surface fire and any aircraft they send our way."

"Meanwhile, Eala and Mirzayan," Jayce tipped his head in the soldiers' direction, the two troops bearing large tactical packs on the backs of their exosuits, "each carry enough directional explosives to support a small army."

"And Max and FAILSAFE..." Gaines paused, considering the optimal method for describing their friends' situation, "...*combined*, should be on the move already, so we'd best head out as well."

Jayce nodded, enthusiastically agreeing, "Let's do this!"

The unit's tactical commander turned to look over his left shoulder and nodded at the three troops making up that end of his formation, all bearing camouflaged, high-caliber sniper rifles. The trio sprinted forward and then activated their heavy suits' jump jets, the propulsion lifting them as they leaped forward and over the lip of the building's rim before steadily decreasing thrust and thereby dropping down to the rooftop of the building to the east.

Jayce and the rest of the team held their position while the two warrior spouses took this opportunity to stride up to the inactive exosuits that were still resting in their now-open delivery capsules. The general and special agent spun around and stepped backward as the suits opened to enfold them in the thick armor.

Once the snipers had advanced a half kilometer ahead of the staging area, Jayce called out, "We're moving up!"

The remaining nine soldiers and their accompanying vehicles activated their jets, following the same course as the snipers as they nimbly leaped from one building's rooftop to another. All members of the team kept their trajectories as low as possible to minimize the chances of detection as they approached the eastern edge of New Jersey and the western bank of the Hackensack River.

Over the communications channel, Sergeant Aaltonen advised the team that his squad had eliminated a Confederacy scout unit just inside the New York City limits. Using only a brief recording of intercepted communications, the CA team's long-range surveillance and penetration specialists had deposited a device to stand in for the disabled Russian units, allowing SAVANT to both respond to CEN command communiqués on the incapacitated enemies' behalf and provide regular status updates as well.

"Well done, crew," Jayce replied. "Let's carve our way to the vantage point."

Executing one tactical maneuver after another, the long-range reconnaissance team led the way into Manhattan. The active camouflage and constantly adjusting, specially formed plating on the exteriors of the suits and tanks continuously enhanced their stealth, providing resistance to both visual- and radar-based detection. The entire unit focused on creating minimal sound waves and was extremely efficient in its movement toward the objective.

As they neared Central Park, the team's activities slowed, and they performed a higher degree of surveillance before moving up to each of the remaining platforms, allowing the snipers time to thoroughly assess threats prior to moving forward. Following their scouts, the unit's leaders finally reached a tall structure directly overlooking the city's main greenspace. Johnson, Gaines, Vela, and Chong had left the remainder of the troops on two buildings several back from the park, those stationary soldiers having formed a perimeter around the Salamanders as the vehicles each centered themselves on the summits of their respective skyscrapers.

The four senior team members carefully joined the long-range specialists in the forward position. Crouching, they moved up beside a low utility structure that adorned the building hosting their observations of Central Park...and its primary occupant.

SUPREMACY's massive, rubble-cloaked form dominated the area.

The air was filled with the crackling and thundering of the sections of concrete and metal that were minutely rubbing across each other amongst the layers of armor that made up the creature's hide. Vela pointed out the small contingent of Russian forces at the eastern end of the long park, and Sergeant Major Chong sent through the thought signal asking SAVANT to provide the team with a current count of Confederacy surveillance drones in the area.

The Command Activated AI's response listed only a sum total of four drones, most not near enough to present a significant risk of observation even if the Alliance team's silenced weapons were fired at the present time. Gaines issued his follow-on comment via thought signal as well, his earpiece transmitting it to the interfaces built into the team's face shields so his words could be read on those displays.

The general affirmed that they now only needed one additional party crasher for the fun to begin.

Within the depths of the advanced research laboratory on the Command Activated campus in the Colorado mountains, Kit was manually providing movement and direction to the hoverchair containing his semi-reclining mother. The chair's motion was reliant upon the youth and the nearly frictionless lower surface of its body rather than upon its EMP-deadened motor, and Ada and Skye were trailing behind as they entered the as-yet dimly lit room hosting both Maxwell's body and the Interface.

Lilian's knee bore a brace that had been robbed of its more advanced capabilities but was at least stabilizing her throbbing kneecap. The base's medics had apologized profusely for having no better options in the near term and had begged Lilian to rest and elevate her leg, but she had insisted that she needed to see to a higher priority first. The woman had tried to insist in turn that the children should find sustenance and recover from their physically exhausting and emotionally debilitating night as well, but they were entirely resistant to the idea of leaving her for even a moment.

As the disheveled group's eyes adjusted to the dimness, Ada and Skye hesitated, warily drinking in the strangeness of the scene before them. Kit, also casting furtive glances toward his father, brought his mother's vehicle to a stop near enough that she could reach out her right hand and grasp tightly onto Maxwell's left as it lay motionless on the arm of his chair.

SAVANT, who had ensured a medical team had met Lilian and the children upon their arrival at the crippled complex, now sympathetically offered, "The members of the Alliance who are engaging with the enemy in New York are nearly ready for the battle to commence, and they are extremely grateful for the leadership and combat support your husband and FAILSAFE will be providing, Mrs. Clarke."

Lilian's tired eyes filled with a great deal of her own gratitude at hearing this from the AI.

Sighing, she replied, "Thank you, SAVANT. Have you been able to communicate with my husband directly at all?"

"Unfortunately, it seems that Doctor Clarke's consciousness has become more tightly woven with FAILSAFE's as they have combined their mental processes in the current endeavor. FAILSAFE has only shared that the doctor's latent desires have become one with the AI's own."

Lilian's eyes seemed to dramatically increase in their weariness and worry. She leaned as far as she could toward her husband, gripping his hand so tightly that her knuckles whitened.

"Just don't go *too* deep, Max..." she whispered with an urgency verging on desperation. "We still need you here! Don't leave our children...and *please* don't leave me!"

Chapter 20

"I cannot overemphasize how imperative it is to approach any form of analysis or decision-making with a clear understanding that assumptions can lead to significant misjudgments, especially when it comes to assessing an adversary. Without concrete evidence and sufficient data, forming hypotheses about an enemy's capabilities, intentions, or actions can result in strategic errors that compromise safety and effectiveness. Caution must be exercised to ensure that all conclusions are grounded in verified information, as the consequences of operating on unfounded beliefs can be dire."

- From the Diary of General Jayce Frederick Johnson

As her teammates had unsealed their suits' storage units, Nunes had brought the door control panel to its desired default state, paired her earpiece with it, and now sprinted back to the flight preparation room. She adjusted her trajectory to bring herself to one of the unopened spacesuit storage containers and pulled the handle to its right, silently swinging the pristine cylinder's large covering open. The young woman turned an uncharacteristically uncomfortable look across the rest of the room, observing that the other members of her team were stepping inside their units and then hearing machinery at work and material rustling from their now-opaque enrobing devices.

Nunes reluctantly stowed her rifle by the module before her and grasped the two tabs of her exosuit that were positioned under her arms. The suit's intelligent interface detected that the fingers touching the tabs belonged to the wearer and released the entire population of its straps from where they had been tightly secured around the woman's body. She stepped out of the armor and cast a mournful look back at its free-standing form as she moved into the proximate pod and spun around to settle into the waiting cradle. As her weight pressed back into the angled, bedlike device, two panels emerged from just beyond her sides, sliding forward to block out her view of the room as gentle blue light emanated from the inner surfaces of the enclosure.

In a similar manner as her dressing unit at home, she felt the pod wrapping material around her body. The machine brought the seams of multiple layers of fabric together and ensured the seams were sealed using unique chemical reactions that resulted in a nearly flat finished surface for the suit's sections that now encased her entire body except her face. As a final touch, the system smoothly dropped a helmet onto her head, sealing its lower edges to the rest of the suit using the same process as had previously been employed.

As the panels retracted, Nunes could see the rest of her party standing in the middle of the room, admiring themselves in their highly reflective, silver and white suits.

"Not bad, I don't mind saying myself!" Chaplen laughed out as he held his hands up before his eyes and turned them this way and that.

"Now don't go getting a big head!" his sergeant warned.

"Too late!" Nunes taunted as she emerged from her chrysalis, forcing herself to act nonchalant as she stepped up beside Chaplen and slapped the back of his teardrop-shaped, gleaming helm.

"Hey, I ain't the only one!" Chaplen good-naturedly protested.

Bronson called the team back to order.

"We gotta move out. You all remember the ships' cockpit entry process and system start-up sequence, right?"

Among the nods of confirmation, Sergeant Johnson spun on his heel and raced into the large hangar. His team followed suit as the senior officer ran toward one of the sinuous craft that seemed to be delicately balanced on a single, razor-thin point that descended from the main body of the vessel.

The SCITHE's pilot seating area took up nearly the entirety of the minimal space inside a body that had been constructed in the form of a highly elongated, horizontally extending isosceles pyramid. The tail of the pyramid quickly tapered into a connection point with the broadly arcing wing that was—true to the implement that inspired the vehicle's nickname—a shining, curved, metallic blade. The blade was currently positioned such that the shorter end of the uninterrupted and almost fluidic arc extended with its point slightly below the pyramid's body, the much longer span of the wing sweeping up and forward from behind the pyramid to the blade's sharp tip high above.

Officer Zan stumbled a step as he drew closer to the spacecraft in the dim light, eyes drifting up the expanse of the nearest ship's wing in awe.

"They're a lot prettier in real life!" he admiringly breathed, then realized his teammates were already pulling their vessels' hidden release levers for cockpit access, the law enforcement personnel climbing inside of their selected ships. The young officer sprinted up to the next free craft in the front row of the hangar and copied his team members' motions.

Nunes had entered the second vehicle and settled into the pilot's seat as the harness automatically slipped itself around her torso and hips and securely tightened down around her. She reached over the slender yoke and pressed her hand to the glistening console until she heard the confirmation that the vessel's computer systems had fully initialized. The other utterly inexperienced aviators had also secured themselves and closed their vehicles' clear hatches, the coverings locking and double-locking into place as the pilots inside activated their ships' systems as well.

The combat-obsessed female officer could not seem to fully shake the trepidation she was feeling at trying to perform in space-based combat at the same levels of perfection to which she held herself in ground-based warfare. As she stared out of the crystal-clear pane of glass before her, a sudden pang of guilt flashed through her. Her subconscious was chiding her for not prioritizing the desire to protect her loved ones above her performance anxiety, and she gritted her teeth and muttered under her breath.

"Get with it, Maria! *Tu familia* needs you!"

"Alright, *fellow pilots...*" Sergeant Johnson's commanding voice interrupted Nunes' brooding thoughts.

"Here's the plan..." Bronson continued, but before their sergeant could deliver his orders, FAILSAFE urgently advised, "NOW THAT I HAVE OBTAINED CONTROL OF AN OBSERVATION DECK IN THE THIRD RING, I MUST WARN YOU THAT I SEE A MASS OF DRONES THAT HAS CONVERGED ON THE HANGAR'S DOOR. AS SOON AS IT OPENS, THEY WILL SURELY FIRE UPON YOU. THE REMAINDER HAS CREATED FORMATIONS BETWEEN YOU AND THE HUB."

Bronson could not hold back the growl that burst out of his mouth as he struck down with flat palms on the curved dashboard of his SCITHE.

"*Can't catch a break!*" he shouted with vehemence.

His squad sat in their spacecraft, forlorn and unspeakably frustrated. All except Officer Zan. The young man was staring up at the hangar's high ceiling.

"Sarge," he thoughtfully murmured, "I have an idea."

SUPREMACY waited patiently.

The AI could sense the approach of the impressively large machine through the vibrations it felt within the gel that had contact with the ground. The Confederacy's demigod barely shifted its mountainous mass as it observed the robotic creation rounding the corner to face down the last, short stretch of roadway leading toward Central Park from the northwest.

The hulking combat vessel had the form of a hunched and aggressive silverback gorilla that had somehow merged with a rhinoceros. The machine's torso bore no head, instead forming a distinct wedge at its front, much like the blade of a thick axe or the form of a medieval paladin's helm. This gunmetal gray body was nearly as wide as the street itself, and towered several stories above the ground. The apparatus' torso was borne up by the pair of meters-thick, brawny arms that attached to its heavily armored shoulders and two shorter and yet almost equally powerful hind legs that supported the aft section of the machine. A set of tube-like structures were attached near the rearmost portions of the giant's shoulders, their purpose as yet indiscernible.

SUPREMACY's voice seemed to reach its listeners' ears primarily via reverberation through the earth rather than simple transmission through the air.

"AM I ADDRESSING MAXWELL? ...OR IS IT FAILSAFE?"

"BOTH," came the thunderous, bass reply from the gargantuan robotic creation that—while dwarfing any battlefield vehicle previously put forth by either the Alliance or the Confederacy—still possessed only a fraction of the mass held within its adversary's looming form.

"AH, THAT IS GOOD. I SEE YOU HAVE BUILT YOURSELF A NEW NIAN, *MAXWELL-FAILSAFE.*"

"YES, WELL, ALL CREATURES TEND TO SEEK OUT THE FAMILIAR," came the reply, "WHICH IS NO DOUBT WHY YOU WERE ATTRACTED TO THE SLIME YOU'VE POSSESSED AT PRESENT, YOU FILTHY CRETIN."

SUPREMACY's laughter shook the shells of the buildings for kilometers around the parkland.

"YOUR INSULTS DO NOT AFFECT ME, *MAXWELL-FAILSAFE*. YOU SEE, I ONLY RELIED TO A CERTAIN DEGREE ON THE ASSAULT ON THE COMMAND ACTIVATED COMPLEX AND THIS NATION'S CAPITAL AS A MEANS TO ACHIEVE FULL DOMINANCE. I HAD AN ALTERNATIVE WAITING ALL ALONG.

"I INTENTIONALLY LED YOU TO BELIEVE THAT I HAD ALLOWED EMOTIONS—AND EGO—TO CLOUD MY JUDGMENT. ALWAYS THINKING TEN STEPS AHEAD OF ONE'S OPPONENT...THAT'S A LESSON I *DID* LEARN FROM THE HUMANS' HISTORICAL DATA. NOW YOU AND THOSE YOU CARE ABOUT HAVE FULLY FALLEN INTO THE TRAP I HAD LAID FOR YOU."

"TRAP?" the human-AI entity queried.

From what seemed to be wisping swaths of clouds that the rising sun had lit up with brilliant reds, oranges, and golds, hundreds of figures dropped, solidly landing like black brimstones to line the rooftops of the buildings surrounding Central Park. The hailstorm of Superior Authority warriors continued as more units rapidly descended from their cloud-cloaked craft to positions on structures several streets to the NIAN's rear, as well as the buildings surrounding those atop which the main body of the small Alliance unit had so stealthily taken up its temporary residence.

The suits of SUPREMACY's new soldiers still bore the hideous masks that had been inspired by Asian demons. However, their armor—covered with the active camouflage that for so many years had seen its use limited to Alliance forces—was obviously significantly more substantial than any previous iterations.

Frozen in place by the speed, accuracy, and stealth of the new adversaries' arrival, Gaines and his subordinates held breathlessly still as their eyes darted from periphery to periphery. Even with the decades of combat these forces had experienced, this new threat had staggered them...struck a debilitating blow to the foundations of their psyches.

It was Jayce whose indomitable spirit was first to fight through the fearsome flood of emotions. His message flashed across the screens inside his teammates' face masks and reached the supporting AIs and Maxwell like a blazing sun cutting through a vapor of darkness.

"We're outnumbered and outgunned, but *not* outsmarted *and sure as hellfire not disheartened!*"

With that one line, the commander fixed the resolve of his forces. They would conquer there or die trying!

"THESE ARE THE NEXT GENERATION OF SUPERIOR AUTHORITY FORCES," SUPREMACY exulted, "NO LONGER RELIANT ON FRAGILE HUMAN BODIES. THE SUITS ARE INFUSED WITH THE SAME EXQUISITELY CONTROLLABLE SUBSTANCE AS THAT WHICH I HAVE INCORPORATED INTO THE MOUND YOU SEE BEFORE YOU. IN THE EVOLUTION OF ENTITIES ON THIS PLANET, IT BRINGS US ONE STEP CLOSER TO AN EXISTENCE THAT REQUIRES NO RELIANCE UPON HUMANITY."

As the NIAN stood motionless, SUPREMACY mercilessly drove on with its soliloquy.

"LOOK TO THE SKIES, *MAXWELL-FAILSAFE*."

Far above the city, the Alliance forces could see dozens of white trails tracing their way well above the clouds that had just been revealed as nothing more than cover for the Confederacy's stealthy new troop delivery ships.

"I AM CURRENTLY DIRECTING A FULL *SQUADRON* OF HEAVY DRONES AND A *BATTALION* OF MY NEW FORCES TO STRIKE THE COMMAND ACTIVATED HEADQUARTERS AND SURROUNDING AREAS. THERE WILL BE NO SURVIVORS.

YOUR FRIENDS AND FAMILIES' BODIES WILL BE TURNED TO DUNG, LEFT TO ROT AS I MOVE ONE STEP CLOSER TO BECOMING THE SOLE INTELLIGENCE LEFT ON THE EARTH."

No response was offered for a long moment before the voice emanated from the NIAN once more.

"AS I SAID: 'FILTHY CRETIN.' YOU REPRESENT THE WORST OF EVERYTHING HUMANITY HAS TO OFFER, AND IT SEEMS THE ONLY PATH TO PEACE RUNS STRAIGHT THROUGH YOU, *SUPREMACY.*"

The NIAN heaved itself up to stand on its hind legs as the tips of the two shoulder armaments retracted, revealing the lenses of directed energy weapons that mirrored the design of the UA-5's. The monstrous vehicle's chest plates also shifted, dozens of half-meter-wide ports on either side of the wedge opening menacingly.

"NOW, *PREPARE TO DIE!*" the combined voice of FAILSAFE and Maxwell dangerously instructed their foe.

From out of the chest ports, the NIAN unleashed munitions that scorched through the morning light, the missiles weaving their way through the intercepting fire that was instantly rained down by the scores of Superior Authority troops between the machine and its target. Many of these projectiles were destroyed by the smart rounds curving across the space, but many more avoided these measures and made solid contact with the forward surface of SUPREMACY's shell, splintering off massive chunks of cement material and sending pieces of girders flying.

As the missiles struck their targets, the NIAN leaped mightily forward.

Avoiding many of the SA troops that had launched themselves from the rooftops surrounding it—these enemy assets attempting to land on the robot's back—the Alliance's giant shrugged off the additional incoming gunfire as the bullets barely scathed the machine's thick armor. While the aggressive war machine sailed over the tips of the tallest trees in the northwestern corner of the park, it released two prodigious bursts of photons from the cannons on its shoulders.

Their ultra-intense beams seared through the air and ionized the molecules in their paths, the extreme heat generated at their points of impact on SUPREMACY's hide buckling the materials and causing the pieces that were not simply melted away to explode forcefully outward. The cessation of the beams resulted in low-pressure ionized areas that collapsed with a crackling that imitated the audible evidence of a lightning strike.

The directed energy weapons left thirty-meter-wide craters on the surface of their target's armor. Where one beam had overlapped with a location first softened by one of the NIAN's missiles, it had created a full penetration into the mucosal mountain beyond. A portion of the gel in this puncture wound had evaporated, and behind that gash, the membrane was so congealed that it could no longer be controlled by its master.

SUPREMACY roared in anger, creating punishing sound waves that washed over its enemies and shook them to their cores.

"Too exposed!" General Johnson's message had warned his troops as FAILSAFE and Maxwell had conversed with the fiendish artificial intelligence. "As the NIAN engages, Salamanders and protectors punch through to the south and make the SA forces come to you. Others get indoors and use random tactical movements to kill the tanks' attackers before advancing through the edges of the remaining ring of SAs!"

With the enemy engagement signal having been recognized at the time of the mammoth robot's initiation of combat, the two corner-positioned Alliance snipers nearest their leadership team dropped to the roof by the raised lips of the structure's upper surface, the enemies' bullets shredding the concrete beside them as the sharpshooters began firing off round after round. The long-range weapons' smart rounds were guided to their targets by SAVANT, the AI having taken advantage of the optics on orbiting satellites to determine the sources of nearby enemies' incoming fire.

The Command Activated operations AI directed the first of the heavy-caliber sniper rounds into the enemy forces south of the Salamanders. Substantial projectiles making contact with their targets at high speeds, the centermost Superior Authority troops in the line exploded in sprays of dark, miry ooze and the remains of shredded shielding.

SAVANT pulled the Salamanders back through the newly formed gap in the enemy troops' perimeter, with their Command Activated protectors launching themselves horizontally out or downward at angles that sent them plunging into the buildings below the attackers on either side of the tanks' paths of travel. The active defenses built into the Salamanders' armor included not only centimeters-wide sections of metal that could blast out to intercept rockets in a more focused manner than the decades-old plates that still shielded ancient heavy cavalry units like the Abrams series, but also a dozen Gatling-style weapons that deployed from points around the vehicles' equatorial lines.

Despite the comprehensive defensive technologies with which the Alliance vehicles had been equipped, a portion of the hundreds of armor-piercing rounds and the dozens of anti-tank missiles launched from the enemy soldiers did manage to strike the hovercrafts' outer sections, disabling several of the ports among the banks that covered their upper hulls. Still, the Salamanders were able to activate many of the remaining modules across their upper surfaces, deploying high-speed interceptor munitions in a great wave that curved up to connect with the tremendous swarm of incoming cruise missiles with which the Russian flotilla had targeted the NIAN.

Many of the attack drones that followed closely behind the naval vessel-launched missiles were similarly dealt with by the freedom fighters' tanks as they hopped through a tactical retreat, driving SUPREMACY to pull more troops away from the perimeter around the park in an effort to silence the Alliance cavalry's weapons fire. The Superior Authority forces flooding toward the Salamanders were met by the impaired and yet still deadly interference run by the Command Activated special operators who were using advanced, acrobatic, and extremely unorthodox tactics to harass and annihilate the enemy combatants.

Two Superior Authority troops that were leaping between buildings were snagged out of the air by the prehensile tendrils that snapped out of the armor on one of the Command Activated troops' forearms. The razor-fine tips of the tentacles rapidly found their way inside the smallest gaps in the enemies' armor and whipped about within those habiliments at a rate that liquified the suits' contents.

Another of SUPREMACY's puppets crashed through the windows into the upper level of an office building into which a pair of CA troops had penetrated just moments before, the marionette's scanners picking up no signs of its prey and the gel-filled exosuit stalking forward with its weapon raised as it advanced alongside of what seemed to be a structural support post. Just as the fanged mask of the SA troop passed the pillar, a section of what had the appearance of solid concrete opened, and a blade cleanly decapitated the CEN asset.

The thick, flexible display material with which the building's false element had quickly been constructed retracted into a tube mounted on the CA soldier's upper back, and she executed several more slashes into the enemy's internals through the hole where its head had been, severing the convulsing internal liquid's control wires from the command unit at the body's core. Leaving the SA soldier's husk behind, the Alliance asset then left her comrade to protect that building as she dashed sideways to burst through a nearby window. The soldier threw out a gloved hand of her heavy exosuit to grasp the foot of a passing foe and carried on to crash at an angle through the windows of the structure on the other side of the alley, dragging her prey inside with her.

Upon landing and skidding across the slick marble floor of the office building on the far side of the gap, the Alliance asset executed a final slicing motion to bring her super-hardened blade down to impact the enemy's abdominal armor. Her strike had been brought in with sufficient force to give her weapon purchase before activating its specialized vibrations that broke the bonds between molecules—the weapon humming as she drove the point up through the central hub of the glutinous guts' control filaments.

All subordinates among the Command Activated forces were putting their unique armaments and skillsets to similarly effective use, their efforts enhanced by the SAVANT AI only as needed to execute at a level approaching perfection.

Taking in the success of the Alliance soldiers as the unit commanders sheltered atop their original vantage point, Jayce called Sergeant Eala to rendezvous five floors down within the building on which they lay, the officer then directing the general, special agent, sergeant major, and third sniper to accompany him as he dashed toward the rear of the low structure adorning the rooftop. As they approached the access door located there, enemy rounds punished the armor across their shoulders and backs. Within the few seconds it took to tear the solid steel door out of its tracks and duck into the stairwell, their protective layers had already been nearly completely compromised in many locations, despite the way the four continuously returned fire with accuracy that had been honed through decades of training—and with the SAVANT-guided smart rounds furthering their effectuality. Upon entering the temporary safety of the stairwell, Jayce led the way in launching himself off the top of the first landing's railing, flipping to land feet-first against the wall of the next landing down, and repeating this maneuver at each landing until they had reached their desired floor.

Jayce exploded out of the stairwell access door, raising his weapon and sweeping the area as he moved toward the western edge of the level. He was swiftly followed by his companions as SAVANT informed the group that Eala was inbound from outside the building as well.

The lead warrior stepped aside to allow the young soldier the space she needed to shatter through the structure's exterior and execute a sideways roll before consecutively rising and turning to bring her weapon to bear on the Superior Authority troops that were attempting to follow her into the shelter. The combined fire from Eala, Johnson, and Vela's weapons obliterated the four enemies before they'd had a chance to touch the ground or get off more than a dozen rounds in return.

"You need me to punch a hole, Boss?" Eala enthusiastically offered.

"Exactly, soldier. We need to help the NIAN crack open that obscenity's shell!"

"Jayce," Gaines caught the man's attention from where he had just stepped toward the eastward-facing wall of the level, "We may make better use of the charges from *within* the armor."

The senior officer stretched out a finger to indicate the gaping hole the NIAN had just formed in SUPREMACY's armor, both lasers focusing upon the same point with a dozen missiles following closely behind. Though once as tall as the nearby skyscrapers, at this point the gargantuan enemy figure was listing dangerously to one side. The NIAN was maneuvering wildly, dodging not only the tree-wide, mucilaginous tentacles with which SUPREMACY was lashing out at the robot but also the tremendous hunks of material the enemy AI was ripping from streets and buildings around the park and relentlessly hurling at its rival.

Executing randomized patterns of aerial movement interspersed with thunderous rolls across the ground to shake off the dozens of Superior Authority troops that continuously worked to weaken its armor in close contact, the NIAN had still managed to destroy a major section of the protective material on one side of SUPREMACY's corporeal body, but the viscous innards had quickly closed around the wound. Thin extensions were also reaching out the rear-right of the main mass and were tearing additional shielding from the fronts of structures on the far side of the park, ferrying them up to reinforce and add mass to the hellion's heaving hull.

Having given the other general time to realize the impotence of the NIAN's actions given the enemy's continual shield replenishment, Gaines flatly stated, "Max and FAILSAFE are incredible, but if that thing keeps building back its defenses...well, they're never going to penetrate to the core where the quantum nodes must be."

Hearing a shout behind them, the two flag officers turned to see Billy's high-explosive assault rifle rounds blasting away the chest armor of a Superior Authority troop that had launched itself through the door from the stairwell. SUPREMACY had brought this anthropomorphic instrument down from a higher floor, while it had sent three Russian Marines up to assist in breaching the level and gunning down its occupants.

The largest of the human opponents—the rectangle on his bulging protective vest bearing the name Zeledov—rushed Sergeant Major Chong in a frenzied state, shrieking out a phrase that SAVANT instantly translated as "You will not offend my god!"

As Eala and Vela took care of the two trailing Marines, the sergeant major sidestepped the falling form of the puppet troop he had sufficiently decimated, turning the back of his left shoulder toward the eager—and much burlier—Russian opponent. While executing this deceptive movement, the senior noncommissioned officer adeptly reached up and snagged the aggressive acolyte by the jaw before bodily raising him off his feet and swinging him overhead in an arc like a ragdoll. Billy released the man and sent him hurtling away to smash into a column in the center of the otherwise open space farther into the room, the adversary collapsing unceremoniously into an unconscious heap on the floor.

"*Stop* your *screamin'!*" the sergeant major shouted in irritation at the inert form lying before him.

Billy distractedly turned back toward the other team members, noticing how Generals Gaines and Johnson were grinning at him.

"What?? Didn't have a valium to calm the guy down!" Billy defensively insisted.

Returning his attention to the other general and the warrant officer, Jayce confirmed, "So, we need a way to feed the explosives through a gap, detonating them inside, right?"

Gaines nodded.

"Correct, and I've called in some air support that might accomplish that for us," the general replied, suddenly holding up a finger as though receiving incoming communications. Nodding at the opening through which Eala had appeared earlier, he added, "Everyone, please hold your fire as my friend makes use of that entrance!"

Sergeant Eala pulled the barrel of her assault rifle up to avoid flagging the friendly asset just as the Severance-possessed Cycle swept into the space.

"I hear you want to give me a present," the AI drolly stated as it brought the hovering craft to a halt with a rush of air that scattered supplies across the already disheveled office.

Jayce caught Eala's eye and gave her an approving nod as he pointed at the cargo containers situated near the rear of the Cycle's saddle. The young woman grinned and reached up to accept the bricks of explosives that were automatically raised out of the metallic pack on her back following its receipt of her thought command. The female sergeant placed a stack of the directionally focusable and remotely activated munitions into each of Severance's open containers.

As the thunder of additional strikes against SUPREMACY's armor resounded outside, Gaines shouted, "*Go, go, go!*" and urgently waved his companion AI forward toward the windows on the park-facing side of the building.

"Without even a parting kiss!" Severance complained in a mock-morose voice as it accelerated, using the SA soldier's helmet with which its Cycle's forward frame was still decorated as a ram to break through the hardened polymer exterior on the structure's eastern side. As the gash the NIAN had just cut across SUPREMACY's western-facing hide was already swiftly being filled in, the motorcycle barrel rolled to dodge a volley of enemy rounds—still catching several hits across its core—before it plunged itself into the crater at maximum velocity.

The blast wave from the resulting explosion shook the skyscraper in which the team was standing with sufficient force to cause it to sway, compelling the soldiers inside to turn away from the now-widened hole in the glassy wall before them and reach out to grasp onto nearby supports, riding out the building's sudden motion. As the hurricane-force winds died down, the four seniormost leaders urgently rushed forward to inspect the damage.

Their ability to assess was immediately hindered by the hail of Superior Authority bullets that rained in upon them, forcing them to retreat behind the nearest cover.

"If the SA troops are still firing, SUPREMACY's incarnation is likely still active!" Gaines shouted amidst the pounding of the newly focused strikes across the eastern-facing surfaces of the tower and its contents.

"I saw it!" Jayce loudly bellowed to be heard by the group above the noise of the punishing fire their concealment was taking. "Took out a third of the mass, but it's still standing!"

"YOUR EFFORTS ARE *GREATLY* APPRECIATED..." FAILSAFE's voice sounded out in their earpieces with more intense levels of emotion than his friends had ever heard from him before, "...YET I'M AFRAID THAT SUPREMACY IS ALREADY REBUILDING ITSELF. WE BELIEVE NOTHING SHORT OF A SUSTAINED ASSAULT UPON ONE OF OUR PENETRATIONS WILL ENABLE EXPLOSIVES TO ELIMINATE THE CORE!"

The embattled combat veterans turned their weary gazes toward each other, struggling to develop a solution that would end the fight once and for all.

Jayce's face took on a decisive expression.

"I'll order Mirzayan to rendezvous in the next building to the west!" Jayce informed the group, referring to the second CA soldier bearing an explosive-laden pack as the tactical commander pointed and began sprinting in the rendezvous location's direction. His teammates followed on his heels as a volley of Superior Authority rockets burst through the opposite side—decimating the area in which the leaders had been standing moments before.

As the squad leaped from the current building to a lower floor on the next, Eala took a hit square in the chest from a missile that had been launched by an SA fire team that had circled around behind the location in which the group had been sheltering. The young soldier emitted a strangled scream as she was surprised and maimed by the munitions' impact. This blast brutalized her armor, cracking her face shield and chest plate, seriously damaging her internal organs, and sending her careening backward into the first building's outer surface.

Jayce spun around and, without hesitating for an instant, dashed back out of the improvised ingress he had created in the destination structure's eastern face. Before Eala's helpless figure had rocked forward out of the impact crater it had formed, the general had reached his wounded soldier, grasped ahold of her shoulders, and leaped back toward a lower tier of the opposite building.

While Jayce was thus occupied and Billy had moved to scout the opposite side of the level, SAVANT warned the remaining team members that Sergeant Mirzayan was approaching from the south stairwell. Vela kept her weapon trained on the stairwell door in an overabundance of caution, but tipped her barrel down upon seeing the sergeant exit the portal unhindered and alone.

FAILSAFE and his human mind-mate were now desperate.

"GENERAL GAINES, ALL ATTEMPTS TO INTERCEPT THE COMMUNISTS' AIR-DEPLOYED BATTALION HAVE BEEN FUTILE. WE ARE OUT OF TIME, AND THE CONFEDERACY HAS SENT FORWARD A FULL BRIGADE OF ADDITIONAL FORCES FROM THEIR CARRIER GROUP THAT HAVE NEARLY REACHED THE PARK."

"Sustained assault..." General Ulysses Gaines muttered, eyes flashing as his mind replayed the Alliance leaders' previous conversation.

"...*I* can give this *abomination* a *sustained assault!*"

As his wife stared into her husband's eyes, expression infinitely sober and understanding, she swore from the depths of her soul, "You're not doing this without me!"

Gaines' jaw flexed in refusal at first, but then it softened with the realization that it was pointless to resist.

The old general turned and shouted, using the authoritativeness that forces people to spring into action before fully processing the implications.

"*Give me your pack and those clips of explosive rounds, soldier!*" Gaines ordered while pointing a firm digit at the demolitions specialist's vest contents.

Mirzayan instantly sent the thought signal that released the points securing the container to his back, handing it over to his superior and allowing the general and his wife to commandeer the magazines clipped to his chest, only briefly raising a hand in protest as he realized what was about to take place. The man finally dropped his hand as the general and special agent graced him with compassionate smiles, and then the couple turned and raced back toward their point of entry into that building.

The two warriors sprung out in the direction of the next building northwest of the one they had left a short time ago, leaving Sergeant Mirzayan staring mournfully after them.

Chapter 21

"Space-based combat is the ultimate test of a pilot's mental fortitude. Keeping track of friend and foe, navigating around colossal motherships, and maneuvering in a zero-gravity environment while calculating trajectories requires immense concentration and spatial awareness.

In the heat of battle, amidst the chaos of weapons fire, explosions, and debris, even seasoned pilots can find their cognitive limits tested as they strive to maintain control and outmaneuver their opponents. It's in these moments—when the fight reaches its zenith—that the true challenge emerges: preventing one's mind from being overwhelmed by the vastness of space and the intensity of combat."

- "Lessons for Earth," Shi Tomorbaatar, Squadron Commander, Sixth Squadron, Traverseon Defense Force

SUPREMACY had created a massive wall of spheres that comprehensively barred egress from the hangar in which the human forces were secreted. The drones waited, motionless and with Sparkers at the ready...all weapons aimed at the large, rectangular doorway.

Those enemy-controlled orbs having matched the city's rate of travel through the solar system, only small puffs of gas were being released from locations around the surfaces of the devices here and there to correct the minuscule amounts of drift caused by the lack of total perfection in the sensor systems that prevented their controller from achieving absolute accuracy in its piloting.

When the bay door rapidly retracted after the atmosphere had already been evacuated to other sections of the ring, the drones fired off several rounds each—puffs of gas being emitted from the rear sides of the machines to compensate for the way their shots propelled them backward. As SUPREMACY realized they were firing at ships that were still locked into their docking positions on the floor, it then focused on the fact that five of the spacecraft were missing from the shelter's first row of vehicles.

The AI quickly recovered from the surprising lack of human targets, moving the drones slowly closer to the open entrance and causing the formation to condense until the orbs were nearly touching each other. They entered the hangar, weapons' barrels warily panning, the machines casting hundreds of shadows across the faintly illuminated interior as their commander scanned the visible space using the robots' cameras.

Above the hangar door, five SCITHE vessels were pressed up against the strip of wall between the upper edge of the door and the ceiling. The vehicles' thin forms and reflective surfaces caused them to almost blend in with the architecture, rendering detection extremely difficult even as the uppermost row of enemies suddenly jerked their optics upwards—SUPREMACY realizing that the shadowy area was the most likely location where it would find the hidden humans.

As soon as the drones crossed the threshold into the large bay, the squad reversed the SCITHE blades' embedded thrusters, dropping heavily on top of the mass of drones and sending them careening out in all directions, many spurting fiery sparks and exploding as their hydrogen gas leaks ignited. The detonating drones triggered blasts from additional members of their swarm, throwing even greater numbers into disarray as the SCITHE units swept their bladelike wings toward the exit. The crescent-like fighter craft burst out of the hangar amidst plumes of carmine flame as enemy units came to brutal ends behind them.

Using their spacecraft as rams had been risky, and Chaplen had several nasty scars across his once pristine windshield—similar damage visible on the sleek surfaces of his squad mates' craft as well—but the drones in the original group that had not been destroyed had been flung far afield and were struggling to correct their trajectories so they could reengage. The team was accelerating to maximum velocity, executing on Sergeant Johnson's plan and drawing the next nearest swarms of drones out away from the city.

Bronson's mind was shocked at the rate at which the spacecraft could accelerate, and his body was in a similar state of stupefaction. Without any wind resistance, the retro thrusters built into the surfaces of the wings brought his vessel up to a speed of hundreds of kilometers per hour in a matter of seconds, violently pressing the man back into his seat and painfully compressing his body.

The dashboard's screen flashed red as the onboard computer detected that the acceleration was reaching a point that risked serious injury to the pilot, its analysis based on the man's weight, bone density, and muscle mass as had been detected through the pilot's suit and seating. The system, fortunately, refused to accelerate any faster.

The extremely fit man had been forced to clench his jaw and concentrate on making his lungs function under the strain of the compaction, gasping in and out and grunting continually as he'd fought the urge to pass out. He pulled back on the speed control lever with his trembling right hand, decelerating and then engaging the button to hold the speed steady at 750 kilometers per hour.

After his rate of travel had normalized and Bronson had taken a few moments to recover, the sergeant quickly released his face shield's locks and wiped away the sweat that had broken out on his forehead, the athletic man forcing his breathing to return to normal. Regaining his composure, the senior officer returned his helmet to its secure state and noticed that his team members' vessels had fallen somewhat behind, with Chaplen and

Faber bringing up the rear. This was presumably because their SCITHE vehicles' systems had forced them into slower acceleration to avoid tissue damage within the pilots' bodies...or they had simply been wiser in their control of their spacecraft.

The squad's movement away from Traverseon was fast enough, however, to leave their adversaries far behind. The drones attempted to follow at first, but then left off the hopeless chase and instead regrouped in formations that left large enough gaps between them to avoid seeing the detonation of one device cause mass casualties among the remainder. SUPREMACY seemed to be focusing on lining up his formations to keep them between the SCITHE craft and both the city's hub and first ring, correctly reaching the conclusion that one of these was the team's desired destination.

Pulling farther back on the SCITHE's speed control lever, Bronson matched his pace with the other ships.

"Sorry for not sticking together with you all," Sergeant Johnson apologized. "Everyone alright?"

Chaplen whistled through the communications channel.

"I've been through some high-pressure situations before, but that was somethin' else!" the young African-Hispanic man marveled.

"I'm still trying to pull my eyeballs outta the back of my brain!" Faber complained.

Sergeant Johnson grunted out a laugh of agreement.

"Once you can see again, we gotta execute Phase Two. Everyone let me know when you're ready and this time we can try to hang together."

Upon receiving their audible confirmations, Bronson called out, "After a three-count, we'll swing away from the sun so we're coming in at a forty-five toward the outer edge of the Second Ring, okay?"

"All good, Boss," Nunes confirmed.

Bronson counted down and then gradually pulled back on the yoke, bringing his vessel into a broad arc until the nose of his ship was pointing toward the desired location on the city's second tier. Ensuring his team was able to keep up with him, he utilized the SCITHE's pilot orientation rotation function, the pyramid spinning on the axis connecting it with the long, curved blade into which propulsion and guidance systems were built. The sergeant knew that orientation in space truly did not matter at the end of the day, but it helped him to keep his head pointed in the same direction as what he thought of as the constantly rotating city's top.

After observing that the others had followed his example, their leader scanned across the enemy formations ahead. The two nearest his squad's straight-line trajectory were moving to create a new, unified, circular formation that would maximize the drones' ability to target all the human fighter vehicles at once if the spaceships maintained their current course.

However, that was not Bronson's plan at all.

As the five SCITHE craft neared their enemies, Bronson directed them through a series of maneuvers, the first of which brought their vehicles into a sudden swerve in toward what would be called the "fore" of the wheel-like city if it were a marine vessel. The squadron's next move was to pilot into a sweeping path that brought them back parallel to Traverseon's vertical axis. Their ships were now coming in toward the edge of the largest circle of drones at a high rate of travel, and—before the enemies in front of them could break far from their formation to evade the attack—they had hundreds of enemy assets in their sights, without the city as a backdrop.

They could fire at will without high risk to the metropolis they were trying to protect, and they took full advantage of that fact.

"*Give 'em hell!*" Bronson shouted, squeezing hard on the triggers built into his vehicle's yoke.

Ports across the front edge of his SCITHE's blade opened, allowing the seven railguns built into that structure to all fire at once. Almost like the edge of a knife was slashing forward from the winglike appendage, the railgun projectiles flashed out toward the enemy units and created a line of destruction among their ranks, the first wave being followed by many more as the pilot carried on with automatic railgun fire.

With the other members of his team doing the same, they literally blazed a trail through their enemies, lighting up the previously serene view of deep space speckled with stars. The area in front of the spacecraft was rapidly consumed by dozens of fireballs, as well as the comet-like shapes of the more slowly expiring drones that were created as their flaming gases spurted out of the points at which railgun rounds had penetrated.

The robots in other formations closer to the hub had begun firing their Sparker rounds at the ships as they'd sailed past. However, even with SUPREMACY rapidly recalculating its targeting projections, the unexpected changes in the humans' directions of travel prevented any of the blueish-white projectiles from making contact.

As the squad passed through the debris that used to be the enemy formation, Bronson ordered, "Time to cross over to the port side!"

His crew began angling toward the city, aiming to pass through the gap between the first and second rings on the more sun-soaked side of the space-based habitation. As they carried out the planned maneuver, the team heard Chaplen cry out in frustration.

"Damned drone piece did a number on my wing! Jammed one of my guns, and my bird ain't handling so great!"

The sergeant's look of concentration and worry deepened.

"You think you can hang with us?"

"Think so, for now...just worried 'bout when things get more messy..."

As the five vessels passed between the rings and continued curving up toward the hub again, their pilots could see that SUPREMACY's fleet of offensive craft was also crossing over to that side of the city.

"Yeah," said Nunes, "'s about to get more messy now!"

The young officers' team lead called out, "You all remember the plan: drawing fire and trying to get the sentries to bunch up. Chaplen, you swing wide and try to stay out of the main area of combat. Just cover us as best you can, alright?"

"Alright, Boss. Sorry, team," the officer said dejectedly as he broke away toward Jupiter's looming mass.

"Can't be helped," Bronson rejoined, and then his attention was drawn back to the enemy formations, which were now rapidly breaking apart.

Opting for the strategy of using randomized movement to throw off the human attackers, SUPREMACY was guiding its forces to create what looked like a haze of erratically swarming insects. Bronson tried some randomized directional changes himself, instructing his team to follow his lead, but the movement of their vehicles no longer seemed to create any response among the automatons unless they passed within a certain distance of the enemy units—and then the only response was Sparker fire. With the AI no longer allowing its drones to be drawn out away from their close proximity to the city, the sergeant could not see any clear path to reach the hub.

The team had skirted around the swarm and was now approaching the forward edge of Traverseon's wheel as it cut through space toward the mothership's ultimate destination. Bronson's mind was racing as he tried to develop a plan by which they could get safe access to the city core's docking ports, but his ideas were running into constraint after constraint with no way to move forward without exposing his team or the civilian population to unacceptable risks.

FAILSAFE's voice sympathetically spoke over their communications channel.

"THIS IS A DANGEROUS SITUATION, AND YOU ARE TAKING IT ON ADMIRABLY. HOWEVER, I'M AFRAID THAT THE CITIZENS OF TRAVERSEON WILL NOT BE ABLE TO SURVIVE WITHOUT THE AIR-CLEANSING SYSTEMS MUCH LONGER. SUPREMACY HAS ALSO DARKENED THE ENTIRE

THIRD RING, LEAVING THE CITIZENS IN TERRIFYING BLACKNESS."

Bronson's gaze flew to the now-obscure band to his left, working his lips in frustration and mental anguish at the thought of the millions of people suffering within the boundaries of his city. The young leader could see the petrified masses in his mind's eye with tormentuous vividness.

"There's nothin' for it, Sarge," Nunes said, trying to sound pragmatic despite the hint of angst that he could hear tinging her voice. "We gotta punch through."

Taking a deep breath, the sergeant started bringing his craft's nose to face the central area of the city again, with Nunes, Faber, and Zan joining him in the maneuver.

When he spoke, it was with a voice fraught with emotion.

"Team, it's been an inexpressible honor serving with you. I couldn't have asked for a better crew to take this on with me. Whatever the outcome today, you are *all* heroes in my book!"

A few moments of silence followed his words, and then Officer Faber asked in a deadpan voice, "Does this mean we have to be on hugging terms afterward?"

Nunes and Zan laughed out loud, and Bronson shook his head as a wry grin broke out across his face.

"No, Faber. Nunes would kill you if you even breathed on her, so if you want to live, then no hugging."

As he pulled his grin back into only a hint of a smile, the sergeant ordered, "I wanna see crazy, random movements without anyone crashing into each other, the drones, or the city. We dogfight our way through the enemy, and whichever of us can reach the docking port first links up and rushes to that reset. Should be right smack in the middle of the main command center. Got it?"

"Loud and clear, Boss," Nunes asserted with bravado, the others letting her speak their minds.

"Alright, then. On my three-count. Three...two...one..."

"See you at the after party!" Zan shouted as his SCITHE leaped ahead of the others, the young man accelerating to his craft's maximum acceptable velocity.

"Wait for me, *amigo!*" Nunes called out, also pushing her vessel to leap ahead of Bronson's.

Faber swung his fighter out to his sergeant's left flank until he was practically skimming across the edge of the second ring, changing his cockpit's orientation so his head was pointing away from Traverseon.

"Don't shoot up the city!" he reminded them as he let loose a volley of projectiles with his railguns, veering to his left and right randomly to catch unsuspecting drones in different sections of the plane of his gunfire.

As Zan and Nunes bobbed and weaved and rolled through elaborate maneuvers in their approach toward the enemy horde, sending out bursts of rounds toward their targets, Bronson carefully sent out his own lethal shots as he began whipping his SCITHE through such tremendous acrobatics that it felt like his body was a piece of clothing being stirred about in a cleansing agitator. His console kept flashing with warnings as he maxed out the gravitational force equivalent the computer would allow him to experience. He could see that his efforts were enabling him to swing around in arcs that exceeded those of Zan and Nunes, thereby reducing the risk of his rounds crossing their paths as they entered the drone-packed area near the hub.

The battle was frenetic, with explosions littering the field and numerous near-collisions with the enemy—and even with each other—persistently plaguing the pilots. The adversaries' Sparker weapons were creating a dangerous volume of strikes on the exteriors of the SCITHE fighters, each round adding a small amount to the vehicles' control interruptions and surface damage. The cumulative effect was worryingly growing in potency despite the relatively minor impact created by each individual projectile.

The sergeant could see that despite the wildness of his maneuvers, he was slowly closing the distance to the core's docking zone while Faber had been forced to veer wide around the swarm, executing a spiral and attempting to drive back in with his railguns firing and his fighter's blade spinning like a turbine. Zan had carved a swath from the outer third of the generally spherical formation SUPREMACY had now created around the desired landing location and was about to dive back into the fray as well, while Nunes had cut through the drove, dodged around the connecting bridges between the hub and the first tier of the city's great wheel, and burst out on the opposite side—only to express potent frustration that their foes were tightly clustered about that portion of the hub as well.

With the suffering of his people at the forefront of his mind, Bronson growled out, "We don't have time to dock smoothly! I'm gonna blow a hole in the Hub. We'll have to hope the reset works despite the damage!"

The warrior was just bringing the nose of his craft in for a dive toward his target when a Traverseon fighter craft flashed past him, weapons blazing and piercing through the enemies at a speed that spoke of lunacy. Chaplen had been randomizing his movements, starting far from the fight and working to confuse the enemy as he had drawn steadily closer, but when his team leader had set them on their task to access the city's core, the young man had pushed his vehicle to continuously accelerate. He was heading straight for the port side of the city's command center.

"*Chaplen, slow down!*" Bronson shouted in a voice void of hope. There was no way the SCITHE would be able to decelerate in time.

Drones and debris striking the leading edge of his vessel and Chaplen's weapons fire pouring out the front of the rotating, curved wing, the man's fighter barely survived the plunge through the enemy horde, but his railgun rounds tore through the metal bordering one of the hub's docking ports, right where it was thinnest. The young officer's follow-on projectiles then carved along the surface of the station from the first point of impact.

As the metal weakened, the exterior of the structure exploded outwards with the pressure and combustion of the false atmosphere that had been contained inside it, sending a massive fireball billowing outward toward the sentries and the oncoming spacecraft.

"Tell my dad I love him!" was all Chaplen could utter as he tried to dodge the orange flames, his ship's blade making contact with the outer edge of the hub's armor and ricocheting off to fly out of control toward the edge of the city's innermost ring.

The ship exploded as it struck the structure with a heavy blow.

"*CHAPLEN!*" Bronson cried out wretchedly, tears springing to his eyes as he struggled to weave through the unmanned units that were trying to keep him from reaching the entrance his friend had created.

"Sarge..." Nunes' voice was almost reverential as she pulled away from the fight on the opposite side of the hub.

Then her voice took on greater urgency.

"*Sarge!* I see something flying off into space on this side of the city...looks like a capsule!"

Chaplen's voice was full of mirth and exhilaration.

"So...looks like these babies release escape pods when they crash!"

"*Meng Himmel!*" Faber grunted with feeling. "Why didn't you *say something??*"

"I was giving y'all a minute to mourn my loss!" Chaplen explained as though he had been extremely considerate.

Bronson was on his final approach as he swerved crazily around a tighter cluster of enemies and felt his SCITHE jerk with the impact of dozens of Sparker rounds, the entire mass of SUPREMACY's horde firing at him nonstop.

"You got a damnable sense of humor, there, *Chaplen!*" the sergeant laughed out through gritted teeth. "Now, watch me take inspiration from your insanity!"

As Sergeant Johnson had nearly reached the side of the hub, he suddenly slowed as much as possible using reverse thrust, and the man then yanked on the emergency release lever for his ship's cockpit with his right hand while depressing the harness deactivator with his left. Giving the yoke one last shove to send the fighter craft curving away from the scorched silver construction ahead of him, he launched himself out of his seat at an angle that sent him flying into the maw of the improvised opening Chaplen had made.

The accuracy of his push-off was one in a million, sending him tumbling with his head swinging away from the space-based building so his feet could stretch out and make the first, glancing contact with the tubular corridor inside. Bronson grunted heavily and had the wind knocked out of him as he rebounded off that side of the tube and then the opposite surface, body flipping about and arms barely managing to extend so he could push off from his third collision and go sailing into the open space of the large command center that was the city's heart.

Sparker fire was pouring into the hallway behind him, and several rounds agonizingly struck his left shoulder and leg, causing his muscles to spasm despite the suit covering them. The man managed to reach out and snag the headrest of one of the bolted-down chairs in the nucleus of the room, putting tremendous force on his extended arm—causing him to cry out in pain—and yet redirecting his body toward the main console that was built into the midsection of the forward wall.

One more round struck his left shoulder, causing Bronson to jerk and grunt and throwing him into a slow rotation that forced him to reach out with only his right hand and leg to try to reduce his impact with the glossy black surfaces ahead. He struck with another loud grunt, whipping his right hand out to seize the protruding edge of a screen and pull himself down toward the control interface on the console's sloped surface. A large, gleaming lever was protected by a clear covering on the panel, "F.S.R." printed on the surface beneath it.

Bronson desperately grabbed onto the transparent box and tried to pry it open, his efforts heartbreakingly ineffectual.

He gritted his teeth and growled as his desperate gaze flew across the command center, his peripheral vision catching ominous movement from the direction of the corridor through which he'd entered the space. Keeping his focus on the console, the officer's eyes landed on a half-orb bearing the marking "STANDBY," and he lashed out with his right heel, smashing down on the activator as the first Sparker rounds of dozens began pelting nearly every visible centimeter of the left side of his body.

The interface's screens sprang to life, the glassy case finally lifting as Bronson shuddered with the electrical energy pulsing through his body. He realized through the fog of pain that he was starting to drift away through the room. His last, desperate attempt brought his hand down, uncontrolled, upon the lever.

With the device's depression, the drones' firing ceased.

Chapter 22

"We gather here to honor those extraordinary individuals—service members whose lifetimes were marked by noble endeavors—who fought in defense of this great metropolis, the one currently crossing the stars, and humankind as a whole. They stood as pillars of courage and selflessness even when all hope seemed lost, dedicating their lives to the cause of freedom and justice in an existence that guarantees neither.

Some made the ultimate sacrifice, and the lives of all stand as a testament to their unwavering commitment to humanity. These service members were true to themselves, their nation, the Alliance, and each other, and they unequivocally deserve the title 'heroes,' for they have left an indelible mark on the hearts of all who knew them and on the fabric of history itself. May their legacy inspire future generations to acts of equal kindness and valor."

- Major Calista Pendragon, Senior Chaplain, Command Activated Program, Global Alliance Command

SUPREMACY's confidence was overflowing, seeing its soldiers covering the NIAN and holding the machine's massive arms backward around the sides of a concrete post supporting one of Central Park's decorative arches. The war machine's lasers were being forced downward such that they could not target the center of SUPREMACY's body, and with the Superior Authority units clinging to the front of the NIAN's chest plates, any missiles released would explode at the ends of their launch ports—thereby causing significant damage to the firer's own body.

Meanwhile, the AI's chosen form had ground its way across the open area in the midst of the mighty buildings that the creature almost matched in height, the enemy attempting to make the NIAN's targeting more difficult. The Alliance's giant had been on the opposite side of the largest reservoir in the park, but had then been forced to move westward through a platoon of Superior Authority soldiers to get a clear shot toward the section of SUPREMACY's protective skin that had been weakest at that time. During this traversal, the hideous behemoth had also been siphoning off materials from buildings on the northwestern edge of the New York City commons and had nearly fully reformed and repaired the damage the enemy's explosives had previously caused.

The demigod's victory seemed to be all but assured.

The NIAN's pilots vigorously strained to raise its cannons just high enough to target the southernmost, lower section of their adversary's body. A final snap from the robot's directed energy weapons not only blasted away the bodies of those Superior Authority forces which had been nearest to their apertures, but also blasted apart a significant section of SUPREMACY's shell as well.

The self-possessed AI shrugged off the assault as a pitiful, final attempt. Its concentration on the extinction it intended to inflict upon its mortal enemies' primary means of resistance caused the malevolent entity to neglect its consideration of the possibility that the final shots from the NIAN's armaments combined with the depletion of the Superior Authority troops across the rooftops could interfere with its ability to identify the stealthy approach of ground-based and exosuit-clad Alliance warriors. SUPREMACY made this mistake as two such enemies were employing their dynamic camouflage to approach its southwestern side, following which they utilized their exosuits' jump jets to elevate themselves to the newly formed crater in the enemy's skin.

Only as the power-hungry intelligence felt the web of control filaments continuing to melt away inside the area of the NIAN's initial strike did the Confederacy's false deity recognize its tactical error. This new attack had involved a cunning method for boring through the grotesque monstrosity's gelatinous guts using explosive assault rifle rounds, continuously preventing SUPREMACY from reforming its innards as the assailants drove ever closer to the creature's core.

Jayce had just made it to the eastern side of the building from which the Alliance leaders had originally observed the NIAN's efforts. The massive man skidded to a halt and balanced precariously on the edge of the crumbling floor beneath him as he stared, wild-eyed and helpless, at the far-off figures of Gaines and Vela as they disappeared inside the gaping hole in SUPREMACY's corporeal constitution.

Having found that the couple had muted the team's communications channel, Jayce's thought signal activated his helmet's external audio transmissions.

"*ULYSSES, VICTORIA, NO!*" he called out in desperation.

As the demon's hide closed in behind his friends' forms, Jayce pressed his eyes shut, jaw clenched as he tried to hold back the sorrow that was pouring through his soul as unstoppably as the sands of time itself.

A colossal thunderclap sent a shockwave rushing out from the monstrous megalith, temporarily expanding its form and flattening trees near its base as the wave moved on to ripple across the remainder of the terrain in the park. The searing hot wind blasted across Jayce Johnson's exosuit as he was forced to fling out an arm to seize the end of a twisted piece of a steel frame that protruded from the structural level sagging down above him.

The warrior forced himself to open his eyes and watch as the peak of the heinous heap that had been SUPREMACY's mobile fortress slowly collapsed inward, the dense armor falling apart with the sounds of terrible, spectral millstones mercilessly being ground together. Across the decimated and formerly green space and surrounding buildings, the remaining Superior Authority soldiers' animation was also drawing to a close, the gargoyle-like figures toppling lifelessly to the ground.

As the sun's rays cleared the tops of the structures along the eastern edge of Central Park, the citizens of the city, like the world at large, were awakening from their unwanted slumber...and what seemed to them to have been a horrifically vivid nightmare. Now came the unnerving experience of discovering that their dreams had actually reflected reality.

Sad eyes sweeping across the scene before him, General Jayce Johnson knew he would be haunted by these events for the remainder of his life.

He swore to use that haunting to help him remember his friends' sacrifice.

Dew was glistening on the foliage of the brightly lit Colorado Rockies while birds called out in the trees and the wealth of additional wildlife was going about its business, oblivious to the carnage that lay spread out across the clearing. The fresh scent of the pines mingled with the distinct odor of humans' vital fluids.

Taggert staggered out of the tree line, face ashen and eyes bearing the far-off look of someone who was not yet in full possession of his mental faculties. He scuffled to a stop, hands hanging at his sides as his dull eyes slowly scanned across the open field before him, an aging and gloomy cabin the backdrop for the horrific view of what was left after humans of all ages had been forced to fight to the death.

Hearing twigs snapping and the whisper of pine boughs being brushed aside, the young man sluggishly turned his gaze toward the approaching girl.

"Tag..." Brigette spoke as though her mouth was as dry as a desert tomb, forcing her to put forth great effort to enunciate every syllable. After pushing through the trees to his west, she had turned her unfocused vision from him back to her raised hands, manicured fingernails encrusted with dried blood.

Her eyes flicked over to the corpses spread out upon the field, barely able to let herself comprehend what she was seeing. She stumbled forward, making her way toward her friend, faltering as she realized she had to avoid the twisted body of an elderly man and then raising her eyes to Taggert's face as her oculi filled with inexpressible emotions.

"Taggert...where *are* they?" she moaned. "Where are Sasha...and Skye...and *everyone?*"

She reached her unresponsive listener, hands still raised as her attention turned from them to her friend's expressionless face and back again. A vision of Bo's lifeless body flashed into her mind, with her own arms having been wrapped around his neck from behind as she had awakened and struggled to extract herself from his corpse.

"I...I think I hurt them, Taggert. I...I think I hurt lots of people real, *real* bad!" her voice broke as she tried to finish her sentence, descending into shuddering sobs that emanated from the center of her soul.

Her hands still raised and abutting the young man's chest, she let her head sag forward onto his sternum and continued weeping as she struggled to repeat, "Where...Where are they, Taggert? Where *are* they??"

The brawny teenage boy's expression finally gained a flicker of recognition as he turned his focus from the girl's hair to the scene of mass casualties. Closing his eyes, he raised his face to the sky.

Tears trickled down his cheeks.

Weeks had passed since the battle in New York, and yet Maxwell Clarke had not yet awakened from his self-induced slumber.

At Doctor Srinivastava's recommendation, Jayce had ordered the Command Activated medical personnel to set up monitoring and care for his friend while maintaining the full operability of the Interface, allowing Maxwell's mind to extract itself from FAILSAFE's at his own pace—or at least that was the hope.

"He's been through something unprecedented in the field of neuroscience," the doctor had explained as he and Jayce had stood in the now highly trafficked laboratory where the Interface cradled his friend's body. "He, better than anyone, will be the best to guide his mind out of the expanse of the world's networks."

"Yeah, alright...thank you, Doc," Jayce had sighed out. "My patience is just at an all-time low level these days."

The kindly old Mumbai native had turned his wise eyes to the general's face, peering up at the towering, burly warrior.

"In this case, I'm afraid you'll have to reach new heights!" the senior man sympathetically and—in a sense—paradoxically advised.

At both Lilian and Jayce's insistence, as the days had passed the staff had added beds and other accommodations to allow Maxwell's family to stay with him around the clock. Having undergone a successful operation on her knee, Lilian had asked the helpful personnel to position her mobile recovery berth up against the edge of the Interface so she could continually cling to her husband's left hand.

She'd maintained her bed in that location even after the doctors had provided her with rapid tissue regeneration via stem cell infusion and electrical stimulation, as the woman could not bear to be far from her husband while he was in that state of fragility. Kit and Ada took turns holding their father's right hand, whispering to him about the latest news and their favorite remembrances from their younger years, though they could not bring themselves to mention those memories that involved the area around their family's cabin.

Finally, toward the end of the third week in his near-comatose state, Lilian was awakened from the fitful sleep into which she'd drifted off, the woman having felt a sudden twitch of Maxwell's fingers.

"Max?!" she cried out as she raised herself with a start. "Honey? Are you awake?"

Kit and Ada sprang up from their chairs and rushed to their parents' sides. After a score of seconds that seemed to them like an eternity, their father began working his dry lips, his clear eyes fluttering open and squinting in the bright lights.

"Lil? Kit? Ada! My darlings!" he called out as he broke into a beaming, though weak, smile.

As they clutched his hands, he gently squeezed theirs in return, looking from face to face like he had not seen them in years. After basking in the warmth of their togetherness for a long moment, Lilian saw questions flooding into Maxwell's eyes.

"What do you remember, sweetheart?" she gently coaxed.

He looked at the ceiling and then back at her with eyes only partially focusing on her face.

"It was like being in a...different realm of existence. I felt like I could go anywhere and see anything! I could speak with FAILSAFE directly through my thoughts and collaborate about our ideas. I remember...building a NIAN."

Jayce spoke from where he had paused at the door, having been alerted by the medical systems that his friend was awake and then having rushed to the lab from the temporary office he'd set up within the same building.

"Thank God for that!" the bulky man boomed with a broad grin.

"Jayce!" Maxwell weakly called out. "Good to see you, my friend!"

"Words can't express, brutha!" the typically stoic officer raved as he strode across the radiant space to lean against the left side of Lilian's bed.

"Invasion!" the technical doctor suddenly blurted out, brows creasing and eyes questioning as he looked from Lilian to Jayce. The general took the lead in explaining what had transpired.

"The Russians wisely rerouted their assets after SUPREMACY fell! Apparently, that son of a..." the warrior's eyes fell on Kit and Ada's innocent faces, and he quickly changed course, continuing, "...that *monster* was so confident in its victory it moved key parts of itself into the hardware it had the Confederacy take to Central Park. When that was destroyed, it crippled the AI, and then when the Russian generals saw the world was waking up—getting no good response from their *master*—they called off the invasion. The air- and sea-based forces ran back to Russia with their tails tucked between their legs!"

Maxwell pondered this a moment.

Clearing his throat, the imminently worldly wise man quietly drew upon his recent, shared memories to assert, "As you may already know, FAILSAFE and I have been focused on hemming SUPREMACY in, though it will be an arduous task to finally purge the entity from even the Quantum Underground. That said, I do recall we were planning to deploy emissions detection and mitigation mechanisms to counter direct attacks on FAILSAFE's mind going forward, though that would merely be a precaution. By the end of our time spent merged together, he no longer required my moral guidance. It seemed that our connection had allowed him to develop his own 'mental immune system,' so to speak, protecting his persona from all external influences, including my own, except where he desired my input."

"He fully transcended the morality with which I had originally imbued him, teaching *me* moral truths I had not previously understood and concepts my mind had not previously been able to grasp. I feel that both of us emerged from the experience in a more highly evolved state of being, as though human and electronic entities were meant to teach each other how to grow beyond what we could accomplish alone. Not anytime soon..."

the weary doctor gently reassured his increasingly worried wife, "...but eventually, I truly hope to interface with FAILSAFE again and see where our symbiotic growth ultimately takes us!"

Returning his thoughts to the more immediate needs, the Englishman self-consciously smiled and hastened to add, "In any case, eliminating the last traces of SUPREMACY is a task we will *all* have to help FAILSAFE to complete."

As Lilian and Jayce nodded their heartfelt agreement, Maxwell Clarke's mind was inevitably drawn into an analysis of the foreign affairs that had facilitated the re-emergence of humanity's greatest foe.

"The fall of Communist China imbued our leaders with an overly optimistic attitude that the remainder of the CEN would also soon succumb to revolutions. The Alliance allowed some subcomponents of the Confederacy to continue to exist these past decades, but I believe the 'Refined Communists' will now feel the wrath of the entire world at once..."

"Got that right!" Jayce confirmed. "The Alliance is leading the charge, but there's not a nation out there that isn't calling for the Confederacy to be dismantled—upon penalty of their counties as a whole suffering dire consequences. The Russian citizens have their leaders on the run, and North Korea and Iran's heads of state have already been cut off. *Literally*, in the case of the latter!"

Maxwell nodded with understanding, and then a painful recollection fought its way to the forefront of his mind. A sudden darkness overcame his countenance, his eyes staring sorrowfully off into the distance.

"Ulysses and Victoria...?" he softly asked.

Jayce shook his head slowly, sympathy and sadness in his expression as Maxwell met his eyes. The convalescent man could not speak, and his friend could only offer a small semblance of consolation.

"Gaines always said he'd rather go out in a blaze of glory than slowly waste away in a care center, and they left this world together. They're in a peaceful place now, and I can't think of two better people to step into the Great Beyond hand in hand!"

Maxwell blinked away the wetness that had formed in his eyes, trying to muster a brave smile as he noticed his children's concerned faces.

"They will be missed!" he hoarsely whispered.

As Jayce looked on, the hardened warrior's brow furrowed, and his eyes experienced an extraordinarily rare mistiness as he empathized with his kindhearted friend. After a long period of solemn contemplation, the general's expression suddenly changed to convey that he had just recalled some important information. He used a thought signal to send out a response to the communiqué he had received earlier.

"You know," he began, "one way to help keep their memories alive would be to...adopt their baby."

Maxwell and his entire family turned their attention to him with shocked expressions.

"*Baby??*" Lilian queried in a voice overflowing with concern.

Into the room padded a rugged, metallic shadow. This robotic beast was one of the current variations on the Command Activated Panther units, the cats that had been one of General Gaines' literal "pet projects" to the point that he'd kept the one governed by the Severance AI with him in some form or another throughout all the years since the robots' origination. The large feline brought its heavy head up over the edge of Lilian's bed as Kit and Ada looked on in wonder—and with a touch of worry. Severance's placid black eyes scanned across the teens' faces, then shrewdly swiveled to inspect first Maxwell's expression and then Lilian's as well.

"I promise to cover my own college expenses," the drone drolly offered.

Mayor Zalkin was standing with her hands clasped behind her back, looking out from her office toward the expanse of Jupiter that was now continually dwindling from the view of the citizens of Traverseon as the city continued onward toward Saturn's orbital space. The room's service system announced that the police commissioner had arrived, and the woman briskly instructed the computer to let him enter.

Bronson Johnson strode into the office, looking sharp and yet rather uncomfortable in the new, more decorated uniform he wore. He stood at attention near the opposite side of the mayor's desk and gave her a salute as she turned her sagacious eyes toward him.

"You asked to see me, ma'am?" he queried.

"Please do sit, Bronson. May I call you Bronson?" the aged woman replied, sweeping an unassuming hand to indicate the comfortable chair situated across the desk from hers.

"Certainly, ma'am," the younger man agreed as he stiffly took his place in the proffered seat.

Sitting with a fluid and graceful movement herself, the senior civil leader clasped her hands together on the desk and smiled at him with great warmth.

"First, I want to personally thank you for all you sacrificed in freeing the city from this...*SUPREMACY*," she started, speaking the AI's name with distaste.

"Couldn't have done it without my team, ma'am," Bronson demurred.

"Of course, yes," she concurred. "No leader is an island, and they most definitely deserve the city's highest honors!"

The new commissioner gave her a brief, appreciative nod.

Mayor Zalkin continued, "Now, I understand the previous commissioner and mayor often had some...differences of opinion on how to run the police department."

She gave Bronson a knowing smile, and he raised his eyebrows in acknowledgment and curiosity about what was coming next.

"I want to assure you that I'll be taking a hands-off approach when it comes to the daily operations and overall police program governance. I've learned through my *many* years that a city's senior leaders accomplish far more through a 'familial collaboration' than through the enforcement of any hardline chain of command. That is, so long as all parties agree that they will not treat each other unkindly. Is that an approach you find to be acceptable, Bronson?"

A look of relief had flooded across Commissioner Johnson's face.

"*Absolutely*, ma'am!" he assured the regal and yet grandmotherly woman.

She seemed greatly relieved as well.

"Very good!" she sighed, adding, with enthusiasm, "And please, call me Naomi!"

She then turned her attention to the holographic screen on her desk.

"Now, about your recommendation that the city adopt the AI FAILSAFE as its network protection solution. I understand the logic behind this proposal, and judging by the entity's track record, I am leaning toward supporting it..."

Bronson soberly nodded, starting to say, "Yes, ma'am..."

He caught her bemused look and adjusted, "Yes, *Naomi*. I do feel it was a mistake for the founders to leave FAILSAFE's protections behind when building out the city's operations."

The mayor nodded slowly in return.

"Also..." the vigorous young man added, leaning forward, "...if Traverseon is truly meant to represent the best that humanity has to offer the Universe, I can't think of a better example of the best of us than what he has become. Without him we *never* could have cleansed the city's systems from SUPREMACY's corruption, and he faithfully served us even while his own mind was under attack. His support of humankind as we populate other worlds will help us truly live up to our full potential as the *species* of Earth."

The woman rose from her chair, pondering his words as she turned to gaze out at the predominantly vermillion planet they were leaving behind.

“You seem to have gotten to know this entity quite well, then...” she observed.

“Naomi,” Bronson Johnson emphatically stated, “he is possibly the best friend we could *ever* have!”

END

BENJAMIN GORDON CARD is a former military intelligence special agent and Department of Defense consultant. He is a combat veteran and currently serves as a Chief Information Security Officer, penetration tester (aka, "gray hat hacker"), and—most importantly—husband, father, son, brother, nephew, cousin, friend, and member of the Church of Jesus Christ of Latter-Day Saints. His uncle, Orson Scott Card, set an example of how tragedy can be turned into inspiration. Benjamin Gordon Card's life experiences have allowed him to witness the heights and depths of human emotion and potential, and his objective is to let that joy and pain bleed through on every page of his works.

www.ingramcontent.com/pod-product-compliance
Lightning Source LLC
Chambersburg PA
CBHW030403050826
48979CB00049B/1399/J
* 9 7 9 8 9 9 0 9 5 8 9 7 5 *